Me, Again

Exercise because
you love your body; not
because ... you're trying
to fix it!

Ann

Me, Again

The untold story of every woman's life

Ann Mody Lewis, Ph.D.

ISBN 978-0-9817191-1-5

Book Design by
Suzanne Leslie - President & Creative Director, Rachlin Design
Nicole Cravey - Graphic Design Supervisor, Rachlin Design

Editorial Consultations by
Cynthia A. Roby
Dr. Anita Davis-DeFoe

Printed by Lightning Source
in the United States of America
Copies of this book may be purchased through www.amazon.com,
Borders and Barnes & Noble.

A. Lewis and Associates, P.A.
Fort Lauderdale, Florida

In Dedication

Have you ever wondered why part of your life stands still, while
the rest of your life is flourishing? *Me, Again* will help you find answers
to this profound question.

Early in childhood, you began to separate from your intuitive self.
Cultural expectations about 'feminine' behavior over-ruled your personal
freedom. You became an "Old Bride" without your consent, because you
were hungry for acceptance and love. *Me, Again* will systematically and
compassionately lead you back to your 'core' by awakening you to unhealthy
and unrealistic cultural expectations. After reading *Me, Again* you will
feel whole, because you will finally realize that to improve your life, is to
learn to see yourself as you really are...a "New Bride!"

This book is dedicated to YOU... the woman who wants her life!

CONTENTS

Stages of **RESOCIALIZATION**

ACKNOWLEDGEMENTS

I owe a huge debt of gratitude to the friends who read and critiqued this work...and to every woman who shared her personal story at the monthly meetings of Woman's Journey, Inc. I am grateful to all of them who encouraged me to keep going, when it would have been easier to quit.

To my mother, Bedelia, who spent hours telling me her story... the "Woman, Now Old." She has become a "New Bride" who inspires me every day of my life.

INTRODUCTION

The lives of men and women are shaped in very distinct ways by an unavoidable invisible force. Betty Friedan called it "a problem without a name." I call it gender socialization. In this book, I will introduce a model for understanding how deeply gendering invades a woman's inner life.

During my years as a psychotherapist and educator, I have observed distinctive patterns in the psychology of women. Her need to be a "bride" is a dream so powerful that she will abandon her good judgment, put aside her dreams, display a willingness to endure years of unhappiness and cling to hope in a hopeless situation. There is a bride in every woman, regardless of her race, color or sexual orientation. The bride is the romanticized ideal of herself and her life. The metaphors "Old Bride" and "New Bride" used in this book will put us in touch with a model to which every woman can relate.

When a woman chooses to marry, her wedding is the celebration of her ultimate dream. It is the dramatic acknowledgement that, at that moment, she is a proper woman because she has found her place in this society as a loved woman. Her culture praises, almost worships her; enraptures her with elegant attire, music, flowers, celebrations, gifts and dance. Everyone collaborates in the adoration of the Bride. At no other time in her life will she be so honored. The blushing, ecstatic bride knows that something big is happening to her and that fills her with joy and hope. But a feeling of dread lies beneath her consciousness as she remembers her mother's life. At that moment, no matter how "New Age" her wedding vows, she is an Old Bride. She now belongs to a man whose name she will bear; to her culture, whose expectations will flood her mind. She will eventually struggle to survive and maybe, disappear.

To be an Old Bride you don't need to walk down the aisle dressed in a white gown and veil and be given away to a man. You simply have to be a woman. I have seen this ideal control the lives of lesbian women who search for the perfect love. A woman needs to believe in the underlying definition of a bride: in order to exist, to be worthwhile, to be a real and proper woman, she must be in a romantic relationship. She must habitually be willing to defer to those she loves and be responsible for the well-being of everyone who touches her life.

A woman who firmly commits herself to social expectations, no matter how unreasonable the expectations feel, is an Old Bride. The Old Bride belongs to everyone but herself.

Who is the
"Old Bride?"

Who is the "Old Bride?"

The Old Bride approaches relationships eagerly and with great intensity. Poised to love without boundaries and give without caring for herself, she takes responsibility for others while ignoring her personal needs. She loves without being appreciated and respects others without having her own uniqueness acknowledged.

When entering into a committed relationship, The Old Bride, when either walking down the aisle or becoming known by someone else's name, is prepared to reenact her mother's life. This ultimately confirms her fulfillment of social expectations for femininity. She then feels beautiful; the envy of other women. Belonging to someone grants her permission to be someone. Her identity has been defined.

Her dedication is so profound and socially reinforced that no one notices when she struggles to survive and, eventually, disappears. In a relationship, she is important. Not for the person she is, but what she does and how much she can accomplish alone. Recognition, for her, is accomplished through the achievements of her husband and children, as she bears the burden of their well-being deep inside her own identity. Because of this contingent recognition of her personal worth, she lives in fear of criticism; being labeled "not good enough" as a wife, mother or lover is her deepest dread.

The Old Bride is unable to verbalize her feelings with any certainty because for years she has forgotten to ask herself, "Am I really happy?" She whispers when she wants to shout and shouts when she is unhappy with her life and cannot envision a way to change it.

She feels trapped by a problem she cannot identify. She may call it marriage, children, men, relationships--but it was always the myth of femininity. The myth, one she learned before she could remember, seems inseparable from her vague sense-of-self.

"Old Bride"

Every woman, privately and in silence, struggles with the Old Bride. She does not realize that this unnamed problem has its origins in a complicated system of what it means culturally to be feminine. She does not realize that from the dawn of her life who she would become has been more important than who she would be. She may be afraid to break the silence of her forgotten self because it not only unveils a life that has become lost, but a future of uncertainty.

The Old Bride dreams that love will save her, making her life worthwhile and complete. She believes that love will add certain credibility to her life which she is incapable of achieving on her own. She builds her life around this dream and has a difficult time protecting herself when the dream begins to fall apart. The Old Bride is noble, strong and loyal; she struggles to maintain dignity and surrenders much of herself because she believes so firmly in the potentialities of others. Everyone relies on and loves her, but she does not feel the love.

Love has made her tired.

To some degree, an Old Bride lives inside every woman. She is unavoidable because the messages of socialization were waiting for her as she passed through her mother's birth canal.

There are serious health consequences to the intra-psychic split that invade a woman's internal peace. I concluded that a problem of this magnitude could not be addressed quickly. It demands a systematic and progressive program of resocialization that would help women reclaim their lives.

Dr. Douglas Brodie, M.D., who has treated cancer patients for more than fifty years, wrote: "Suppressed anger seems to be, by far, the most common emotional feature of cancer patients, in general."

Anger is the most prohibitive emotion for women.

He continues, "that this anger" has usually been suppressed for so long, that patients either can't bring it out, or don't even realize that it is there.

"Old Bride"

The relationship between cancer and personality type has existed for centuries. Dr. Brodie, who specializes in alternative and integrative treatments for cancer patients, identified certain personality traits that are consistently present in the cancer-susceptible individual. All seven traits can be correlated directly with the Old Bride syndrome, the first three being particularly applicable and poignant:

1. Being highly conscientious, dutiful, responsible, caring, hard working and usually at above-average intelligence.
2. Exhibiting a strong tendency toward carrying other people's burdens and taking on extra obligations, often "worries for others."
3. Having a deep-seated need to make others happy; being a people pleaser and having a great need for approval.
4. Often having a history of lack of closeness with one or both parents. Sometime later in life, this can result in a lack of closeness with their spouse or others who would normally be close.
5. Harboring long-suppressed toxic emotions such as anger, resentment and/or hostility. The cancer patient internalizes such emotions and has great difficulty expressing them.
6. Reacting adversely to stress, oftentimes becoming unable to cope adequately.
7. Showing an inability to resolve deep-seated emotional problems and conflicts, usually arising in childhood and often even being unaware of their presence.

While these general commonalties have been noted, this does not in any way suggest that these personality types, personal experiences or life circumstances constitute or contribute to the direct cause of cancer. They remind us, however, of an important truth: our emotional life deeply affects our physical health.

Numerous demographic signs of long-term stress would be exposed if a woman's life, at every stage, is studied. Stress emerges dramatically during adolescence and becomes complex as her role multiplies and she struggles to survive.

"Old Bride"

Through research, I uncovered a statistic stating: "Female students, over the age of twenty-five years, often referred to as adult or reentry students, have become the fastest growing population in institutions of higher education." (Carney, Crampton & Tan, 2002)

Many of these women are single-parents, a demographic indicating women's persistent psychological resilience. Their desire to live, even under great stress, is the New Bride wanting to survive and flourish. This paradigm shift to grow, reach out, appreciate one's uniqueness and understand the entrapments of socialization creates health on multiple levels: physical, mental, emotional and spiritual.

It is possible for the Old Bride to become the New Bride. Not because it is New Age thinking, but because she wants to be healthy and alive. Resocialization requires women to overcome painful self-examinations and catharsis.

Resocialization offers real hope for those with the courage to walk the difficult path of waking up. Dr. Brodie refers to the "willingness to expose and address deep-seated emotions to resolve long-standing conflicts" as the keys to true and lasting healing.

Every New Bride was once an Old Bride. This transformation is by choice; perhaps the most important choice she ever made. Wanting to be a New Bride is the first step toward resocialization.

Who is the
"New Bride?"

Who is the "New Bride?"

The New Bride approaches relationships realistically and with a healthy desire for equality. She wants to love and is willing to ask for the love she requires. She approaches conflict head on in order to establish trust and boundaries. Her positive self-perception demands respect; she takes responsibility for her own personal development. She can openly acknowledge her accomplishments.

Having understood and grieved the tragic influences of cultural demands, she is bold about reexamining her life, her feelings, her values and her priorities in order to enjoy a full life. She is mentally alert to the traps that could paralyze her life and resists them without guilt. She, therefore, speaks on her own behalf whenever necessary and will not allow the voices of others to silence her own voice.

Although committed to her husband or life partner and children, she authors her own life and understands and believes that her personal love for life is the greatest gift she can share with those she loves and influences. She does not question herself in the face of conflict, criticism or adversity. She accepts those painful passages as part of the human experience and the natural evolution of relationship development. These passages, for the New Bride, become an opportunity for developing intimacy.

The New Bride is comfortable with her body and is vigilant about its care. She wants to please herself because she cares for and respects herself. She can, with grace, accept her changing body as she appreciates the richness of her inner world that has become so magnificent. She honors and shares her wisdom without using it as a tool of control; connects with other women because her own story is seen and reflected in their lives. Her female connections expand her identity as woman. She uses her sexuality creatively, allowing her body to tell the story of her loving soul.

"New Bride"

The New Bride is happy to be a woman, because she is happy with herself. Love has motivated and energized her; challenged her and helped her to realize the global influence of her unique self. She allows herself to be loved because she knows she is worthy. By loving and being loved, she invents new excitement in her life until drawing her last breath.

When our inner spirit is found, we have a stronger immune system, lower blood pressure, fewer visits to the doctor and a general feeling of well-being.

A recent study that received great attention from the media revealed that journaling and connectedness significantly reduced symptoms of rheumatoid arthritis and asthma. Dr. Candace Pert noted: "When emotions are expressed all systems are united and made whole."

The New Bride buries the self-criticism, the blaming and judgmental attitudes she once absorbed through socialization. And, just as important, she forgives her oppressors because forgiveness is an act of creation. She remembers that they too are victims of an oppressive system that attempts to divide humanity into two distinct and separate groups. This system of gender polarity, although real, is untrue. She is now free to invite and inspire her oppressors to reinvent their own lives, to seek what is true and to organize their lives around it so that their humanness becomes more important than their separateness. She can now live freely.

Ann Mody Lewis, Ph.D.
Author of Me, Again

How Has Socialization Affected You?

Detecting the ways social conditioning has infiltrated your life is difficult because we all take for granted the uncomfortable conflicts, personal subjugations and unworthiness that haunts us. This simple survey divides your life into six categories. In each category, there are twenty behavioral and/or attitudinal questions. Respond honestly to each. You will not be scored or criticized. These questions will help you to know why you should read this book.

Self-assessment questions for you to answer privately

Your "Self" Perception:
- Do you have a hard time believing you are beautiful?
- Do weeks go by without any time dedicated to your favorite pastimes?
- Do you struggle with buying yourself gifts?
- Are other people's dreams and pains more important than your own?
- Do you cry alone?
- When you feel exhausted, do you allow yourself to rest?
- Have you ever given yourself a birthday party?
- Do you fear the judgment of others?
- Have you stopped singing in the shower?
- Are you reluctant to join women's groups?
- Do you often wear dark clothing?
- Do you find yourself preoccupied with how you look or how much you weigh, rather than how happy you are?
- Do you believe that you have the right not to be perfect?
- Did you change your style of dress after you were married?
- Did you give up your career to raise your children?
- Do you try to protect your husband from the stress of parenting?
- Do you resist telling your children, husband or partner what you want from them in your relationship?
- Do you feel that you are the only parent who knows how to care for your children?

- Do you avoid social activities because you don't think you're interesting enough?
- Are you afraid to admit that you were sexually active before marriage?

Your "Self" and Your Body:
- Do you eat a healthy diet?
- Do you insist on applying makeup before leaving the house?
- Do you suffer silently when others joke about your thoughts or your body?
- Do you make negative comments about your body when others try to compliment you?
- Are you constantly on a diet?
- Have you given up desserts?
- Do you avoid wearing tight clothes?
- Do you take time for annual physical exams?
- Do you exercise at least three times per week?
- Do you keep a file of your medical records?
- Have you neglected taking a daily multi-vitamin or other supplements?
- Did your mother or father make negative comments about your body?
- Do you need someone to tell you that you're beautiful?
- Are you critical of your appearance?
- Have you just felt the urge to dance lately?
- Do you remember your last manicure, pedicure or massage?
- Do you resist telling others what hurts or bothers you because you do not want to bother them?
- Are you tired most of the time?
- Do you feel that you are not using your personal talents, intelligence or creativity?
- When you have a psychological problem, do you seek help?

Your "Self" and Relationships:

- Do you feel guilty about showing anger?
- Do you avoid making assertive decisions because you do not want to risk upsetting someone who you depend on or love?
- Are you currently experiencing emotional, physical or sexual abuse at home, in the workplace or institution and have not told anyone?
- Are you assertive enough with your mother to set firm boundaries?
- Are you afraid to complain about your unanswered needs because you're uncomfortable with conflict?
- Do you find conflict uncomfortable and do whatever you can to avoid it?
- Do you tolerate insults, humiliating remarks and name-calling by others without expressing your anger?
- Do you keep your children's struggles a secret because you're afraid you'll be judged as an inferior mother?
- Have you neglected your need for close female friendships?
- Do you relinquish your suggestions or needs readily when they are challenged by others?
- Are you bored in your relationships?
- Are you living with someone who abuses drugs or alcohol?
- Are you living with someone who is depressed?
- Are you living with someone who is not romantic?
- Do you fantasize about a life you'd rather be living?
- Does your partner give you gifts spontaneously or on special occasions?
- Do you feel a responsibility to mother your spouse?
- Did you hide the woman you "used to be" from your partner to be?
- Do you make time to spend with your close friends?
- Do you let your family and friends know that you are unhappy in your relationship?
- Do your children carry your name?
- Do relationships feel burdensome to you?

Your "Self" and Career:
- Are you presently in a career of your choosing?
- While at work, are you expected to perform demeaning and unrelated tasks?
- Do you feel that your work is as important as your husband's or partner's?
- Are you staying in a job you don't like because you are afraid you won't find another?
- Do you eat healthy food during your working hours?
- Do you avoid making friends at work?
- Do you go to work when you're sick?
- Have you neglected to build a personal retirement fund?
- Do you feel that your husband or partner appreciates your financial contributions?
- Do you talk to your children about your job?
- If you are a lesbian, are you "out" at work?
- Do you feel as though you must manage all of the household responsibilities yourself, even if you are working full time?
- Is it easier for you to be underpaid than to ask for the wage you deserve?
- Are you doing more work for the same pay?
- Have you, for a number of years now, surrendered your career to care for children or aging parents?
- Have you been denied a promotion because you are a woman?
- Do you fear taking time off to care for your children or personal needs?
- Are you afraid to set boundaries with your male supervisor?
- Have you reported a male co-worker who has been inappropriate with you?
- At the end of your workday, do you feel rushed to get home because your family needs you?

Your "Self" and Money:
- Do you allow your husband or partner to use your credit because they have abused their own?
- Has ending a relationship resulted in you suffering financially?
- Have you found it difficult, perhaps even impossible to set financial boundaries with someone you love?
- Did you sign a prenuptial agreement that awards you nothing in the event of death or divorce?
- Would you engage legal counsel to assist you in the resolution of financial matters?
- Are you sure about your financial well being in the event of a husband's or partner's death?
- Have you written a will or trust that dictates how your assets should be distributed upon your death?
- Are you too embarrassed to discuss financial issues with those whom you do business?
- Do you feel that getting paid for your services makes your services less sincere?
- Are you reluctant to deposit your paycheck into your own bank account?
- Do you have credit cards in your own name?
- Are you afraid to ask people for the money they owe you?
- Are you putting too many of your personal needs aside because there isn't enough family money?
- Do you spend money freely on others and deny yourself gifts?
- Do you have full knowledge of the family assets (location, value, etc?)
- Do you know how much money you will need to retire comfortably?
- Have you contributed to Social Security throughout your working years?
- Do make "deposits only" into a conjoint bank account?
- Do you allow your husband or partner to claim control of the money you earn?
- Are you the beneficiary of your husband/partner's life insurance policy?

Your "Self" and Family:
- Did you surrender your surname when you married?
- On the day of your daughter's marriage did you sit in the pew while your husband walked your daughter down the aisle?
- Are you frustrated with housework because you have to do it all?
- Do you feel burdened by the responsibilities of parenting without a participating partner?
- Are you afraid to end an unsatisfying relationship or marriage because it will hurt your partner?
- Do you hate to clean, but do it anyway?
- Do you hate to cook, but do it anyway?
- Do you take full responsibility for the welfare of your children?
- Do you feel guilty when you get angry at your children?
- Do you give up doing the things you enjoy because you feel guilty about having fun?
- Are you ashamed to talk about problems your children might be having because you blame yourself?
- Do you feel totally responsible for running your family household?
- Do you get the respect of your in-laws?
- Do you expect your husband or partner to respect your family?
- Are you satisfied with the amount of time you spend with your biological family?
- Have you experienced the termination of a relationship without the support of your biological family?
- If you are a lesbian, do you talk freely about your life with your family?
- If you are a lesbian, do you and your partner spend holidays separately with your biological families?
- Do you value having a comfortable relationship with your spouse's or partner's family?
- Are you threatened by your husband's relationship with his mother?

Story of a Married Woman

When the alarm clock went off with its familiar buzz, Nina leaned over and quickly turned it off. This was her morning ritual, one which allowed her husband some extra time to sleep. Ironically, her own body ached for more sleep, but the well-trained woman she was, wrapped herself in a robe and walked barefoot to the kitchen.

She made coffee for herself and her husband as well as breakfast for the three children. The thought of preparing eggs and bacon on a weekday morning was simply too much. She settled on oatmeal and toast. As the oatmeal simmered, she attempted to wake everyone. She hated it. It was the same thing every morning. Calling everyone and getting no response became routine. "Come on. Get going. You're going to be late."

Her husband, Joe, came into the kitchen and waited for the cup of coffee she prepared for him. Then one by one, the kids slowly arrived with uncombed hair, untied sneakers, homework not found. How could she pull it together? she wondered. As they ate breakfast, she quickly made their lunches, a meal that she knew they'd find boring despite her efforts to keep it healthy and interesting.

Joe read the paper and made a halfhearted attempt at meaningless conversation with the kids. "Do all your homework?" or "Hey, did you see that the Rangers won last night?"

How did he guard himself from the responsibility of making it all work? How did that get to be her job, solely her responsibility? She'd often fantasize about what would happen if she couldn't or wouldn't do it anymore. She always dismissed such ideas quickly because she didn't know the answers, and besides, it WAS her job. Why wonder "if." Besides, if someone would magically wave a wand and she didn't have to handle all this, what would she do? This was all she knew.

After Joe left for work and the kids rode off on the bus, Nina poured herself another cup of coffee and began to plan her day. She glanced through the morning paper hurriedly because she didn't want to waste time reading when there was so much to be done. She cleared the kitchen routinely and then made the beds. Her daily high was seeing order throughout the house; order that gave her a sense of control and accomplishment. Strange, she thought, that such a trivial matter became the substance *of her self-esteem. Did she need less to feel more she wondered, or was she becoming less? She remembered clearly how proud her mother was of her home, her cooking; her various roles as mother, wife and civic volunteer.*

As a child, Nina always watched her mother intensely, knowing that she was looking into a mirror that reflected her future. Oftentimes what she saw filled her with an excited expectation, but more often, what she witnessed was puzzling. This created a subtle unrest that she could not identify or even begin to understand. Her mother always appeared busy, yet not at peace; her restlessness reflecting unresolved anger. While quite social, she often appeared lonely. And while the bustling and fussing about the home indicated a great deal of caring for and loving her family, there was something about her mother that cried out, "I feel unloved!"

Growing up, Nina wondered about the constant anger between them. It erupted frequently over trivial matters. Her jeans were too tight, her hair was a mess and her room wasn't neat. She was eating too many desserts, talking on the phone too long; she wasn't dating the right boys. The annoyances seemed irresolvable.

Her brother, on the other hand, never had to deal with that level of scrutiny. He just existed and seemed to enjoy not being the center of their mother's attention. He was free to come and go. To simply be.

What was it about her that so annoyed her mother? What caused the constant watching and maneuvering? Was her mother's criticism a sign of love and protection or was it a display of her total dissatisfaction with who Nina was as a daughter? Throughout her life Nina was unsure; always wondering about the unrest between them. The mother and daughter were definitely intimate strangers. She never got an answer.

Story of a Lesbian Woman

They sat on the beach watching each wave gently slap the shoreline. Neither felt a need to converse. Finally they were as connected in their silence as they were in conversation. They both fought hard to reach this peaceful place. They watched their children, now 19 and 17, chase each other in playful competition. They are my children now, she thought, and Sara is my life. Her mind drifted back to the memory of her past life and the new life she now shared with her new family.

Sports were Thea's deepest love. She participated in every sport she could squeeze into her busy schedule, and excelled in most. Her family's lack of interest in her athletic achievements was a disappointment. Even when ribbons, plaques and banners accumulated in her bedroom, she received no acknowledgement. They wanted her to be an academic wonder, but she was too busy.

Miss Mench, the physical education instructor, welcomed her into the office every morning with the other students. Thea's presence had no particular purpose. She'd always worked hard to gain Miss Mench's admiration. She felt a certain attraction and connection, but didn't understand its meaning.

Sometime during her sophomore year, Thea's body became fabulous. Her firm muscles gave her hips and legs the fullness of a young woman. Her breasts, round and full, complimented the goddess curves of her total body.

Thea fell in love with Adam. He was dark, handsome and delicious. They kissed for hours on the front porch, a passion screeching to a halt when her mother flashed the porch light on and off. She could feel him against her, but had no desire for penetration. The possibility of pregnancy frightened her. How would or could she handle the shame of pregnancy outside of marriage? Contraception was never discussed; fear overruled her desires. At some level, she seemed disconnected from her desire for a full sexual experience, yet loved all the sensations that enlivened her body.

Thea always thought of her life as a blast. Even as she struggled with her family, since her earliest years, she loved the outdoors. Her best friends were Joseph and Tom. They built huts and organized a civilization in the woods that allowed children the *freedom they needed to imagine. During her early years, her mother accepted her best friends and the disinterest in traditional little girl toys. "Tomboy is only a stage," her mother often repeated.*

Somehow Thea felt it was a threat, but she didn't challenge her mother's wisdom. Her father didn't seem threatened by her tomboyish ways. On the contrary, she followed him as he replaced things around the house and built furniture in his woodshop. Her father seemed to enjoy their friendship and that made Thea feel accepted; that she had his approval.

Her parent's behavior toward her changed, as did her body. Womanhood seemed to eradicate her right to be free. Unfamiliar expectations now seemed to govern her relationship with her parents. Her mother was suddenly more critical of her friends; often complaining about how she walked, what she wore and who she was dating. Her father began discouraging her from coming to the woodshop or fixing the cars. The two became strangers in the odd world of "becoming a woman."

Thea faced the mystery of her changing relationship with her parents with some compliance, subtle resistance and later, outright rebellion. She was alienated from them as she loved them, struggling to understand their need for her to be someone who was different from the person she knew herself to be. Was their image of Thea more credible than her own? Many times their needs superseded her desires.

The old jeans that Thea loved so much became the focus of great controversy with her mother. They were too tight, too old and unladylike; the tank tops were too revealing. It didn't seem to matter that everyone at school looked like Thea. Her hair should be longer, her mother lamented. "How are boys going to be attracted to someone that looks like you?" She insisted that "boys want to date a lady."

During the week, Thea wore tight skirts and short-sleeved tops her mother purchased during her many shopping excursions, but the weekends were "hers." She decided that wearing tight jeans, tanks and flip-flops were her right. As long as she had a date on Friday or Saturday night, her mother seemed to tolerate the altered weekend dress code.

Her father was less explicit about the changes that were occurring between them. He became less affectionate, and when he was, it was a quick and emotionally disconnected hug. "Who didn't he trust?" she wondered. "Was it her or him?"

Occasionally he echoed her mother's demands, but without conviction. Thea felt her father's emotional confusion and suffered through his new detachment. When she tried to join him as he repaired the car or in his woodshop, he became irritated. He always complained that her mother needed help and that's where she should be. Thea didn't comply. She convinced him that a good wife could never know enough. It was strange how the word "wife" brought her parents comfort.

Thea knew that boys were her best friends. She loved doing what they did and their determination to be free. She identified with their competitiveness; it made life more interesting. But now that breasts and skirts were part of their friendship, they began to view her differently, desiring more from her than she wanted to give. They seemed to want what she represented more than who she was and that, she felt, made her an object. That infuriated her. They, too, are ruled by another code, she thought. It was mysterious, unfathomable and alienating.

With Adam it was different, although their relationship was not as complete as he wanted it to be. She loved him. They were buddies and could be sexual without intercourse. Together they took long bike rides, played pool, ate pizza and kissed. After Adam got his car, their passion became more intense. It took all of her determination to prevent intercourse, yet she wondered what it felt like to be totally free. That would have to wait until marriage.

Story of a Black Woman

"IT WAS DURING PREGNANCY THAT SLAVE PARENTS REALIZED, MORE THAN EVER, THE GRUELING AND DEHUMANIZING CONDITION OF THEIR LIVES."

As far back as I can remember women in my family have struggled to survive. They managed to do so by a repression that would have crushed the spirit of ordinary people. Yes, my female ancestry was strong, spirited, fiercely creative and wise. The story of my great, great grandmother Tashi set the stage for our black nobility. Let me share her story with you.

Tashi and Pello were slaves on a large plantation in southern Georgia. They met in the cotton fields. They knew each other through their glances and the stories they passed to each other through friends. Pello loved Tashi though he never spoke to her. He knew that the master regularly summoned her from the fields and she complied without resistance because she knew black women had no choices.

Tashi had one son from the master, a boy she cherished. When she was summoned, her son stayed in the fields and was cared for by the other women who understood Tashi's life. She was beautiful and intelligent, but that was not why she was summoned. Pello knew she had no choice and neither did he. His love for Tashi transcended her bondage. He loved the part of her that the master did not know or care about. Even though Tashi's sexuality was abused and defiled, she remained the virgin of her own life and everyone knew it.

Twice each month all of the slaves were allowed to gather in a distant field to eat, dance, sing and hear each other's voices. No white person was around. The women cooked special foods and the men organized the benches, musical instruments and homemade beers. It was during these festive occasions that Pello approached Tashi.

Pello was strong, proud and humble. His quiet courage had been long noticed by Tashi. They danced together and sang the spirited songs that separated them from the bondage of their lives.

After a year of watching each other, Tashi and Pello were married during one of the Saturday night festivities. They knew their marriage meant nothing in the white world; it wouldn't be recorded, noted or celebrated. Pello knew their family would never include his name; only the names of Tashi and the children she bore. The couple knew that their children, at any time, could be sold off to other plantation owners; that they may never be able to live together because the master would be threatened by their union. Although Tashi and Pello were the master's property, their hearts belonged to each other.

Tashi and Pello had one child. During the pregnancy, their anxieties mounted. If a son was born, he would be taken away because it was profitable to the master and because it would have castrated Pello. It kept him a slave and that was all. He could never defend or protect his wife or children. If they had a daughter, she would be sexually exploited. It was during pregnancy that slave parents realized more than ever the grueling and dehumanizing condition of their lives.

Tashi secretly wanted a daughter because she would have more years to teach her to be self-reliant, emotionally independent and strong. With these traits, her daughter could survive emotionally. She could teach her to carry on her cultural pride. "My daughter will represent the continuity of life and hope," she would say. In most cultures, a son is the dream of both parents, but every slave parent knew that their son would be sold off by age twelve. He would grow up not knowing his family because it was nearly impossible to deliver news. Every son was doomed to loneliness and an imposed detachment.

My grandmother told me about Tashi and Pello many, many times. I listened to stories I'd heard before because they represented a secret code that helped us remember that our personal freedom and our personal pride transcended political systems and cultural immaturity. When I asked my grandmother questions about Tashi and Pello, she always had an answer. She spoke as if she knew them, as though she had picked cotton, danced in the distant fields or was summoned by the master. I came to realize that Tashi and Pello were myth and reality.

Story of a Woman ... Now Old

"AS SOON AS I WAS ABLE, I LEARNED TO HELP MY MOTHER CARRY THE BURDEN OF HER LIFE."

I am 91 years old now. As I reflect, it is hard for me to believe that I have journeyed through so many years. My life has been filled with family: ten brothers and sisters, a family created from my marriage to John and my family of friends that hover over me during this time in my life. Ninety-one years is a huge collection of memories. Where shall I begin?

My mother, Anna, came to America with her two older sisters and their husbands. At eight years old, she said her final good-byes to her parents in Lebanon.

She never attended school in America. Instead she spent her days occupied with household tasks that she cared nothing about. All of her life she spoke only Arabic. At age 14, she married my father, happily, as if it was her preordained destiny. My father was very strict, battering her many times.

She was a beautiful woman, my mother. Her full, round face was framed by curls of wavy dark brown hair. Her eyes were strong, yet gentle; her facial features, strikingly beautiful. Those who saw her never wanted to look away. She was easygoing even when my father was unrelentingly demanding.

No matter how much needed to get done, my mother had little interest in housework. From an early age, I learned to take care of her responsibilities to save her from abuse and to make her life easier.

My mother became pregnant right away and was pregnant every year until her death at age thirty-two. She bore ten children. My father's resentment of my mother's gentleness motivated him to make frequent and unreasonable demands on her, hoping to change her kind nature. Often sick from both pregnancy and the unhappiness of a lost life, my mother sought to cloak her sadness behind a smile.

We lived in a small mill town in upstate New York. Our neighbors were mostly Lebanese immigrants; others were a mix from other countries. My father's two older brothers built a large apartment house in our small town. All three of our families lived there together. Each a successful farmer, my father and his brothers retired early. The complex was only for the family, and strangers were considered to be anyone not in the family. This included folks like the English settlers who lived across the street, the Polish family who ran the repair shop at the foot of the hill and other Polish families who sold us raw cow's milk--milk that we used to make our own yogurt and cheese. Food was purchased in bulk and distributed to the three families.

Although each family had their own apartment, so much of our lives were lived communally. Doing anything alone was unthinkable and deemed a breach of family loyalty. A small store was attached to the apartment building where food supplies were stored. Behind the store was a pool hall and card room. Most evenings the men congregated in this room and smoked.

During the spring and summer, the women gathered on the benches lining the front of the apartment house and pulled peas and beans away from the vines. I remember huge piles of vines awaiting our eager hands to harvest their fruit while my mother and aunts talked about their children and the food they prepared. Competition over recipes was fierce, and noticeably, my mother didn't have much to contribute. I don't think she cared much about recipes and she was probably ashamed to tell anyone she was battered by my father. They had to know, I thought, but no one intervened. Was their silence an indication that my mother's treatment was expected, or worse yet, deserved? I silently waited for my mother to share her story, but she never did.

I was my mother's second child and the oldest daughter. As soon as I was able, I learned to help my mother carry the burden of her life. My father kept me home from school most of the time to help my mother manage the household tasks and cook. We spoke only Arabic to each other.

For me, school quickly became irrelevant. When I was there, my bilingual background made learning difficult. I felt strange among the kids my own age; I was much more mature. My attachment to my mother's life made me different, causing me to feel out of place with girls my age. Sometimes, in subtle ways, they made fun of me. My clothes were too old, my hair, too long; I wasn't interested in playing silly, meaningless games.

I felt lost in school. Because English was rarely spoken in my house, reading was a particular problem. I began to feel like I was just born stupid. I believed that school had no place in my life, just as it had no place in my mother's. I was my mother's daughter and that was all that mattered.

My mother needed me, particularly to do the jobs that overwhelmed her. I always knew when she felt overwhelmed because she rested for long periods. She cried, and though I could not see her tears, sadness filled her eyes. Seemingly always pregnant, her energy was sapped, leaving her life to feel out of control.

I loved my mother immensely. We were mother and daughter, two friends trapped in the same world. Completely insensitive to my mother's suffering, my father's only solution was to keep me home to assist her. And so it was.

I learned to be a wife, a mother and a traditional woman, all while still a child. I don't remember having a childhood, especially after age thirteen.

WAKING UP

—∞∞—

I understand how limited my personal life became as myths of femininity overwhelmed my identity.

How We Think

"Waking up psychologically is not easy... especially, when sleeping feels natural and protective. This awakening is a choice."

It is vital for us to understand that throughout our lives, as women, each of us has lost a part of ourselves. Our personalities were influenced by a force few recognize: socialization. It permeates our inner and outer world at every stage of our lives.

During childhood, we are uncertain about who we are and consequently, look to adults and institutions for guidance. As children, we were vigilant about watching and listening to the adults who directed our uncertain hearts. Motivated by love and a need to belong, we willingly complied with all the directives defining acceptable behavior for little girls. Without knowing what was happening to us, our lives were influenced by the most powerful cultural force: socialization. Or simply put, "learning to live within the culture of our birth."

At each stage of our life, the messages of socialization change and intensify. As we mature, the messages, for us, may become uncomfortable, feel imposing and unnatural. Yet we continue to comply because when we don't, we are punished in a variety of ways. The process of socialization goes on and on without any conscious scrutiny by the socializer or the child who conforms. You may have felt your life slipping away from you as a child, but didn't quite know how to manage your doubts. You may have felt like you did not have the right to question what was presented to you as fact and as absolute. Now is the time to question the messages of your childhood history because questioning is an important part of maturing. Understand that now is your time. Cherish this invitation because it will bring great gifts to your spirit. This work will bring you home to your deepest and truest self.

To change, to burst out of our "good-girl cocoons," we must first identify the socializing forces in our lives: the people and institutions that have shaped our opinions of ourselves. We must discover all the ways in which our personalities were influenced by the social expectations of others. In so doing, we come to understand who we really are as unique individuals. We discover that we still retain social messages so deeply imbedded inside us that often we can't distinguish them from who we know ourselves to be.

Giving up our true selves for the sake of others is often a slow, silent and painful process. Most women mask the pain, hide it, rationalize it, or ignore it. The internal pain of the compromised, denied person who exists within us is hidden by our over-identification with others. In the roles we assume as Jimmy's wife, Andy's mom or Charlene's daughter, the real "us" gets lost.

Waking up psychologically is not easy, especially when sleeping feels natural and protective. We are made to wake each morning to begin our day. This waking up psychologically is a choice. It is progressive, more often happening in the presence of other women and in the privacy of your own heart. The pace at which you proceed is yours to choose. As long as you are committed to finding yourself, reclaiming yourself, knowing yourself and enjoying your life, you will wake to a new dawn of consciousness. You will be supported and encouraged by your sisters, but the work is yours and so is every victory. At this stage, you are simply challenged to realize that your life was never entirely yours, but it can belong to you again.

All of us cannot wake up at any given moment. For example, we can identify a problem, but not resolve it. We can feel badly about a problem, but not have the ability to change it immediately. We can identify a problem in our relationships, but not know how to redesign our interactions. Waking up does not require immediate change, although it does require recognition, identification and a desire to know more. At this stage, you may be curious. And that is good. Eventually curiosity must yield to commitment so you can belong to yourself again and become the bride of your life. At this stage, you are beginning to enter the bridal chamber of your soul. While you are within its protective walls, you will prepare yourself to be a bride of your own, one who is not given away, but a bride who gives herself life in all its forms. Congratulations, bride-to-be!

As socialized women, it is easy for us to perpetuate our own oppression by believing the messages and the messengers of sexism. Sexism is what we end up with because of gendering. Gendering is the process of socialization that divides the human race into two groups based on their sexual and physical differences.

Men and women differ biologically and gendering presumes that they are different psychologically as well. The end result is that biology assumes both psychological and behavioral styles that are expected to become our destiny. For years researchers have struggled to prove that a radical difference between women and men exists. But no real, substantial difference has been identified.

Maleness is assigned human traits such as strength, power, privilege, entitlement, intellect, analytical, rational, expertness and so on.

Feminine traits are assigned to women. Gentleness, kindness, loving, forgiving, soft, nurturing, dedication, loyalty, weakness, emotionally needing protection and the need to be directed are accepted as healthy and normal for women.

The division of human traits is dangerous and entrapping for men and women throughout the world. What a man does is respected and honored. What a woman does is minimized and devalued. The uneven distribution of power between masculine and feminine traits polarizes one from the other, making them opposing rather than complimenting traits that are a part of every one of us. Each of us will be asked to relate to the impact of socialization in a personal way, and at the same time, recognize the damage it causes women the world over. One author called this stage "before the dawn." It is very apt.

As you become aware of the universality of gendering, you will recognize it in every aspect of daily life. You are encouraged to waken yourself first. You may be tempted to want to change it all.

We can begin to recover our lost selves by discussing how lost we've felt. You may be tempted to deny that socialization affected your life; we all like to be victorious and not feel like a failure. If you find yourself in denial, maybe that denial protects you from what you don't want to see. Just remember that denial is a false protection. You haven't failed yourself because you were socialized, you simply did not have a choice. Now the choice is yours. The time for resocialization is now, and it occurs every time we recognize the hidden ways we have struggled to survive: emotionally, cognitively and interpersonally. We can recover our lost selves every time we become aware of how silence and invisibility have affected us.

We call this resocialization. We remove the messages and negative programming that came in from the outside and replace it with a newer, healthier design for our lives. When we speak of resocialization, this is what we mean.

When we try to understand and justify the behavior of those who oppressed us, it keeps us bound to the oppressor. If we are endangered, we don't try to figure out the motives of the perpetrator. Our minds immediately focus only on our survival, and so it should be when seeking to rediscover our true self. We have spent our lives trying to figure out other people so we could survive, when in fact, our survival and our opportunities for personal fulfillment are based on understanding ourselves first. Being comfortable with our own experience serves to expand our ability to know others without struggling. Being able to explain the behavior of others will eventually become secondary to feeling comfortable with our own. The more we feel, the greater our self-awareness and self-acceptance, and the more exciting our journey will become. It is a time for healthy separation.

This emotional separation, the stepping away from others, is the necessary first step in our personal journey to wholeness. Before we can truly bond with others we must know ourselves. As this journey to self-discovery commences, there will be people in our lives who may try, out of their own neediness, to sabotage it. However, as we begin to rethink our lives, we recognize the comfort found in discovering our own wisdom.

Each one of us is asked to remember an inner life that now seems lost to us. We call into consciousness forgotten dreams and life experiences. By hearing our own voices talking about forgotten dreams and the significance of our personal journey, we begin to break the silence of our forgotten selves. With the encouragement of other women, we can regain our own strength and enjoy social union.

With power, we no longer minimize the tragic effects of socialization. We stop treating our dreams as though they really didn't matter. We stop saying, "It was OK." It isn't acceptable to be minimized or denied. Our dreams do matter because they are the cornerstones of our identity. Without them, we become spiritually broken, living a life void of joy and meaning.

We have become very adept at being many things to countless people; this all in response to their expectations of us. Taking a deliberate stand to separate what we know of ourselves from what others expect of us may be uncomfortable. We have to be prepared for resistance and resentment. The people around us have become accustomed to us handling most, if not all, of the responsibility for maintaining the relationship. But we must remain committed to this quest for personal fulfillment as it leads to our liberation. Our self-actualization and social equality will be realized only when we are liberated from unrealistic cultural demands.

The process of socialization is deeply personal, but in the broadest sense, it is also political. All women are affected by socialization. It extends to women of all cultures in which the expression of women's power is suppressed. For years women have written about the invisibility of our power, but we have lacked the influence to reverse the discrimination that has become such a part of our social status. If you need quick proof of how unequal we are treated, ask why, with fifty percent of the population being female, there has never been a woman president! As long ago as the 1848 Seneca Falls Convention, women used the term 'resolve' to invite all women to secure for themselves their sacred human rights.

Before we can be freed from an enemy we must know who and what that enemy is and where this enemy lives in us. Our enemies have been social mores, behaviors and expectations that caused us to discount our unique gifts and talents. Silence is our first and perhaps greatest foe. It holds back the Self we want to enjoy. It limits our power, which in so many ways, we have silenced.

We silence our bodies by always trying to be thin. We silence arguments for fear of criticism. We are sheepish in exercising our leadership because we are taught that power and femininity are opposing qualities. Each segment of silence that we break will propel us into a new awareness of our personal magnificence.

How We Feel

"Our feelings have an intelligence of their own, and oftentimes, are the
truest part of our authentic self."

Recognizing the magnitude of our socialization may be overwhelmingly frustrating. It may seem too horrible to believe, too generalized to overcome and too complicated to resolve. We must fight against the fear of feeling overwhelmed. Because we have suppressed and denied so much for so long, when feelings finally surface, there is a flood of dictating emotions that we fear will overtake us. Our feelings, however, are the most honest part of our existence. When we experience our own feelings and witness the feelings of other women, resocialization is happening.

We may feel frustrated as we realize the extent of socialization, but this frustration can be comforted when we understand that our sisters in China, Africa, Russia and countless places around the globe suffer as well. We can't personally right the wrongs of the world, but be clear about this: You are the world.

Global awareness, however, is the avenue toward developing a connection with womankind. Gradually, global empathy and unity will become a permanent part of our awareness. By connecting to womankind, we foster a sense of community among women. It makes other women, many who we do not know personally, known to us.

The first step is to break our long silence and the place to begin is with one another. By giving voice to our frustration, we will build courage. It is important to use our connection with womankind as a source of comfort and to extend that connection to the women within our community. Be willing to receive, as well as give, comfort. Open yourself up to both the possibility and understanding of other women as contributors of your growth.

Women have intense feelings about love. We believe in the power of and have been confused by love, often believing that in order to love properly we have to totally surrender ourselves. We have dedicated our lives to our parents, families and friends and even to our employers. We are well practiced in the art of empathy, meaning the ability to understand and identify with another's feelings. We are expected to hone that skill to perfection. When do we understand and identify our own feelings? Empathy does not include internalizing responsibility for the problems of others or feeling an urgency to find a solution. Empathy must include believing that everyone can find their way to peace. Are we capable of self-empathy?

At this stage in our lives, we must begin to develop self-empathy. By understanding the powerful impact of our culture to limit the development of a true self, we can begin to feel the reality of our own loss. As we move from one stage to another, we will become moved by our emotions. Eventually, we will come to realize that our dedication to others has often been abused; caused us pain. To face the realization honestly, takes courage. We may want to turn away from the admission of self-destructive love, but we cannot because that admission is part of learning healthier ways to love.

Our Western culture has made feeling a shameful behavior. We are told as children not to cry, not to question, not to be angry. "Get over it!" has become the motto of adjustment. Statements like this can generate shame, and shame keeps us silent. Be clear that what we withhold can make us sick and depressed. Getting over anything must include feeling it for as long as we need, for as long as it takes us to regain our personal sense of joy. Our feelings have an intelligence of their own and oftentimes are the truest part of our authentic self. To disregard them is to kill the wonder of our humanness. Both men and women suffer from the shame of feeling.

Your body needs to feel, even when we refuse to acknowledge those feelings. You cannot allow your intellect to lead your emotions into a silent, shameful captivity. Use all your powers to fight this unhealthy trend that separates feeling and thinking. They need not be mutually exclusive. We can feel and think at the same time, which only makes us fully present at any moment. We need to think about our feelings, but not deny them. Thinking about our feelings is different than feeling them. When we feel, we express the deepest part of who we are. Feeling requires trust and a willingness to let go of the prohibitions to be vulnerable. This personal surrender is often referred to as an inner-child experience, because like a child, our emotions pull away the mask of our lost adult self.

A subtle form of gender discrimination is labeling women as emotional and then expanding that idea with the belief that emotions are a sign of weakness or out-of-control behavior. It is the way our culture disowns the powerful wisdom women bring to our environment. In actuality, our ability to feel, our intuition and our sensitivity to the world around us is a gift to be cherished and respected. Our goal is to respect and trust our feelings.

Whatever our feelings, we must let ourselves feel them because they are ours. We can't build a castle over quicksand. If we are to build something strong in our lives, we must first put down a solid foundation. Suppressed feelings could sabotage our lives if they are unacknowledged and we simply build over them. How do we become comfortable with our emotions?

First, we learn to name them, understand and talk about them with other women. By listening to other women share their anger and confusion we develop a compassion for the child we were and the woman we are. Our own experiences will be validated by listening to our sisters. This listening helps us break down the wall of silence, isolation and self-denial that socialization expects us to maintain. Too many women think their feelings are sick, unhealthy or even crazy. It is only through sharing with other women that we discover how similar we are; that our thoughts and feelings are not at all alien.

Waking up emotionally at this stage may cause us a tremendous amount of conflict because we are now asked to pay attention to ourselves, when it is still our habit to focus on the needs of others. As we move through the various steps, these critical stages in our journey, talking about what we are experiencing is essential. As we talk about our life, and are listened to, our own voice gradually emerges. The acknowledgment of our pain opens the door to healing.

We must realize, however, that another person is unable to feel our personal pain as we have. They may say, "I know," but they really can't know our pain because our pain is part of our journey. The pain of others can touch the pool of repressed sadness that lies dormant with us. Their listening can awaken our unclaimed self. It is important not to interpret another woman's sharing, implicitly or explicitly, in order to save her from her pain. This does not mean we don't support each other. We both support and encourage each other simply by listening. To be the architect for our own life is an invitation to live completely.

We must learn new words to describe how we feel. How often in the past did we substitute acceptable ways of speech: "I'm annoyed," "That bothers me," or "I wish you wouldn't," when we really wanted to say, "I'm angry," "What you're doing is unacceptable to me," "I don't want to." We will talk more about how we feel and less about what we think. Our feelings may be judged, but as long as we are the jury, we can exonerate ourselves from silence.

Our feelings simply are, and must be, acknowledged directly. Think of them as belonging to our new Self, our true Self. Freedom comes from accepting and expressing our feelings.

Let's begin speaking out about our emotional captivity. "Captives no more" must be our determination. Slowly and deliberately we weaken the force of shame and guilt with direct communication that will not be silenced. Direct language is the language of power. Direct language does not depend on another person to know our mind. Only by revealing what is on our mind can we enjoy the emotional freedom we were born to have. Silence will yield to self revelation and self discovery. Our new voice will generate a joyful relief from emotional repression.

When we examine our lives and our history, standing firmly in the foreground of those responsible for our socialization is our mother. She brought us the message of womanhood, the same message that was given to her. She taught us what would be expected of us as women. It was the only message she knew. She didn't know that women can, and must, change the message.

Our mother was the first woman we watched and listened to as we journeyed to womanhood. We listened to her voice, one that may have echoed her lost-self, before we could listen to our own. A voice yearning to be helped filled with criticism, anger, depression and frustration. When we recognize our mother's role in our socialization, we may become angry with her for allowing it to happen; anger often conflicted with guilt for having those feelings. Remember that in order for resocialization to happen, feelings must be acknowledged.

And, to finally emerge from the shadow of our good woman role, we have to silence our mother's voice so we can find our own. This is not to deny her, but to understand her life in its political and personal context. As we do this, we will no longer feel sadness or grow to develop feelings that caused such resentment toward the first woman in our life. This empathetic process of letting go is done lovingly and clears the way for our real Self.

Our mothers struggled with a discontent they didn't understand. Every time you feel resentment, remember that you have a golden opportunity to rewrite the script of womankind by coming alive yourself, finally honoring the woman within, the woman you were destined to become before being bombarded with stereotypes and cultural expectations. As we grow to understand our mothers as women, we will gradually feel a lessening of sadness, misunderstanding and resentment.

It is your courageous self that enables you to make the changes your mother could not envision. It is this courageous self that even dares to scrutinize the aspects of life that your mother dared not challenge, instead learning to accept things as they appeared to be, choosing to simply live a life dominated by settling. This courageous self unlocks your capacity to question, to explore, to seek to know and embrace your true identity. When we speak out for change, we are stepping out of the prescribed role of silence. Others may judge us harshly because they have profited from our silence or they clearly recognized our power and worked tirelessly to extinguish it fearing the tremendous impact it could have, uncomfortable with how inadequate it might make them feel. These are the people who judge us harshly because they may refuse to believe that womanhood includes personhood and that silence should not dominate a woman's persona.

In a letter published in Ms. Magazine, a woman, obviously on this type of journey, wrote: "I am making major changes in my life. I am working very hard to be as good to myself as I am to the other members of my family. Today though, when I asked my husband to pick up his dirty clothes from the floor, he asked me, "Why? You've always picked them up!" What should I have answered? How can I explain that I won't do this anymore?"

The answer was really good: "The next time he asks that question, tell him, "That was yesterday!"

How We Are With Others

*"It is up to us to take responsibility for our lives and our own right to equality...
and as we do, the walls of gendering will come tumbling down."*

Gendering is a progressive and systematic process. As we grow from girl to woman, the love-starved world sees us as mother. Our lives begin to be shaped by the world's need for love, which motherhood represents. Inside this illusion of motherhood, we are expected to be an endless source of love, concern and loyalty. We come to know the power of womanhood through the insatiable need of others. They motivate and consume us. Even when others are unwilling to do for themselves, we step in to fill the gap. We know our love makes others prosper and feel victorious. What we may fail to see is that our intervention stunts the other person's process of maturing.

There are many of groups like ALANON and Co-Dependents Anonymous, etc., attended by women who've come to realize that by trying again and again to fix their husbands or lovers, they were, in fact, enabling them. The realization of enablement behavior is vastly different from stopping it. Many women enable their partners because they are unable to use their personal power to set healthy boundaries. They over identify with their partner's problems as if it was their own. This over identification absorbs them like a sponge absorbs water. This is a good time to remember that we come to relationships with an unhealthy willingness to dedicate ourselves to our loved ones without reservations.

As little girls, we are given toys that prime us for the role of caregiver: dolls, irons, cups, saucers and play kitchens, all to simulate our role as caregivers. When our play becomes real, we struggle to protect our own identity because the way we play indicates how we will live. This socialization of our play is destructive.

Although our personal identity is ever-changing, the journey of evolution is halted when our personal power is challenged by someone we love. Our devotion to be relational can too often become sacrificial. Without intention, we become partners in a dysfunctional relationship and struggle to survive. Neither society nor women themselves have any understanding of the price we pay to fulfill the role of mother. We ignore the vague restlessness kept dormant deep within our souls. We become fragmented and exhausted as the world feeds on the breast of our motherhood. Now is the time for us to understand that it is not our mission to absorb the dissatisfactions of a world starved for love. It is time for us to recognize our own need to be loved.

If we are to be free, what is vague must become clear and what is clear must be understood. Caring and loving are beautiful qualities we need to cherish. However, we need to clarify the nature of giving and receiving. Giving has a reciprocal effect; in giving to others, we receive. We receive by seeing the demonstration of our power in the other person. We receive by seeing the impact that our love and caring has on the other person. As we receive, our capacity to give is expanded. A relationship based on one-sided giving will be unbalanced. It is the lack of reciprocity that often controls our relationships and keeps the imbalance in place. This imbalance is supported by our culture, which teaches that only women can give properly. In living up to that belief, our giving consumes us and we lose track of our worthiness to be loved.

By listening to other women, we come to understand that we share pain with all women. Their voices help shatter our wall of loneliness, denial and self-doubt. As we listen to women express how their dreams were crushed, their hearts broken, feelings denied, we feel angry. We are angry for them and angry for ourselves. Anger is not something to avoid. Anger demands that we pay attention to ourselves and it should propel us into action.

As we overcome our inclination to minimize or trivialize the tragic effects of socialization in our lives, we can feel both anger and grief. Why? In those moments, we poignantly come to recognize that our selfhood has been compromised and devalued. We grieve because a force outside ourselves had so much power over us. True realization of loss will forcefully send us to our feelings. We may feel shame when anger and pain drive us out of hiding, but resist the temptation to hide because shame has no place in our recovery. We cannot grow without honest reactions. We have been taught that good girls don't get mad. Counteract that message by remembering that healthy girls must get angry.

Anger calls us to the power of self-determination and at times is an essential component of maintaining our dignity. It gives us the power to set healthy boundaries, to be free. Through this honesty, we validate and learn from each other's anger. Oftentimes women are silenced and relieved to witness the anger of another woman. It is the changes born of anger that tell us how to carve out a clear and conscious self and a safe world for women.

Our mothers, grandmothers and all other significant female role models taught us the value of caring. But caring, as they understood it, did not allow for the accomplishment of their own dreams. We watched their intelligence used only vicariously through the men in their lives, as they tirelessly addressed needs of others, often relegating their own needs to positions of unimportance. We have watched them become lost to their own talents, grow angry and depressed because they were lost and didn't know why life was so hard for them.

As modern women, we have gone to great lengths attempting to reconcile our conflict with our mother's message. As the daughter, we may have had uneasy feelings as we witnessed our mother's unhappiness—a prescription for our own lives. A part of us wanted to disassociate from her, thinking that it would save us from her fate. We didn't want to mirror her subservience, but at the same time, we loved her for what she gave us. We want to honor our mothers by replicating their lives, but in doing this, we may be dishonoring ourselves.

Honor your mother by understanding her life. Honor yourself by thinking beyond her limitations. Honor your mother by moving away from limitations that dominated her life. If you can live this life courageously, your mother may actually learn from your modeling new behaviors. Could we please our mothers and ourselves? Could we do it all? We tried.

Resocialization will come to mean doing what we are comfortable doing, recognizing when we are tired, frustrated, when too much is not healthy for anyone, especially us. Even when our fatigue is labeled as inadequacy we must pay attention to ourselves. We can no longer live as though our energies are boundless.

Because we focus on giving to others and spend inordinate amounts of energy figuring out how they feel, we expect others to be as sensitive to us, knowing how we feel and what we want. We are given the unrealistic expectation of being able to know what others need. We take this cultural assignment seriously because we feel that we must earn our worth. We work hard at it. In some cases, it becomes a continuation of our childhood omni-potence. Remember when you were a child, you thought you could do anything and everything was your responsibility? Even when you didn't understand a problem, you tried hard to figure out how to solve it, and believed you could. This addiction to feeling responsible for others, for creating rightness in their lives is a complete distortion of our relational-self. Relating to others is never supposed to mean the negation of anyone's personal search or the oppression of our own. A relationship, by its very nature, should be expansive for everyone. If we believe this basic philosophical position is true, then we will work to make it happen day by day, moment by moment.

Expecting others to know our feelings may be our escape from self. We avoid speaking on our own behalf because we're afraid to be assertive, to be judged harshly, to be vulnerable or rejected. These fears are a consequence of socialization. Remind yourself over and over again: it is your privilege to be who you are. The world will be richer because you have become a person who has blended the giftedness of your child with the wisdom of your adult. No one is like you. So resist the encroachment of feeling oppressed by love. Let yourself love – speak out in a loud, clear voice wherever you can. Every time you do this, you will be awakened.

We connect in our sharing and listening. Feelings, long-forgotten, will reawaken in us a creative destiny. When we truly listen to another woman and witness her pain, we are also witnessing her rebirth. We don't need to take away her pain because it is part of her recovery. We don't need to offer excuses, solutions or explanations as a way of fixing her. We need only believe she has the power to change and the wisdom to learn from her own life experience. Touching, interrupting, questioning and advising her are a distraction from her message. Remember, comfort is given by our very presence. The power of presence is immense. Our physical presence and emotional availability are powerful agents for healing. Respect her by showing her that this time an outside influence will not dictate the direction of her life.

Our respectful communication with each other may be our first experience of true equality, which can become our new destiny. But the creation of equality, a new experience for us, is difficult because inequality has become a way of life. We must want it, look for it and create it in the circumstances of our lives. We can create equality in relationships only when we are actively involved in defining the balance of relational power with another person. Balance means the relationship itself is a representation of you and another. Your voice is essential in that purpose. Sometimes we must struggle bitterly to find equality in relationships. As we struggle to find a relational truth, we are born and equality is realized. What a great victory for the individuals involved, and what a powerful testimony to the relationship they share.

We come to believe that social equality is not only possible, but imperative. Change begins when we join our voices with other women who are also reexamining their lives and critically examining the makeup of our culture. The first step toward that goal is to realize that the old way of sexism has not worked for women or men. The next is to realize that as women, it is up to us to take responsibility for our own lives and our own right to equality.

"And as we do, the walls of gendering will fade."

Stepping out of our prescribed, traditional role can cause conflict in our interpersonal relationships. At this stage, it may only be our recovering sisters who appreciate the journey we have begun. The people closest to us, the ones we love the most, may feel the most threatened. Be forewarned and not discouraged. They may not be able to applaud our growth because they are stuck in their own social perception of what we ought to be. Their challenge will become the test of your commitment. Other people's fear of change cannot hold us back from our journey. Eventually, they will learn that as we reclaim our personhood we will increase our capacity to love them. By setting our own healthy boundaries in the relationship, we will be modeling to them how to set their own. Equality must be everyone's right and everyone's responsibility. It is a quest that requires vigilance, introspection and love. It requires that we respect ourselves, so that we command respect from others. This collective empowerment not only can, but will, change the world!

JOURNALING

1. Review your responses to the Self-survey as they indicate a part of your life that you may be neglecting. In what category did you indicate the most self-neglect? What is it about that particular aspect of your life that makes you feel compromised? Take each item that indicated a problem and write a paragraph defining your internal messages. For example, if you answered "No" to "Do you feel beautiful most of the time?" you might say, "I worry about my weight and the wrinkles on my face" or "I worry about how attractive I am to others." It is your internalized messages that are keeping you from knowing how beautiful you are. Unfortunately, our culture defines beauty in a very superficial manner. Use this procedure to journal about each of your compromised thoughts in all of the categories. **WRITE!**

2. Expectations from others can dominate our lives because we learn early on that those expectations are supported by cultural beliefs. Oftentimes our internal messages are different than our behaviors. This separateness between our internal life and our external behaviors indicates a splitting of ourselves; like dancing a waltz when you're feeling jazz inside. An example from the Self-survey might be: "Are you doing more work for the same pay?" Your response is "Yes." Deep down inside, how do you feel about this problem? Are you angry but feel ashamed to ask for an adjustment in your wages because of the additional responsibility? Women often feel guilty asking for money. Ask yourself why. Take an item from the Self-survey and write about your splitting. One example that is clear can put you in touch with a huge pattern of splitting that is taking away your authentic life. **WRITE!**

3. List four parental figures who acted as role models throughout your childhood. After each of their names, note their expectations of you. Some of their expectations may have helped you and others may have echoed cultural demands that grew to be uncomfortable as you matured; developed self-awareness. Which messages continue to influence your behavior, beliefs and your attitude toward yourself? These are the messages that still have mastery of your identity. Which of these expectations must be altered or disregarded? **WRITE!**

4. When it touches our lives, the reality of cultural discrimination becomes poignant. It is then that what is political becomes personal. Have you ever been unjustly treated at work, by the legal system, doctors, the police, or in your church just because you are a woman? Select one specific experience and write about it. How did you handle the problem? Were you aware of what was happening to you? How did it change you and your life? WRITE!

REFLECTIVE CINEMA

Movies that reinforce the themes of this stage recommended for viewing:

- Real Women Have Curves
- Revolutionary Road
- Being Julia
- The King of Masks (sub-titled)

STEPPING OUT

- Ask a friend out to lunch to talk about your mother's life. You both bring a picture of your mothers.
- Select a movie from the suggested list. Invite four friends to view the movie and discuss its messages and dominant themes.
- Admit to your spouse or partner how angry you've been with something they do repeatedly without any knowledge of how much it angers you. Be specific.
- Take a fifteen-minute nap when you get home from work. Note your reaction after reading this suggestion.

Story of a Married Woman

Part of Nina's weekly routine was to spend one afternoon with her friend Sue. Sue wanted to spend the entire day with her, to have a "girl's day," but Nina resisted such an excessive demand on her time. Even the three hours they spent together challenged her sense of commitment to her family.

Sue gently pointed out to Nina that she was making marriage the entire purpose of her life. Nina didn't see her total dedication to her family as a failure and resented Sue's interpretation. She admitted feeling overwhelmed at times, but believed that was the price of love.

They usually met at the community park. As they took a quick walk around the two-mile course, they shared details about their lives. But Sue did much more of the talking, she chatted openly about her relationship with her husband, Erin. According to Sue, Erin was a good cook and good lover; he actually prepared most of the family meals. She talked about every aspect of their relationship without reservation or shame. Nina felt that Sue's openness was close to sacrilegious and at times, shocking.

She could never match Sue's stories or her bold honesty so she listened passively offering neither insight nor reflection. Silence became her protective cloak, but it was not a peaceful silence. Nina often felt defensive with Sue, even when she knew it was not necessary. What was she defending, she wondered? Was she defending her family, her marriage or her life?

Nina knew that Sue could not understand the fact that she accepted her life as it was. She did not need to examine it or understand it. She thought of it as natural and normal. The difference in their viewpoints about marriage made Nina unwilling to be closer to Sue. She circumvented any conflict with complacent agreements and common clichés that dismissed any real intimacy, but was always polite.

Since Sue's lack of comprehension for what Nina held sacred made Nina unwilling to expand their friendship, she wondered why she was devoted to these weekly rendezvous. Perhaps on some level she didn't understand; she needed the anger and the discomfort it generated. Maybe she needed this woman to remind her that there might be a small morsel of life left that had not been consumed by her marriage. Maybe there was a hint that somewhere, there was another door.

On this particular day, as they walked around the park, Sue invited Nina to attend a women's support group. At first, the idea was unthinkable. For starters, it was to be an evening meeting, which represented time spent away from her family. Whatever privacy she had was scheduled during the day, a time when everyone was busy and, she felt, her privacy would not deprive them of her attention. How could she get everything done in time to leave? What would she tell Joe? Would he think of her as one of those women libbers? Wouldn't he assume this was a betrayal; a dissatisfaction on her part with him, the marriage or the family? He would certainly think this meeting was in direct opposition to their family cohesiveness and their marital relationship.

Emotionally torn as she tried to decide what to do, Nina felt panic and shame about her inability to accept Sue's invitation. Although she knew it would be refreshing to have an evening to herself, she felt guilty. She was interested in the group's purpose, but she didn't want to be identified as a feminist. The new thinking this group represented might challenge the order of her life, threatening Joe's supremacy.

She never had trouble caring for her household and family while Joe occasionally traveled for business or when he and his friends spent one weekend a month fishing and camping. She never questioned the inequality of their free time because she was a woman and her life belonged to her family. Joe worked hard and deserved the free time. Nina's justifications were indisputable: the children needed her and she knew how to care for them; she knew what they liked to eat; what to do if they were sick. She knew their friends and their friends' parents. Her children relied on her for their well-being and happiness. Her focus on caring for them flowed freely from her generous heart without reservation.

But Sue wouldn't let up. She called her every day to discuss the support group. Nina couldn't believe how pushy Sue was being, constantly explaining all the reasons why the group would be good for Nina.

What surprised Nina was not Sue's behavior, but her own. Why was it so difficult to make this decision? Finally, after weeks of Sue's badgering, she accepted the invitation. She told herself she'd attend one meeting. That was probably all she'd need to dismiss the idea of belonging to a community of women. And besides, what was she supposed to do there? Learn to talk the way Sue did? Nina found it interesting that she was both frightened and excited.

Joe wasn't happy about Nina leaving the house at 6:30 on a Thursday night. The kids weren't bathed, the dishes weren't put away, but he accepted the responsibility for this one night. For him, "household stuff and kids" were too much after a long work-day. Nina openly acknowledged that it was a disruption of their agreement, leaving her to feel torn between Joe's non-supportive attitude and Sue's demands. Who did her life belong to, anyway? How could going to a meeting cause such internal consternation? Obviously the meeting had a symbolic meaning in her life that she had not figured out yet.

Joe never liked Sue. He felt that she was an unfit mother and wife. Her kids, he thought, riding around the neighborhood on their bikes after school and weekends without supervision, were undisciplined. They always needed haircuts and their clothes never seemed to match. She knew Joe was right, but Nina loved her children. They were creative, spontaneous and friendly. Joe felt that Susan's husband, Erin, was pussy whipped. What successful husband had time to shop for groceries and cook? Joe was sure that Sue hadn't learned to cook because she didn't want the responsibility. The couples occasionally socialized together, but Joe's resistance was too much for Nina to manage, so she rejected most of Sue's invitations.

Sue assured Nina she didn't have to join the group. It wouldn't cost her money and she wouldn't have to speak. Sue's reassurances left Nina wondering what the benefits could possibly be if she was not required to actively participate. As she walked into the meeting, she was greeted by other women who seemed to understand her discomfort. She was relieved to learn that there were other women there for the first time. She wondered if they too came with the idea that this would be their first and last meeting. Did they have to struggle with relationships and time to get here? How did they justify an evening just for themselves? Being there, Nina felt, was self-indulgent.

A candle was lit and the statement of purpose was read. Nina listened to the silence as she watched the flicker of the candlelight. Sitting there, a strange sense of peace came over her that she hadn't felt in a long time. Her things-to-do list crowded her consciousness liked flood waters, something she always accepted as a positive indication of her dedication to purpose, love of her family and the fact that she was so needed and so necessary in their lives. It was a life that seemed imprinted in her very soul, and yet, a part of her yearned for more.

As she listened to other women talk about their lives, she began to feel less lonely. She didn't share her own story because she felt it would be boring. She looked across at Sue, who was having a good time. Nina realized that Sue shared without self-censorship. She seemed free in a way that was enviable, but foreign. Nina felt a new

*curiosity about Sue and a new respect. Now Sue's life was a little more understandable;
she came here to refresh her spirit and become a student of her own life.*

*There lived somewhere deep inside of Nina, the young and free inner woman who she
had long abandoned. For the first time in years, Nina had a glimpse of her forgotten self.
She had a revelation: it was Sue who saw her inner self and the possibilities that
surrounded her. Sue was the only one in her life who offered affirmation that there was
more to Nina than the life she was living. It was Sue's deeper wisdom about Nina's life
that made her patient, persistent and a committed friend even when Nina rejected her
invitation for intimacy. Every time they met, she expected that Sue would not call again.
Part of her was relieved, and another part of her did not want to let go, as if she was
waiting for life in some mysterious way.*

*The two hours passed rapidly. The meeting was drawing to a close and everyone
was holding hands. Someone was saying something about dedicating the energy they'd
collectively generated into the world of womankind. Womankind? That was a strange
word. Could these women possibly understand what she was feeling? Did they all suffer
in the way that Nina was suffering: silently, privately, personally, deeply and emotionally?*

*She never really thought about the importance of other women. She always kept
apart from most other people. When she did think about other women or women in
general, she assumed that most were equally as dedicated and busy with their
relationships and families.*

*On the drive home, Nina was quiet. Her evaluation of the evening was limited by her
inability to continue attending. She was sure that some women, maybe most women
could profit from the monthly get-togethers, but she was living in the real world. How
could she change what seemed to be preordained by generations before her? Isn't the way
she was living, the way women were supposed to live? Did she have the right to want
more? Did anyone have that right? The idea of making life changes seemed inconceivable
and exhausting. She thanked Sue and walked into the quietness of her home where she
knew how her life would be; a place where she knew and understood the rules.*

*As she crawled into bed, Joe turned over and folded his body into hers. She felt his
quiet dependence and desperate possession of her life.*

Story of a Lesbian Woman

"WELL INTO THE NIGHT, THEA'S EXCITEMENT KEPT HER IN A STATE
OF ALERT, EXCITEMENT, FEAR AND WONDERMENT."

Adding to the confusion she was experiencing with her parents was Thea's own confusion about herself. She found herself behaving differently around her friend Amy. Amy was different than Thea. She was very comfortable with being a lady even though she was athletic and wore torn jeans. She seemed to get away with more than Thea. Why was she more convincing? Convincing of what?

Although Thea and Amy had been friends since fourth grade, something was changing between them. Thea was acting differently around Amy, almost flirting. She found herself physically attracted to Amy. "Was this a phase, too?" she wondered. They found more occasions to touch one another and hugged longer when saying good-bye. Thea found herself fantasizing about Amy. She created stories that were romantic and passionate in which she was always the heroine of love and Amy was her conquest.

Thea's relationship with Adam continued, but began to feel different. Adam was totally frustrated about their sexual life, as Thea's resistance to intercourse was not negotiable. "I'll wear condoms," he offered after she told him about how threatening her parents were about the possibility of pregnancy.

"It is impossible," she protested. "I am supposed to be as close to the Virgin Mary as possible." As far as Thea was concerned, the only likeness she could come up with was an intact hymen, whatever that meant. So that was the way it had to be.

During their senior year, Amy and Thea were on the All-Star High School Basketball team that traveled to compete with other regional teams. They were proud of their status. One Saturday night after winning the State Finals was a night Thea will never forget.

All of the team members partied at a nearby pizzeria that had a live band. The girls on the team danced with each other to keep them safe and because their boyfriends were not around. Thea took every opportunity to monopolize Amy's time. They moved as rhythmically as they had played that afternoon. They looked at each other during the dances, forgetting they were both girls.

A longing that was undeniable developed between them. Thea didn't understand the intensity of her emotions, but dove in anyway. "What is Amy feeling?" she wondered. Luckily, they were rooming together that night in a very ordinary motel. After the door was locked, Thea suddenly felt uncomfortable with the tension between them. "How will the sexual tension be resolved?" she wondered. "Should it be satisfied?" Being romantic with Amy would be as far away from the Virgin Mary as any girl could get, even with an intact hymen!

They quickly undressed, brushed their teeth and crashed into bed. Although Thea had seen Amy naked many times in the shower room at school, on this night, she had a new attraction to every part of her body. It was as if she was seeing a woman's body for the first time. "Is it shameful to be so excited?" she wondered. Excitement overruled every need to think!

They both laid motionless beneath the covers waiting for some intervention to bring them together in love. After Amy turned off the light, the darkness magnified their passions and immediately sent out its magical power to eradicate distractions. Their need to touch was too compelling to deny. With an unrecognized boldness, Thea silently turned to her side and cautiously slid her arms over Amy's body. She wanted to ask, but how could she? Silence ruled the moment and seemed to be a more effective mediator than words she didn't know. As she slid her body on top of Amy's, she was certain that she was breaking through a barrier that could change her life forever.

Amy responded immediately. They kissed softly, then passionately, then feverishly. They touched each other's breasts. Thea sucked as a child. They never stayed in one position very long. The excitement of discovering a body like their own mesmerized them with a mutual heightened awareness. They were both wet with passion. Thea wanted to talk, but Amy slid her hand over her mouth. Thea's fingers gently entered Amy as they both groaned in orgasmic rhythm.

Suddenly, without warning, Amy pulled away. "We shouldn't continue. We can't continue," she said. Thea was afraid to ask why. She was grateful for what they had shared and knew that it meant something profound. She was not afraid – at least not yet. Well into the night, the excitement of feeling complete kept her in a state of wonderment, excitement and fear. After hours of tossing from side to side, they slept peacefully, not knowing what the morning would mean to each of them and their long friendship.

Story of a Black Woman

"MY MOTHER SPOKE TO ME CONSTANTLY ABOUT BEING FREE AND, IN THE
SAME BREATH, REMINDED ME THAT I WAS A BLACK WOMAN."

Tashi's story was never recorded. Most slaves were forbidden to read and write, so spoken-word and songs carry their truths from one generation to the next. Historically, motherhood has been an important role for black women. From precolonial Africa, where children were highly prized, the roles of childbearing and child rearing were taken seriously and valued.

My mother, Reta, was a descendent of Tashi's daughter, Medora. Medora was born into slavery, but spent most of her life in the free world of the white men. Like her mother, Medora took pride in the legacy of culture, strength and survival. She dreamed of a different life for her children as she taught them to cope with the hardship of discrimination.

My mother spoke to me constantly about being free, and in the same breath, reminded me that I was a black woman. I thought if I kept my life close to the black community, I would be safe and unchallenged. In day care, all of my playmates, like me, were black children. But, when I entered kindergarten in an integrated school, I faced a different world. I was made aware of differences. Were we supposed to stay in separate worlds because of the color of our skin?

My mother, who always worked hard, cleaned the homes of two families and cared for their children when needed. She worked long hours outside of our home, and my sister and I missed her. As far back as I can remember kin--women who are not biological mothers but play a mothering role in raising black children--cared for us in my mother's absence. In our culture, children are seen as part of and belonging to a communal network that extends beyond their natural parents. That community is always made up of women who are sensitive to the needs of their sisters.

My parents did not spend many years together. When I was four years old, my father left my mother unexpectedly. One day, my mother came home after work and found a fifty-dollar bill on the table with a note that read: "Good-bye. Hope this helps." The family problems were holding him back from becoming successful. He blamed my mother for being too demanding. I can still remember how sad my mother was. She was scared and confused by my father's unexpected abandonment. I didn't understand that he wasn't coming back. I thought he just needed a vacation from us.

My grandmother came to live with us right away. Her presence seemed to comfort my mother. My grandmother did not have to be asked to help; she simply knew my mother's needs. She gave up her job and rented her home to come and live with us. I knew my grandmother had to give up a lot of her life to save our lives and help my mother. Was the sacrifice making her as angry as my daddy? I worried about her becoming fed up with us and, like my daddy, leaving. Every day when I got home from school I looked to see if there was a note on the kitchen table from my grandmother. The only way I could help was to be good. I worked hard to anticipate the needs of both my mother and grandmother. I listened to their instructions. I tried to be as grown up as I knew how to be. At first, they were excited that I could do adult things. Soon excitement yielded to expectations. It was as though I was on a treadmill that kept going faster and faster without my permission. I was proud that I could keep the pace, but the pace was consuming me. Reconciling child with adult became as confusing as reconciling black and white. I must have done a good job, because my mother and grandmother bragged to everyone about how good I was. That is how I learned that being good meant doing good. Even when I didn't want to.

Story of a Woman ... Now Old

"ALL POSSIBILITIES FOR A CHILDHOOD VANISHED FOREVER ONE
AFTERNOON WHEN I WALKED INTO THE KITCHEN AND FOUND MY
MOTHER IN A POOL OF BLOOD."

It was clear that my father considered marriage a rite of ownership of his wife and the female children she bore. His attitude was apparent by his sexual demands of my mother; demands that left her constantly pregnant. Her young body had no time to recover after deliveries, so each pregnancy resulted in dreadful, prolonged physical exhaustion. Her children loved her, but we could not protect her from the burden of being my father's wife. My love for her motivated me to help her in whatever way I could. As time passed, I became consumed by the responsibilities that flooded my mother's life. At first, I wasn't aware of my lost childhood. I was eager to help my mother, brothers and sisters in whatever way I could. The closeness to my mother messaged my loss.

In this role I learned how to get my siblings ready for school. I knew the location of their clothes and shoes. I was aware of their food requirements and when they wanted attention. I comforted them when they had a problem or other unmet needs. I even knew how to do laundry and cook; I became highly functional because I needed to be. My competence was an outgrowth of giving life. Everyone relied on it, including my mother in her loving, good-natured way; my father, in his critical way and my siblings in their desperate childhood needs.

Our apartment was probably less than one thousand square feet. The kitchen was our family's hub. The kids were crammed into two bedrooms that were wall-to-wall beds. The boys were in one room and the girls in another. Two kids had to sleep in one bed. The entire family shared one bathroom. There was no place in our apartment to relax; we were there to eat or sleep. Our closeness blossomed around the kitchen table during and after meals.

By age thirteen, there was no more time to acknowledge or relish the childhood left in my life. In early June, all possibilities for a childhood vanished forever one morning before I left for school. My mother told me she was not feeling well. I stayed behind to care for her and my younger sisters Marion and Ellen. After making the beds, I walked into the kitchen to join my mother who was trying desperately to wash the dishes. I found her standing at the kitchen sink with a pool of blood heart her feet. I panicked, and followed her instructions to call my aunts. My aunt Rose moved swiftly, telling me to take my sisters and leave the house. "This is nothing for you to see," she dictated.

Not knowing exactly what was happening and full of fear for my mother, I took Marion and Ellen for a walk. We saw my Aunt Rose, my father and Uncle Moses driving past us taking my mother to Memorial Hospital. At the time, I felt assured that they would take good care of her.

At thirty-two years old, my mother was pregnant with her eleventh child. That morning she was taken to the hospital. I remember feeling a strange sense of separation when they told me she would be staying. How could I help her if she was away from me? This deep feeling of helplessness kept me awake the entire night. I didn't know then that she would never return.

For one week, I visited with my mother every day with my baby sister, Marion. My father allowed me this freedom because on some level he appreciated the bonding between my mother and me. While I visited with my mother, Marion played in the nursery. All of the nurses loved her. At first, my mother seemed okay. The nurse explained to me that the fetus died inside of her. My mother was bleeding constantly. Her doctor was out of town so they packed her and waited for his return. It all seemed logical. During that week of waiting, my mother's entire body was poisoned from the fetal remains. I had no idea that my mother was gravely ill and neither did she. My only indication of the seriousness of her condition was the odor that permeated her room. As the week progressed, the odor of her poisoned body became overwhelming. Each day I shared with my brothers and sisters information about my mother's condition. My brothers didn't visit her. In fact, they never saw her again.

On the morning of June 28, after breakfast, as I dressed Marion for our visit to the hospital, my Uncle Moses entered the apartment and told me that my mother had died. Died?! What did that mean? I'd heard of death, but never knew its finality or its permanence. No one expected my mother to die. I had packed a lunch of all her favorite foods: yogurt with barley, pita bread and cooked greens. What would I do with her lunch now? In disbelief, I placed her lunch in the refrigerator.

As I walked through the kitchen, I could feel her around me; I still saw her standing at the sink and felt her laughter in my heart. My brother Eddie was graduating from eighth grade that day. We had planned a celebration for him. Hearing the news, he refused to attend graduation. My brothers and sisters, all so young, gathered around me. I felt their fear and confusion without knowing how to fix it. I could not protect them from this loss. It was my loss too, but did I have the freedom to grieve because my brothers and sisters needed me? Attending to their pain gave me no time to think of my own. They were too young to know about death and I was too young to explain it. What did it mean to my sisters, never to learn about her life, never to listen to her wisdom, never to watch her grow old?

What would it mean to my youngest brothers Tony, Teddy, Albert and Tommy, who would feel the premature loss of their mother's love? How would it affect their relationship with women? A vacuum was created in our lives that would take a lifetime to understand, and perhaps, never heal. We all sat in the kitchen where our mother gathered us so many times and grieved her absence, a loss we felt, but didn't understand.

Because my mother was in the eighth month of pregnancy, her unborn child was buried quietly in the family plot. She was named Fanny. We did not attend the services of this child who was unknown and unloved; she joined my mother in the kingdom of saints.

The week after my mother's death was a maze of confusion of which I only remember short moments. We cleared out one bedroom where the casket was placed. Chairs lined the room for the steady stream of mourners that came through our small apartment. It is customary for her female family members to express their grief through wails and loud chants. I shuddered as I listened to their voices, which screamed out the sadness we all felt. Finally, my mother's body was brought up the stairs into the room her children prepared for her. As I approached her casket and knelt before her, I found it difficult to open my eyes. When I finally did, I saw my mother's beauty instantly, so still, so young, so far away from all of us. I knew my mother so well. We shared life together. How could I share her death? I couldn't avoid the deepest feelings of loss. The void I felt was so profound it took my breath away. At times, I feared it would consume me. Could I survive this? After three days of mourning, my mother was taken to the church and the cemetery. I don't remember a moment after I stepped away from her casket.

Now the energies of survival and nurturance emerged in me like a raging volcano because our family had to be saved. There were ten of us left. As members of the family decided which child they would take in, I protested, cried, and realized that my brothers and sisters had really become my children, even before my mother's death. I pledged my

57

life to keep us together. My father knew how capable I was because for years he had been demanding it of me.

After a few weeks it had been decided that I would be in charge of my orphaned siblings. I knew I could do it because their care had become my life. A life filled with self-sacrifice and love. My brothers and sisters looked to me like abandoned chicks. My mother's life vanished so swiftly, marking the final ending of childhood, but her presence kept us together because she had made us a family.

One morning while I was alone, I walked to the refrigerator to remove my mother's lunch. In sacred remembrance, I kissed it before throwing it away.

AVOIDING THE TRAP

─❦─

I will come to realize that I am more dynamic when I avoid the social entrapments imposed on my life.

How We Think

"If we are to be free, what is vague must become clear."

We've probably entered this program of self-discovery not knowing what to expect, with curiosity being the main motivator. Now we begin to realize the depth and breadth of our transformation. We can feel how deep and deliberate resocialization is when confronted. Our decision to find a new way to be is not easy, but it will create beautiful results. It is a spiritual ascent that leads us to the person we truly are.

Here in Stage Two, we will examine the main divisions in our lives. Our internal struggle is to maintain identity as we rush to satisfy the insatiable demands of others. We are pulled in so many directions without ever finding a safe place in any of them because none of them are our place. We are daughters who try to respond to our mother's beliefs and overcome her critical view of our lives. We are adolescents struggling with our bodies because they don't conform to unrealistic images of the perfect body. We are young women who enter relationships with men who expect us to emulate their mothers and win back for them the lost intimacy they were forced to surrender prematurely. We are mothers who bear the burden of the outcome of our children's lives. Our children pull from us a seemingly endless energy. And certainly in our mothering, we are critically watched and judged.

We are employees who work in jobs that usually don't value our intelligence, gifts or loyalty; we are expected to serve and be unassuming. As employed single mothers with unequal pay, we are expected to care for our children. As lesbians we are forced to hide our lovers because loving another woman is contrary to traditional family values and our mother's dreams for us. As lesbians, we often stifle the pain of being around other people and are unable to speak the simple, satisfying word: "we." As widows or divorcees we are lonely, untouched and often feel incomplete, even unnecessary in our identity. As we age

─

and become elderly, we often live alone. The children and the people we've loved forget our sacrifices. All of this sounds painful, and it is.

An essential part of resocialization is reclaiming the dignity and sacredness of feminine mythology. There was a time in human history when being a woman was seen as divine. There was a time when God was a woman; when our love and vision touched the hearts of every man, woman and child. She was called Goddess, Lady and Mother of All. She created life and nourished life. What She did was cherished. The diversity and richness of her images conveyed the feminine experience that had depth of meaning, awesome power and profound value. Sexuality, menstruation, birthing, mothering, menopause, aging and power were areas of her life that were valued by Goddess-worshipping people. To return to these ancient myths, to reconstruct their meanings in our own lives and in our own time is the purpose of resocialization. Creating a positive image of women in our own life is connected to feeling positive about ourselves.

What we learn to reject about ourselves is what was once holy. What we've learned to hide, because of shame and unworthiness was once celebrated openly. Blood was sacred in Goddess spirituality. What we learn to see as the curse was once seen as the blessing. Menopause was seen as the withholding of her magic blood for longer and longer periods and finally forever. Then her creativity was directed toward feminine wisdom, which was used to counsel and teach. Aging was not deterioration, but rather the accumulation of the femininity from deep within her. It was a time when she was truly one with herself.

Goddess spirituality dates back to at least 10,000 B.C.E. and continued for 7,500 years. Around 3,500 B.C.E., patriarchal invaders moved into Asia and Europe, bringing with them the ideals of dominance and unhealthy uses of power. Goddess spirituality struggled to survive for thousands of years, and still does today. We all know that struggle because it has existed in our individual lives. Most of us are not aware of female history or spirituality. Look for books and teachings to bring you back to a time when your life was a Vision.

Whatever is feminine is devalued in most cultures, and we must acknowledge this personal victimization in order to be free. We'll recall circumstances in our lives that made us feel helpless, hopeless and overwhelmed by self-incrimination. This discovery helps us reawaken the little girl we have always carried inside us, but abandoned years ago. Only we can change her karma–the experiences of her life. This will be our greatest accomplishment. By using our power to restructure our perception of life, our forgotten identity will be reclaimed. Our souls will become a unified whole and a safe haven for our spirit.

How We Feel

"Your feelings will call you to realness and authenticity. They will lead you to a part of yourself that you have forgotten."

Honoring our feelings is all about being comfortable with our humanness. Our determination to be guided by what we feel is important at this stage because feelings are, and were, our first source of truth. Inside each of us is an inner wisdom that combines our emotional awareness and our innate sense of who we really are.

As we mature, our desire to love and be loved became more important than connecting to our innate wisdom. Gradually, we neglect to ask ourselves how we feel about what we do and about the direction of our lives. We stopped asking ourselves about how we feel in our relationships. A terrible thing happens to us when we stop listening to our inner voice: we disappear emotionally; we begin to feel robotic and out of touch with our uniqueness. We silence our inner dialogue when it doesn't conform to external demands. We silence our inner dialogue when we don't take the time to listen and acknowledge the emotional messages our bodies are sending.

These acts of self-abandonment are so destructive because what we articulate about ourselves is crucial to our being-ness. While we may not remember a time or moment when we disappeared, what is important now is that we begin to recall the moments of self-dismissal. Without this internal dialogue, what we know never gets connected to our truth and gradually we become lost, confused and possibly depressed. Socialization lays the groundwork for depression, meaning to press down, in women. Depression, a fear of becoming who we are authentically, becomes a way of life. It happens when our life is unknown and not understood. We become depressed when we stop believing that we have choices. It is our life uncelebrated; it can manifest itself in so many ways, but essentially it is the unbecoming of life. It happens to the bride who belongs to someone before she could become a bride to herself. Resocialization is the conscious rejection of all the unhealthy cultural expectations that socialization creates.

Our feelings are unique. They don't have to be like the feelings of other people. They should be beyond judgment. Our feelings are neither good nor bad. They just are. More importantly, they can lead us to our truest wisdom. We don't need to control our feelings by denying, repressing or rationalizing them. We can only heal from emotional pain by honoring them. Feelings are not signs of ignorance or mental illness.

Feelings make our lives interesting. Our feelings have a history and a purpose in the here and now. Acknowledging them will lead us to a strong self-confidence because they connect our past and present, and can predict our future. Knowing the voice of our mind, the voice of our feelings, and the voice of our personal determination will set us free. By acknowledging our feelings, and more importantly, allowing ourselves to be guided by our emotional knowing, we will recover our lost self. By using our personal determination to bring our truth back to life, we've redirected the course of our future. As women, reconnecting with our emotional life satisfies a profound hunger to reclaim a self that is more important than cultural dictates because it values all of our experiences. It is our uniqueness that allows us to take our authentic places in this world, in this way; our lives have deep personal and political meaning.

Returning to the image of the Goddess will make us proud to be women. By doing so, we can be proud enough to acknowledge a female power that is not derived from a patriarchal vision of women. We can learn to be proud of our bodies and our feminine will. This heritage of pride has been unknown and lost to most of us. We have felt the loss without knowing its origin. Loving our feminine heritage is an essential link in our recovery because it connects us backward and forward to women across time and cultures. It brings to our culture positive images of our power, our bodies and our wills. To honor the Goddess in each of us is to imagine ourselves whole. Now is a time to release the self-rejection we have internalized. Hide no more. You are holy and worthy of celebration.

How We Are With Others

"Other people's fears of change cannot hold us back from our 'journey.' They will learn that as we reclaim our personhood, we will increase our capacity to love them."

$\mathcal{B}$ecause we are so relational, we are always connected to many people at the same time. The nature of our connections is intense because we believe in the power of relationships. This multiple-relationship stress contributes to our personal fragmentation if it is not resolved in a healthy way. Forgetting ourselves is too high a price to pay to stay in a relationship. When we approach relationships so eagerly that we lose sight of our own needs, we end up feeling drained, frustrated and depleted. Failed relationships for women become their greatest source of depression because socialization would have us believe that we are to blame. This is the time for us to begin examining ways we struggle to stay in relationships. As we struggle to survive, we tend to the needs of others without question. We are challenged now in the deepest way to incorporate our own life into the relationships we share. The challenges may sound like this: "Do I have the right to have something for myself separate from my family?" "Do I have the right to have a relationship outside my family that makes me feel good?" "Do I have the right to make myself happy?" "Do I have the right to be different or greater than my mother?" "Do I have the right to be angry with my father for not relating to me?" "Do I have the right to tell someone I love that they are hurting or disappointing me?"

We all know these questions, because they come from the doubting child within us.

The unhealed daughter is full of yearnings, hurt, sadness, rage and emotional hunger because her legitimate human needs were not satisfied in her relationship with her parents. The unhealed daughter has always wanted to feel honored, praised and special; first and at the center of someone's life. The unhealed daughter who never got what she needed from her mother or father may remain forever stuck in loneliness. She may spend her life dismissing her emotional needs by pretending they were of little importance and that she was unworthy. This vague sense of nobody-ness undermines even the strongest of women. The vagueness of self is epidemic in the women's community.

We bring our unhealed child to romantic relationships to heal ourselves. We pretend our lover will love us as completely as we love them. We idealize our romantic relationships as a place where our dreams will come true. The Bride in each of us longs to be someone's princess because we are seen as wonderful. We try to find our lost mother or our lost father in those we love and care about so intently. There are many positive ways to approach the unhealed child in ourselves. First, we must identify her needs and accept them as legitimate. This first act is painful because it points to actual losses that are part of our historic truth.

Emotional grieving clarifies our identity; expands our capacity to receive. This is best achieved in supportive relationships, identifying with the Women's Movement and becoming knowledgeable about the history of womankind. The unhealed child within you can help build a legacy of pride for other women and a model of political passion that will help create a different kind of world; a world in which women are respected, valued, known and where bonds between them are greatly emphasized and vital. Our unhealed child can be extremely creative if she has a will to live. We become the birth giver, the mother of our lives as we heal. Our mothering began with our birth or adoptive mother, but it must grow beyond her and into our own wholeness; one that envisions a new reality of personal love and compassion.

How we relate in our relationships will change as we appreciate who we are. Our relationships are a wonderful way to evaluate our recovery because nothing is truly learned until it is lived. As we alter our personal perceptions, our behavior will slowly adjust. Like a zooming camera lens, as we get closer to ourselves, our vision becomes clearer.

Mediating relationships is stressful, especially when our role in relationships changes considerably. Therefore, at this point in our program of recovery, learning to control stress is vital. It involves thinking about what we are doing and how we can best act on what is happening to us. Stress management is a form of self-love. It requires respect for our own rights and the rights of others. It does not compromise the dignity of either party, but may call for a compromise that exemplifies that both parties are satisfied. This is not an impossible dream. Every problem has a solution, and the solution is within us. The universe, in fact, offers infinity solutions.

An ideal to keep in mind is interdependence. The opposite of co-dependence, interdependence implies being healthy enough to be vulnerable, while at the same time remembering that we are worthy, confident and complete. Interdependence protects the self from becoming lost in the concerns of others. We approach others, but with an expectation of mutuality. We must be willing to negotiate through the duration of the relationship to achieve balance and equality. Relationships become a model for growth, an opportunity for receiving as well as giving.

Interdependence is created as equality is defined and established in a relationship. One of the most tragic effects of socialization is how undeserving of equality women feel. Throughout history, a few courageous women have fought politically to establish our equality, but we all know that women, even today, struggle with basic human rights, politically and personally. Now, let's think about how fundamentally important equality is in our lives and what is required of us to maintain it.

The roles that become the axis of our lives indicate that we belong to those we love, to those we serve or to anyone who needs us. Sometimes the message is subtle, and others, blaring. But it is always demeaning because femininity is thought of as inferior to masculinity. Women become emotionally trapped in this primal diminishment early in their lives. Our destiny has been to be responsible for the quality of life rather than the equality of life. So now, we must ask ourselves, "do we deserve equality?" And, if so, "what does equality look like?" Vigilance about equality is a necessary first step to gaining it.

Spend some private moments now and write down all the reasons you deserve equality. Ask yourself if your beliefs are manifested in your daily life.

- Do you state your rights to others?
- Are you willing to struggle in order to establish equality
  in relationships?
- Are you aware of how angry you are when treated unfairly?

- Do you feel taken advantage of by your family, your employer and your friends?
- Do you feel guilty when you say "no?"
- Do you feel compelled to say "yes" when you feel "no?"
- What prevents you from negotiating equality in your life?

In order to avoid the necessary conflict to establish equality, oftentimes we try to make our equality someone else's responsibility. We can mistakenly presume that they will know what is right for us. This kind of presumption can put our well-being at risk. Our path to maturity requires that we take responsibility for who we become. Emotional discord will immediately alert us to the presence of inequality in our lives. We cannot, of course, create equality in this world by the sheer thought of it, but we can do something to remind ourselves of how deserving we are of equality, even in the most unequal situations.

Believing in your equality is the beginning of world transformation. It is more important than any political movement because without your internalization of equality, no movement is truly effective. Our decision to struggle against inequality becomes our personal healthy rebellion.

JOURNALING

1. Women are good at promoting, protecting and respecting the rights of others. How about your rights? Write a personal Bill of Rights. Begin with "I have the right to _____." Repeat this phrase with each declaration. Identify at least twenty rights you deserve to enjoy. Share your Bill of Rights with another woman. Listen to her list. Be specific. **WRITE!**

2. We often postpone our personal desires because we are too absorbed in making the dreams of others come true. What decisions or dreams have you been postponing for some time in the future? Make a list of your postponements. After each, write the reason, real or imagined, for the postponement. **WRITE!**

3. During this journaling exercise, you will be searching for hidden meaning to your behavior. Doing something or not doing are behaviors. What is stopping you from making your decisions or dreams come true? What are you saying to your Self about your Self when you do not acknowledge or implement your dreams or decisions? **WRITE!**

4. Your dreams forward your life. For each decision or dream from the previous exercise, ask yourself, "How important is this decision or dream for me?" "How is it going to affect others?" "How will it change my life - and do I want that change to occur?" "What is the worst thing that could happen?" "What is the best thing that could happen?" **WRITE!**

REFLECTIVE CINEMA

Movies that reinforce the themes of this stage recommended for viewing:

- Shirley Valentine
- Fire
- Elizabeth
- Elizabeth: The Golden Age

STEPPING OUT

- If you know a gay woman, ask her about her life. Share with a friend your struggle with giving yourself personal freedoms.
- Speak with your mother about her life; find out what she did with her life before marriage. What parts of it, what dreams did she surrender?
- If your mother is still alive, take her on a date.
- In 1848, the Seneca Falls Convention was held and the Declaration of Sentiments and Resolutions was accepted. This document reminded Americans that women had been omitted from the concerns and safeguards of the original U.S. Constitution. "We hold these truths to be self-evident, that all men and women are created equal--" Read this document.

Story of a Married Woman

"BEFORE NINA COULD ACCOMPLISH HER GOALS, HER FUTURE HAD BECOME THE FULFILLMENT OF EVERYONE ELSE'S DREAMS."

The next morning, she found herself feeling uneasy, disappointed. Her spirit filled with trepidation. She wasn't sure just what had happened the night before. Her simple outing and the struggle she went through to arrange some personal time awakened her; opening her eyes to a puzzling question. The women she listened to made a difference in her world. Did her family see her differently? Did they notice a change in her? She expected them to show some interest in how she felt about the meeting. No one bothered or was particularly interested enough to ask, not even Joe. No one looked deeply enough to see the personal her. Everyone continued to move in their own little orbit. In truth, Nina's behavior was no different from what it always was every morning. Whatever changes she felt on the inside were invisible to everyone else. That morning, her invisibility was painful.

As Nina completed her morning chores, she remembered stories heard the night before and compared them to her own life. She remembered the closeness she'd felt sitting in a circle of women who were so comfortable talking about themselves. Nina wondered how she could reconcile what she'd heard about resocialization and equality with the life she had gotten so used to, with the only life she had come to know. How does a person who has stayed in the shadows so long step out into the light?

The concept of equality was unimaginable; it seemed like something only a very powerful, unattached person could accomplish, but not her. To Nina, it was like a fairy tale that makes you feel politically correct, but one that you don't believe for a second actually works out in real life. Despite this, Nina felt a stirring; a reawakening of abandoned dreams. Radiating throughout her being, she felt excited as if something was about to happen, but she didn't know what it was or how she would respond to such unanticipated shifts in consciousness.

When she was a young girl, Nina's mother wanted her to earn a bachelor's degree, even going so far as to recommend education or nursing because it would give her something to fall back on when she became a working mother. Nina resisted what she considered a boring choice and instead pursued her dreams. She majored in economics.

If asked, "Why," Nina would have responded that she was working toward a position focused on developing and managing the affairs of a start-up corporation. She had confidence in herself as a creative business manager.

During her junior year at the university she met Joe, who was studying engineering. She was attracted to his character and determination to succeed. Their high levels of ambition created a strong bond between them and led to similar paths, common dreams and long nights filled with vibrant conversation.

From their first date they spoke easily about business, politics and possibilities of every kind. Like childhood playmates, they enjoyed each other. He was a sensitive lover who seemed to understand a woman's body. They were both happy. They traveled whenever they could and shared a healthy community of friends. Just before graduation, Joe proposed marriage. Nina was surprised, but accepted immediately, not having any idea how profoundly marriage would change her personal life.

Looking back at those times from the perspective of the present, Nina could not explain why she had so readily accepted the proposal. Her way of doing things was never hurried or spontaneous. She was practical, precise, steady and realistic. This incidence of haste was totally out of her character. She remembered, however, how the thought of being a bride, someone's wife, and eventually a mother, seemed to overtake and overshadow her rational thoughts. It squelched any part of her that clung to thoughts of her own future. Becoming a bride seemed to make her personal dreams unrealistic and unimportant. Nina didn't resent this sudden and total alteration of her life, she was ready for it. She wasn't sure when the readiness began. Now, she was puzzled and confused. Why did her dreams change so suddenly? Why did all the other goals she'd worked for and dreamed about become lost and pushed aside? All of the job prospects that seemed so promising and exciting had no longer held her interest. Her family was delighted with Joe and encouraged the marriage. Before Nina could accomplish her goals, her future had become the fulfillment of everyone else's dream.

Recalling those events, Nina asked herself wryly, "Whose dream owns me now?" When she was young, when the wedding plans began, her life was taken out of her control. It was as if she no longer had any right to a personal life. What became of her life during the wedding preparations seemed to have nothing to do with the dreams she'd talked about for years at the university. Where was Nina? She felt a bit like Dorothy in The Wizard of Oz. She was no longer in Kansas, a place she loved. She became lost in a foreign land. Everyone seemed happy with this new turn in her life, especially, her mother. They enjoyed a closeness that they had never known. Her father was happy with Joe, calling him "another son." When Nina would think of her aspirations, a future career, she told herself that was giving up so little to get so much in return. Nina rationalized that she was giving up on dreams that were unrealistic. She told herself that the wedding and the marriage were real and her life was becoming what it was always supposed to be. Joe's family helped them buy a new home with all the furnishings. With no rent payments, it was not difficult for Joe to support the two of them. Joe felt there was no need for Nina to work and she agreed because she wanted to be free enough to make a life for her family. It would be her most perfect creation. Designing her home was thrilling. It was fun to discover how talented she was with color, decor and selecting home furnishings. After her first child was born she realized what a good mother she was. It came easily to her. Nina seemed to naturally evolve into the perfect woman, just like her mother always wanted her to be.

As time passed, Nina stopped examining or talking about her feelings or what she wanted. Life began to become more and more routine. What was there to think about or examine? Things just had to be done, didn't they? Her thoughts and feelings seemed less and less significant. What became important had very little to do with how she felt about it. Eventually, she stopped paying attention to her own thinking. She stopped realizing that her thoughts and feelings were a part of her life. And as the thoughts and feelings faded, so did Nina. Occasionally, when deep, personal feelings did emerge, like uninvited strangers that threatened the order of her family life, they were squelched immediately. Feelings unnerved her and frightened her.

She could not honor these personal feelings, and at the same time, maintain her life of caring, loving, serving and enjoying her family. After a while, these feelings stopped. Or, at least, she got so good at denying them, that they stopped reaching the surface of her consciousness. Life might have been robotic, but its familiarity brought about a quiet comfort. She loved without reservation. She loved without question or negotiation. She poured herself a cup of coffee and thought about what had happened to her, what she had chosen and what she had given up. It gave her a headache. She suddenly had a flash of insight. For the first time in all the years that she had known Sue, Nina suddenly saw why she had resisted a deeper friendship with her. Sue had not lost herself. Somehow, she had managed to keep her dreams and still love her family. She'd been able to successfully resist the complete subordination of her life, a state of being that Nina now found agonizing. Nina felt hurt, envy, fear and anger—a range of emotions foreign to her. She told herself to snap out of it. Sue might not have had to give up all the things she had, but Nina, trying to hold on to some dignity and sense of worth, told herself that she was more committed to her family than Sue. She had made the ultimate and true sacrifice: being the bride, mother and home-maker.

Story of a Lesbian Woman

"DID SHE WANT ANOTHER BOYFRIEND OR WAS SHE "GAY?" THE WORD
MADE HER SHUTTER ALMOST AS MUCH AS THE THOUGHT OF PREGNANCY."

The next morning, Thea and Amy dressed quickly and joined the other team members as if it were a normal day. Thea wanted to talk to Amy, but conversation was prohibited by their lack of privacy. She wondered if Amy needed to talk as much as she did. She felt shunned when Amy sat with another student on the bus ride back to school.

As they walked around the track field, Thea asked Amy about their night together. "Amy, it was just an experience!" she revealed. "I missed David." Was that all it meant to her?! How could that be? Their friendship continued, but it was never the same. What they shared and what it meant separated them. Suffering replaced their passion and made Thea feel like a stranger with her closest friend. She felt lost and confused. Maybe it was just a terrible mistake. Did she want another boyfriend or was she gay? The word made her shutter even more than the thought of pregnancy. She now felt emotionally lonely and alienated from everyone. Her mother encouraged her to be a girlfriend to some handsome boy. Her father distrusted most boys. Her friends expected her to marry Adam someday. If she was ever fortunate enough to remember who she was, would that young woman fit into this world?

The summer after her high school graduation seemed endless. She worked at a new movie theater. As patrons moved in and out, she wondered if any of them were gay. She wanted to find out what it meant to be gay, but how and where? She accidentally discovered the section on Gay and Lesbian studies at the public library. It took her several weeks to approach the two shelves of books. She planned her approach at a time of day when the library was least occupied. She made sure she brought her backpack and could use the self-checkout. Her first choices: Are You Gay? and Rubyfruit Jungle. Like a thief in the night, she slipped out of the library with her precious cargo. She read late into the night with her bedroom door locked. Each week she repeated her quest in search for answers. Her mother asked why she needed her backpack every day and why she was spending so much time in her room. It always irritated her that her mother wanted to know her secrets. Thea never realized how difficult struggling to be normal could be. She continued dating Adam weekly, but they both knew that passion was no longer present in their relationship. His friendship remained a comfort to her and sadness to him.

Her parents drove her to school to begin her freshmen year in college. As they drove away, she felt a deep relief from having to hide what she was discovering about herself. She desperately needed the anonymity college provided. No one knew she was possibly gay. Not her parents, her friends; not being known created its own hell. As she went through the student handbook, she discovered information on a gay support group that was held every Wednesday evening. She couldn't believe it! Could she get there without anyone seeing her?

Sitting in a circle with ten other students who supposedly were gay was jubilant, but it didn't erase the shame of being there as one of them. The fear of telling others that she was gay was so overwhelming that she wondered if she could say anything at all. Even speaking her name was a challenge. Silence made being gay seem unrealistic. How could she find her way in a world that imposed such rigid rules about her life? She needed help. The next morning, she thumbed through the local phone book to find a therapist. She couldn't go back to the group unless she knew she was gay. All of the books she read, the people she watched; even her intimate experience with Amy didn't convince her of her gayness.

She sat on a soft loveseat across from a counselor explaining why she was there. "It was fun, but I don't think I'm gay. The shame of this lifestyle is too difficult to bear! How could I tell my parents and friends?" she explained. It took her weeks to realize that making love was not the same as being in love. She hoped the therapist could help her unite the parts of her that seemed to be flying off in different directions. The possible realization that she was gay was a part of herself that she must acknowledge and explore. Never before, did she feel so isolated and lost.

During her freshman year, she looked for other students who might be gay. She watched how they dressed, how they looked at her, who, if anyone, they were dating. The search was futile and made her feel lonelier. She became more withdrawn and secretly desperate for connection with anyone she could talk to freely.

Thea presumed that therapy would be an accepting place where she could talk freely about the many fears and confusions that were paralyzing her life. During the first session, the therapist listened patiently as she confessed her gay curiosity. She explained that she didn't feel personal shame about being gay except in a world that expected her to be heterosexual. *She was relieved when her therapist assured her that he could help. She thought that meant encouragement and support.*

During the second session, the therapist asked if her parents knew she was gay. She said, "No! Not yet!" He replied, "That's good!" Thea felt instantly uncomfortable, but couldn't identify her uneasiness. During their third session, she was asked to watch a video describing a type of therapy that would cure her of her homosexuality. She didn't think she needed a cure, but was willing to yield to his professional opinion. The whole idea of not being gay seemed like a life raft drifting in a turbulent sea of personal confusion. It would rescue her from the shameful task of telling her family and friends that she was different. It was a big attraction that was undeniable. She agreed to the therapist's plan to rescue her from being gay.

The first two meetings were held at a local church that used conversion therapy as a way of cleansing the human race of homosexuality. She was totally disgusted by the judgmental attitude of the presenters. "It's your choice," they insisted; "Sin or Salvation" was their motto. She never thought of being gay as a sin or herself as a sinner. Thea's confusion did not eradicate the healthy ego her parents always fostered. They may not approve of her homosexuality, but she was certain that they would never sanction this campaign of shame or anything that would fundamentally hurt her in any way. How could she deny fundamental parts of herself? She wouldn't! She couldn't! She quit!

In desperation, she returned to the gay support group and told them what she was experiencing in isolation. This sharing actually redirected the rest of her life and adjustment to being gay. She was directed to a gay therapist who helped her through the maze of isolation and social stigma that she needed to face. After two months of therapy, Thea came out to her parents. It was the scariest experience of her life because her future family life would be changed and definitely uncertain. Nothing in life prepared her or her parents for this moment in time.

Her mother had the most extreme reaction. She blamed herself for being too tolerant of her tomboyish behavior. Her father blamed himself for not being closer to her during adolescence. How could they tell my grandparents and their friends? How could they accept a woman as spouse to their daughter when all of their lives they planned on being the parents of a bride? The thought of not having grandchildren was a near-death experience for both of them. Now guilt displaced shame. Even though her therapist prepared her for the grieving of her parents, it wasn't easy witnessing it. She watched them agonize in their adjustment as she did: There was nothing she could do to save them from this pain. Thea was never heavily invested in traditional dreams for her life. They were just part of the expectations that came out of nowhere and took center stage without her approval or consent. Her own grieving, that she was disappointing her parents, overwhelmed her at times, especially when she realized the loss of acceptance, admiration and connection she would endure because she would never become a bride, a wife and a mother.

Now her parents were pulled into her shame. It took courage to face them. She wanted them to confront their prescribed shame boldly; overcome it courageously as she did. She was forced to recognize that her parent's shame and loss looked different than her own.

Thea's father worried. Who would financially support his daughter? He realized that he would never walk her down the aisle. He would never have the son-in-law he expected to amplify his masculine presence in their family. Now, her father's purpose in her life was totally unknown. Could she be Daddy's little girl if she loved another woman? How would he be integrated into her new life? Neither of them knew. The uncertainty of their lives was painful to endure. Perhaps heterosexual certainty was the greatest loss of all. It would take her parents a long time to adjust. Her only hope was that this devotion to family loyalty and love would keep them close, while they seemed so distant. Her therapist recommended that her parents join the group, Parents and Friends of Lesbian and Gays. They accepted the information, yet rejected the idea.

During her last years at college, she dated several women. She fell in love twice, but the love seemed more motivated by sexual passion than enduring connection. Each relationship taught her the meaning of being gay and the meaning of love. Quickly and painfully, she discovered that realizing she was gay is distinctively different from living a gay life. She hated going to bars but felt that if she didn't, the community of gay women became invisible. Was this blind search for meaning what her parents meant when they said, "Oh honey, it is such a hard life."

Story of a Black Woman

I missed my father! That was my biggest secret. After several months of waiting, my father didn't return. He didn't write to me or call. I missed him anyway. I wanted him to come home so my life would be complete, so my mother would be happy, so my grandma could have her life back. I felt guilty about missing him. I should be mad because he did a bad thing to our family, but I couldn't be mad, because he was my buddy. I remembered the times he would take me to the convenience store at the end of our street for ice cream. I could have as many scoops as I wanted. I always chose three scoopers, because that was all I could manage. Even when the ice cream dripped down my hand and arm, my father didn't seem to mind. By the time I got home, I needed a bath. My mother scolded my father about his permissiveness. But he didn't pay attention to her. I wondered why he didn't help me with my scoops and he didn't pay attention to my mom either. My daddy called me Sweet-Pie. I wasn't sure what a sweet-pie was, but I loved the sound of his voice and the alliance it created between us. My daddy was really the only man in my life. My grandfather died before I was born; my grandmother never remarried. She brought up my mother alone, like my mother was doing with us. I wondered if that happened to all black women.

Even my friends didn't have a full-time daddy. I heard bad things said about not trusting a black man to stay around. That couldn't be true! My daddy was probably becoming a big success without us holding him back. Someday he will return. I just knew it! My cousin Leroy had a full-time daddy. I loved watching them play together. I watched their relationship with both an intense interest and a silent jealousy because I wanted a daddy to love me in that way. When I grow up, I thought, I will marry a man like Leroy's daddy. That was a promise I kept secret.

It was surprising how much I knew as a child. It was a different knowing than I have now. I was so aware and so sensitized to everything around me. There were so many mysteries that were like part of a puzzle floating in the air, waiting for me to pull them together. I tried to pull the pieces together even when they didn't fit.

After one year of being away from us, my father returned home. I don't think my mother expected him, because there were only four pork chops in the pan. My grandmother wasn't happy at all. My mother seemed relieved and angry, at the same time. He didn't have a lot of money or gifts for us. I was so excited to see him, but held it back because I didn't want to betray my mother or my grandmother. My father broke the terrible silence with his exuberant personality. He hugged me first, throwing me high into the air, then my sister. He turned to my mother for acceptance and she gave it to him. I was relieved that she wasn't angry, yet I wondered why. My grandmother's coldness suggested disapproval of my father's intrusion. I have come to realize that the strength of black women includes an incredible tolerance for the irresponsible immaturity of black men.

My father stayed with us for six months before a note was on the table again. I didn't see him then until I was a young adult. His absence created a vacuum in my life that I still don't understand. Throughout my life, I felt an emotional hunger that shaped my relationships with men. I now know that father-hunger is a silent yearning for a father's love.

Even when my father was home he was a master at pulling disappearing acts. A night or two of staying out made us all tense and confused. Throughout my life, he always caused a commotion wherever he went. He used his lean, athletic body, his six-foot frame, his creamy light skin, his perfectly aligned white teeth and impeccable speech to hustle everyone into his control and became a legend in his own mind.

My mother did not want to see the deception, but after many disappearances and broken promises, she began to see him clearly. My grandmother didn't have patience for my mother's denial. She struggled to hold in her anger but when she couldn't be silent any more, the two women fought. I worried when they fought, because their relationship was the foundation of my life. For me, my mother and grandmother became mother, father, adjudicator and God's angels, all rolled up into one.

After he was gone, our little family became peaceful again because we were liberated from the barrage of empty promises. I missed my daddy, even when I knew it was better that he was gone.

Story of a Woman ... Now Old

"I WANTED MY BROTHERS AND SISTERS TO KNOW A "MOTHER'S LOVE"
AND NOW, I WAS THE ONE ... THE MOTHER."

I learned the meaning of my mother's death in so many ways. Often, silently and privately, I cried for the woman who was only a child herself when she became my mother. After it was decided that all ten of us would remain together, I had to permanently withdraw from school. I wanted to keep my family together, at all costs, yet I still wanted to be a child. I wanted my mother to bake bread with me. I wanted so many things that I could never have again. My father explained to the judge, in my presence, that I was simple and therefore incapable of learning. The judge asked me if that was true. My humiliation became my power: "Yes. I am simple." Those words accomplished so much. Now, I was my mother's surrogate and in her honor, I gave my life freely, joyously and with complete dedication to my family. I wanted my brothers and sisters to know a mother's love, and now I was the one, the mother.

My father, who was emotionally unavailable and disconnected from us, seemed more so now. He was gone all day and roamed the streets at night, coming home early in the morning to sleep. He did nothing to ease our pain. Everyone excused his outrageousness because he was grieving. "Didn't anyone expect him to be a parent, even now?" I wondered. Six months after my mother's death, my father traveled to Lebanon. During the two years he was gone, he never wrote to us. He never told us how long he would be away or when to expect him home. We were truly alone, abandoned during the darkest time of our lives. Even though other family members surrounded us, their presence was little comfort.

Our only friend and father figure was my paternal uncle, Moses. He watched over us, making sure we had what we needed. He did his best to silence the criticism and scorning that came from other family members. Without a mother and father, we became unjustly criticized and made fun of by others. Being fatherless and motherless stigmatized us; left us unprotected. It made me more determined to fight for our dignity.

The ten of us became a unit as never before. Eddie was fourteen and I was thirteen; Tony was twelve; Teddy, eleven; Leona, ten; Katie, nine; Albert, six; Tommy, five; Ellen, four and Marion was three. We were all bewildered, but determined to be a family, and survive!

The unending needs of the family dictated the course of my day. I woke at three o'clock each morning to bake bread. I baked using forty-eight pounds of flour twice per week. The burden of this task was so much lighter because my uncle Moses helped me most mornings, lifting the heavy bag of flour, emptying it into a huge metal kettle, readying it for mixing. After the dough was mixed by hand and everything was put away, he left. He cared for me in so many ways. At seven o'clock in the morning, I woke my brothers and sisters; gave them their breakfast and sent them off to school. The first year of my mother's death, while I took care of the house, Marion was home with me. Ellen's first day of school was traumatic for Marion. Together, we walked her to school, but when it was time to leave, Marion cried uncontrollably and refused to leave. Nothing I did consoled her. Finally, the teacher said, "Let her stay with Ellen." As I walked home, I felt a deep loneliness without Marion. She always needed me. She kept me company as I cleaned the house every day. Her personality was so lively that it massaged my pain. The family formed a protective bond around her. She loved each of us in a unique way. It was as if she had some profound understanding of our sadness and was determined to heal us with her love.

At midday, I stopped my cleaning to prepare lunch for my family, who walked home from school together. Soup and sandwiches were always waiting for them. Seeing them all take their place at the table comforted me. Now, I had fewer moments of missing school because I was so busy. My life had outgrown school, but my heart was still that of a child, a very strong child.

By early afternoon, I was totally exhausted so I napped. Usually, Marion napped with me. As I lay my head on the pillow, I took pride in my day's accomplishments. We were surviving; I was holding our family together. Our lives had a new order that we each created in the absence of my dear mother and my father. I would rest now before cooking the evening meal.

The evening meals were important because everyone was hungry and gathering around the table was the most comforting experience we had. I cooked huge amounts of Lebanese food. If I made pork chops, I had to cook the entire pork loin. If I made French fries, I prepared ten pounds of potatoes for one meal. My brothers often would sneak behind the stove to grab hands full of fried potatoes before they were served. My pita bread was an important part of every meal. Most of our food was arranged in a piece of homemade pita bread. Eating in this way is a Lebanese custom. Now you know why I baked using more than one hundred pounds of flour each week.

Enough food, enough company, enough caring, enough love. That was my life and I dedicated it to being enough. Enough to fill the gaping emotional hole created by my mother's death and my father's unanticipated and unexplained absences.

CLEARING MY MIND

———∞∞∞———

I am determined to release myself from the confusion and uncertainty myths of femininity create in my life.

How We Think

"We carry deep inside of ourselves the legacy of our mother's life."

At this stage, we face the fear of letting go of traditional ways of thinking and acting. It is an awkward and difficult position, because new behaviors are not yet comfortable, but old behaviors are becoming less believable. The challenge of our new future is learning to trust ourselves with the unknown. The unknown may feel scary and empty, perhaps even too frightening to consider. But emptiness holds a vast potential of which you, at this moment, are unaware. Emptiness and the unknown, force us to rely on our internal resources of strength and creativity, sources we left behind many years ago as a young girl who wanted to fit in and belong. Think of the unknown as the becoming of your life. You are the artist creating a life design that you don't completely understand at this moment, but your spirit compels you to explore and discover. You can allow the unknowingness to unfold as you begin to channel your spirit and affirm your identity. Now that is an exciting prescription for life! The future evolves one moment at a time. So, be in the moment!

Sometimes, it is painful not to know about your life and its future. Facing an uncertain future is a good time to employ your spirituality as a source of strength and inspiration. There can be a lot of knowing in the emptiness you feel if you trust and believe in the potentialities of silence, stillness, and life itself. These are invitations to self-revelation as you journey to rediscover your true self; preludes to a self you left behind. Remember a time when your life was predicted by others and you felt compelled to live it out according to their dreams because you didn't want to disappoint anyone? Remember how lost you felt at times when their dreams became more important than your life? They were designing your life with great enthusiasm, and you let them because you loved them. You trusted their authority more than your own. Now love yourself. Now love your life. Now respect your journey. It's more important than your destination.

Our family and friends may not appreciate the new priorities we have set for ourselves. When we speak in the first person, they may accuse us of being selfish. This type of accusation, which makes thinking about ourselves shameful, is a poignant example of how deeply socialization affects us all. Paying attention to ourselves should never be perceived as neglecting another. Paying attention to ourselves benefits not only the individual, but the relationship network you share. When we are accused of being selfish, it is usually because our accuser is feeling deprived of our attention.

Co-dependent thinking is pervasive in our culture. This makes it difficult for women to separate self-care from loving others. That thinking presumes that an individual's right is superseded by the needs of others. We must remember that when we lose ourselves, we depend on others to define us. We become immediately over identified with their needs. The co-dependent self has a desperate attachment to other people's dreams. They become a substitute for our own existence, a hiding place from the challenges of life that we may not want to face.

The co-dependent self, which lives a life of deferment, is directly caused by cultural conformity, not addiction. These messages that presume self-abandonment are unhealthy and must be silenced one at a time. The world needs you to be yourself because your giftedness is unique. When you break free from cultural prohibitions that restrict who you are, you are at the same time extinguishing co-dependent expectations. Resocialization, then, counteracts social-conditioning. It is your call to live as completely as possible.

As we release ourselves from emotional restrictions, we'll understand how our lives were diverted and derailed by cultural prescriptions that made no sense. We will have a more enlightened awareness of socialization. In the past we have listened to others, and now, we must listen to ourselves. The pain that socialization has caused then becomes clearer.

The progressive nature of socialization heightens during our adult life. We suffer the most during those years because so much more is required of us, and we struggle to survive personally. Our mothers dictated and modeled the course of our adult roles. Now it is time to critically and lovingly examine our relationship with our mother because she was, and maybe still is, the main socializer in our lives. No matter what kind of mother she was, our emotional life with her lays the foundation of our personal identity and emotional knowing. Our relationship with her began during the hardest years of her life. Too many of us remember our mothers as unhappy, angry, frustrated and perhaps economically dependent. We may presume that her unhappiness was simply her natural disposition. Many daughters grow up not liking their mothers, and almost always, not understanding them. Understanding our mother does not excuse her from the responsibility of her actions, but it does soften our judgment, and at the same time, helps us to understand ourselves.

Our personal reconciliation depends on developing a deeper understanding of our mother's life as daughter, woman, wife and mother. Reexamining our mother's life in the social context in which she lived it, is an essential part of our personal peace. In order for us to claim our cognitive and emotional freedom, we must expand our understanding of our mothers.

Investigating the truth of your mother's life will begin with her life as a child and her relationship with your grandmother. If you can discuss with your mother her own childhood, it will create new relationships between you. Your mother will know that you are interested in her life, and initially, perhaps more interested than she is in remembering. She may be reluctant to talk at first, because it is so painful for her to remember. But gently reinitiate your interest each time you are together. It usually becomes less threatening after each truth-telling experience. Find out about the significant women in her life. Remember that your mother's childhood is an invisible part of her relationship with you. We carry deep inside of ourselves the legacy of our mother's life, and she, never having felt that her life was important, may have never had a safe place where she could critically examine and grieve it. Our mothers may still be held captive by social myths and misinterpretations of what it meant to be a woman.

The purpose of truth-telling, a feminist term that encourages women talking to significant others about their lives, is simply to understand our mother so we are able to appreciate the human and social conditions of her life. It is not our job to teach or preach a different way for her to live or to condemn her inadequacies. It is possible that we can demonstrate and encourage self-determination for our mothers by living it ourselves. By freeing ourselves from the oppression of our mother's life prescription, we may also free our mothers by the power of our modeling. By taking leadership with her, we can create a more balanced, functional and mature relationship. Mothers and daughters can grow together. And as they grow, they may see the separation that socialization created between them and recognize the years of closeness they lost. A new future can be established by designing a different style of relationship, not as powerful mother and little daughter, but as women who are eternally connected by birth and life. Knowing your mother's story is knowing her life.

Another way of strengthening our pride in female identities is through exalting the history of womankind. Female writers can quench our thirst for knowledge about great women who stand in obscurity after contributing to every phase of history. Their obscurity will further explain to us the path of our lost self. Women, who reclaimed their lives, will share their victorious and courageous journeys with you. Let them teach you one clear fact: a lost self can be a found self through the sheer determination of your will. Throughout history, many courageous women dared to step out of the confines of socialization and fight against the unequal status of women. We've known many of them by name, but we may not know their lives. Knowing their lives will help us appreciate their humanness; the same humanness we struggle to accept. Admire the courage and singular vision of great women. Let their wisdom enlighten you and their courage, motivate you. There is a rich assortment of feminist literature presently available.

How We Feel

> *"Gradually, we neglect to ask ourselves how we feel about what we do and about the direction of our lives."*

This program of resocialization is about your life, so we must identify the complex and diverse ways that socialization affected our emotional being in order for resocialization to be influential in reshaping your life. Stop now and answer these questions: Did you leave dreams and ambitions behind because you tried to be a good girl, a good woman, a good mother and a good employee? Of course you did! We all did! Remember those abandoned dreams, those dreams deferred and those dreams we did not even dare to think of as real possibilities. No matter how outrageous they may seem, share those dreams with trusted female confidants. Allow yourself to feel the pain and disappointment of losing them. Allow yourself to grieve not only for yourself, but for your mothers and grandmothers who also left their dreams behind. Grieve for all the women who have touched your life and who never claimed their own identity, never determined their own destiny.

Real grieving only takes place when we connect our insights with our emotions. As you talk with your mother, you realize that the part of your mother who didn't think her dreams were important is the same part of her that discounted your dreams as well. She simply applied to your life the same attitude that victimized her own. Our mothers, without knowing why or how, were the bearers of cultural continuity. By leaving their dreams behind, they pushed their identity into the background of silence and often subservience. Even daring women who faced the confines of socialization suffered under the yoke of socialization. There were no exceptions, and that is a grieving matter.

We must be gentle with ourselves when we feel sad, it indicates progress. Sadness has a way of slowing us down because it takes energy to grieve. It makes us stop to reflect on the meaning of our inner conflicts. Our sadness is saying, "We have a lesson to learn now." Our pain is not a mistake, it is a messenger. We don't rationalize our pain away, and we won't minimize the sadness we feel because we are afraid to be vulnerable. Instead, when you are sad, you look for safe places to be and safe people to be with during those moments. A safe place is a place where you can be exactly as you are. A safe person is someone who can remember her own sadness as she witnesses yours. She knows the hidden wisdom that your emotions hold. She does not try to rush you or rationalize your feelings. She is quiet with you. The healing process takes place by surrendering to the vulnerable child inside of you. We must take care of that little girl the way we have taken care of others. Only when the inner child is safe and secure can she be free.

Socialization has also shaped the lives of every man we've loved and known. How socialization affects their lives is distinctly different than how it affects our own, and because men have more social privilege, their victimization can be harder for us to detect. To have knowledge about male socialization is an important part of our resocialization because it is another way we identify the subtle conformity socialization creates in human development. We will be less likely to participate in the dysfunctional drama we create with men if we are aware of the different messages that subjugate a man's life and the unhealthy privilege that shelters them from taking responsibility for their own spiritual growth. Every kind of relationship we have with a male person offers an occasion of resocialization. By understanding how socialization affects both sexes, it can no longer remain the hidden agenda making men and women intimate strangers.

Social prescriptions for men are rigid and do not respect their emotional or spiritual needs, as emotionalism and spiritualism are deemed feminine qualities. It is a way that men are shamed into rejecting whatever it labeled feminine about them. Socialization demands that men, very early in their lives, avoid whatever is feminine because it is devalued and an indication of weakness. Because of this suspicion of the feminine, young boys lose closeness with their mothers prematurely and are too often emotionally abandoned by their fathers. They enter relationships with women with tremendous mother hunger, the craving for the attention they lost as a young boy because they gave up nurturance to be a man.

Women are often trapped into compensating for the huge legacy of loss men experience. We try to do the emotional and spiritual work for the men we love. We excuse them from the adult responsibility of being responsible for their behavior. Women often love men as children, rather than equal adult partners. Because we want to fix them, we are motivated to give them unconditional, positive regard. What that means simply is that they work less for approval, and yet get more of it. It also means that we are willing to live in denial of our unhappiness with them. We cannot, simultaneously, be the mother they lost and the lover they need. They are two different loves. We are motivated to forget about our needs because our male partners have so many needs that demand our attention. We need to remind ourselves that every son must claim the right to feel, to love and to be human, if he is ever to establish a real connection with life. If we truly want a balanced relationship with one male partner, we must stop trying to control them, stop taking responsibility for them, stop excusing them and stop feeling sorry for them.

In relationships, true balance is accomplished only when we respect others and recognize the limitation of our own personal power. Rather than trying to complete or fix others, we should instead trust their own wisdom and power and encourage them to use it. Allowing others to struggle with their own emotional and spiritual development clears the way for more supportive communication, such as empathy, encouragement, admiration and personal sharing. Once we accept the healthier boundaries of our power, we'll feel less stress in relationships and have more confidence in the relationships we share. This emotional unburdening is one more avenue to freedom.

How We Are With Others

"Our relationships are a wonderful way to evaluate our recovery because nothing is truly learned until it is lived."

Relationships can be wonderful opportunities for personal growth. However, in order for our relationships to be healthy, we need to, on an ongoing basis, evaluate what they are doing for us. Are we becoming a better person as a result of these relationships? Are they addressing our needs? Are the people in these relationships responding to us? Are they listening to us? Are we truly being loved? We won't evaluate our relationships realistically unless we believe in our right of choice. Believing we have choices gives us the inner power to influence or change our relationships if we so choose.

When we fail to respect ourselves or our right of choice, psychic chaos results because our denial requires us to repress our feelings and deny our pain. Our self-awareness gradually slips away. We eventually feel trapped in unhappy relationships without a voice to bring about effective change. Feeling that we don't have choices is a subtle but profound result of socialization. We came to believe that the course of our life was designed by some powerful outside force and that to deviate from that prescribed path would result in devastating loss for ourselves and those we love. Choice, we fear, will bring about such catastrophic losses that no one will be able to recover from and nothing will be gained from the use of our power. That is the stranglehold socialization has on our lives. It controls us from the inside out. Feeling that we have choices is an essential part of our existence because it paves the way for our becoming, and leads us out of entrapping, destructive and stagnant relationships or situations. Choice keeps us at the helm of our own destiny; invites us to evaluate life as we are living it; keeps our life open to possibilities. It keeps us spiritually alive. We have to believe that choice is our perfect right in order to employ its diverse and powerful contribution to our life. It allows us to dream and to activate our anger when necessary to bring about change.

Most of us deny ourselves the right of choice because we feel overly responsible for the destiny of others. Our lack of choice can create feelings of hopelessness in our lives, which is one of the main components of depression. No outside person or institution can convince you that you have alternatives if you don't believe you deserve them. Removing the walls that socialization has created inside of you is possible, and it may be the first choice you make to recreate the rest of your life. Rely on the modeling of other women for inspiration. As you read or listen to their stories of courage, anticipate reclaiming your own right of choice. If you recognize the value of choice, even vaguely, it will begin the enfolding of your liberation.

It's perfectly normal to critically examine the relationships that we're forming or the relationships in which we are involved. We do not need to stay in unhealthy, self-deprecating relationships with anyone, including family members. One of the most subtle social influences tells women that they should be nice at all times, and that nice girls are not critical. When we find ourselves being more devoted to being in a relationship than being happy, our healthy, critical self has become lost. Our self-awareness slips away, and we live without being connected to our surroundings and the people in our lives. We stop enjoying life because the life we're living is not connected to our emotional truth. We become less and less real while we pretend to be truly alive. Being busy can often replace being happy. Denying ourselves the right of choice diminishes our essential power. Be clear, there is no life without personal choice. There is only conformity, and that is a psychic death to our inner life. Self-silencing is not the purpose of our lives, nor should it be a part of our relationships.

We have to involve our partners in our frustration, unhappiness or disillusionment. We must initiate a process of dialogue that reaches outside of ourselves. Resist privatizing relationship pain. Self-actualization is not an experience we attain and then coast along, enjoying its accomplishment. Self-actualization is an ongoing invitation to live and enjoy the fruits of your talents, your intelligence and your emotional development. Self-actualization is often realized during difficult times because it forces us to move outside of our denial, our comfort zone or perceived limitations.

Like so many other aspects of our lives, self-actualization is a journey, not a destination. Sometimes the journey of self-actualization is bright and glorious, and at other times, it's dark and lonely. During the dark times, it may be difficult for us to believe that anything is being accomplished. Our dark moments are more difficult to believe in because they hold confusion, fear, loneliness and an uncertain outcome. But darkness actually holds a great deal of promise for all of us, because it is during these moments that we fight for our survival as we define what we stand for. In order to survive darkness, we are challenged in the deepest way. It may require that we alter parts of our thinking, feeling and social connections in fundamental, and sometimes radical, ways. If we embrace that challenge, the course of self-actualization is set. The process of becoming will self-perpetuate because we will be more convinced that darkness and light are part of personal growth.

The privatization of our relationship pain is yet another subtle effect of socialization. Because women are thought of as the supreme architects of relationships and the keepers of love, they suffer when relationships go awry. Dysfunctional relationships become our personal condemnation when privatization is our style. Privatization isolates us from healthy resources, and we become victims of shame that tell us that we should not be having this problem. Whatever we privatize we hold in silence. Silence can be a blessing, but the silence resulting from privatization is a self-entrapment that stifles the forward movement of our lives, and as discussed earlier, our self-actualization. When we hide our pain, we are also hiding our true selves from those we love. Relationship journeys grow through conflict resolution. In healthy relationships, conflict offers each partner the opportunity to reach deeply within him or her to find a loving solution. However, we have to prepare ourselves because some partners may try to thwart our efforts to resolve any problem. In fact, they may resent both our leadership and refusal to be victimized by the problem. If this pattern persists, break the silence of privatization and seek help from professionals and friends.

When toxic silence is broken, we feel immediate and profound relief. We are comforted and become stronger because we are not alone. Nothing can stop our forward movement toward a fuller life—something we must seek in all the circumstances of our living.

JOURNALING

1. Cultural messages come to you from the media, your family, your friends, school and religious institutions. Examine the ways you were exposed to cultural conformity in the past. In what ways do messages of cultural conformity reach you today? Do you resist them? What is your level of resistance? What do you need to do to resist allowing these messages to dictate your life and the abandonment of your dreams? **WRITE!**

2. Divide your life into these stages: Early Childhood, Middle Childhood, Adolescence, Early Adulthood, Late Adulthood and Old Age. Next to each stage, list how you changed yourself in order to feel accepted, right, proper, or what you thought was normal. Be specific. **WRITE!**

3. Were the changes you noted in your previous writing attributable to your desire to belong? How did the changes make you feel about yourself? How did they influence your self-esteem? Were you chronically dissatisfied with your body? Did dieting become a way of life? Did you become desperate about having a relationship? Did you hide your body? **WRITE!**

4. Critically examine your relationship with your mother. What do you know about her relationship with your grandmother? Write all the information you know and a list of questions about your mother you would like to have answered. If you do not have this information, seek it from your mother or relative who knew about your mother's life. What patterns begin to emerge as you write? How have these patterns influenced your life, your viewpoint and expectations? **WRITE!**

REFLECTIVE CINEMA

Movies that reinforce the themes of this stage recommended for viewing:

- Christmas Story
- Diary of a Mad Black Woman
- Under the Tuscan Sun
- Billy Elliot

STEPPING OUT

- Read a book describing the socialization of man. Examples: **Finding Our Fathers; Mothers, Sons and Lovers.**
- Ask your male partner, male friend, brother, or father about how being a man became more important than being happy and whole.
- Ask your father about his life; his boyhood, his relationships with his mother and father.
- Invite a friend to lunch. Talk to him or her about what you always wanted to do, what you always wanted to accomplish; what you postponed for love.

Story of a Married Woman

"MAYBE ALL HER DREAMS OF BEING IMPORTANT AND HAVING A
BUSINESS WERE ALL THE WHILE JUST FILLING UP TIME AND SPACE
UNTIL 'THE RIGHT ONE CAME ALONG'"

She rushed through her to-do list. She would reward herself afterwards with a few minutes of stolen time to read her magazines and **The New York Times**. *This quest for private time motivated her to work quickly and efficiently. She couldn't relax until the house was in order. Everything had to be in order. She often thought how much easier it would be for her if she could convince everyone, including Joe, that keeping things neat and clean is easier when everyone works together. But she never complained about their lack of organization because she knew everyone thought it was mainly her responsibility.*

Finally finished, she picked up the magazines and browsed through articles and features that put her back in touch with the world. She wondered if there was a way to reconcile the real world to the world of her life. She'd once dreamt of doing so much, being someone special. Was there a way to integrate both worlds? Her world at home and her world of ambition? There had to be a way, but she could not imagine how it would work. She knew that many mothers worked, yet she believed that a working mother had to substantially compromise her mothering. In the end, her child would pay the price for her fulfillment and that was something with which she was uncomfortable; unwilling to embrace.

Like her suppressed feelings, thoughts of getting back to her dreams, or, the world out there, seemed threatening. Even on the rare occasions when she'd taken small financial consulting jobs, she was constantly preoccupied with worry about the kids, Joe or the house. The constant stress of these mental and emotional intruders deprived her of any enjoyment or satisfaction, so she rarely accepted offers from friends and local companies that requested her business knowledge. A quiet sadness came over her when she thought about her life. Once again, she remembered how quickly she'd accepted marriage. She wondered why she hadn't taken more time to think about it. Why didn't she work for a few years before marrying? Why didn't she travel? Why did she dismiss her dreams without counting the cost? Had she done it simply to agree to whatever Joe wanted? Had she really been so disinterested and uninvolved with her own career and identity that she accepted marriage because she would have otherwise thought of herself as a nothing? A nobody? Was that why she let Joe talk her into marriage and motherhood without a reasonable time to think and consider her options? Maybe, even as she had been working toward getting her degree and having a career, the idea of marriage had been lying there dormant the entire time. Maybe all her dreams of being important and having a business were all the while simply filling time and space until the right one came along.

Thinking of those lost dreams, Nina felt as if she were grieving for a lost friend. Hope is painful to surrender. Even as she admitted to her loss, that she felt sad and angry, she felt guilty about her private rebellion, even if the rebellion were silent. She felt as if she should not be having these thoughts. She loved Joe and the kids. How could she have done what she wanted to do? How could she have kept her ambitions and still have enough Nina left for them? She wondered if they had any idea what she had given up. She wanted them to know. Maybe what bothered her most was that she had sacrificed so much and they didn't get it; they didn't understand it or acknowledge it. She felt taken for granted, and that hurt.

She also had to admit that in all her relationships, not just with Joe and the kids, but with everyone, there was an imbalance. She constantly struggled to please others. She smiled when she wasn't happy. She spoke softly when she wanted to shout. She was always pleasant, gracious, polite, accommodating, agreeable and comprising. What she now realized was that the pattern of dissatisfaction, of unfulfilled wishes and needs, had become so unbearable that she became more and more withdrawn, increasingly private and lonely. If you ask for and expect nothing, you won't be disappointed, you won't be hurt. The more private Nina became, the safer she felt. Her world was narrow, but manageable. Sadly, it was only on the rare occasions when she accepted a financial consulting job that she felt any satisfaction. It was during those infrequent occasions that she felt like a person. She was Nina; not someone's wife, mother or child. During those times, she felt closest to herself.

Story of a Lesbian Woman

"She seldom brought her girlfriends home to meet her parents, because she knew how bewildered they still were with a gay daughter."

Thea's life had become privatized without her knowing or choosing it. The years of shame kept her from telling anyone at work about her gay life. Even after all the members of her family knew, she still had to face the frontiers of everyday life as a gay woman, a woman who had chosen not to become a bride.

After graduating college, Thea was hired as a financial manager in a large investment firm in New York. She was sure she could compete with the big boys, and she did! Her profits climbed during the second and third years of investing. Everyone was happy, yet her co-workers were absolutely threatened. They began their campaign to disgrace her by asking about her personal life and made it difficult for her to refuse company outings. They challenged her success by continually raising her quotas. She was working more hours and earning the same amount of money. It was painful to speak with her parents about her private life because although they were happy with her financial success, they were still in this-is-just-a-phase mode. They didn't seem to notice that she was struggling with a problem of workplace discrimination and frustration in her personal life. They actually encouraged her to remain single. It infuriated Thea, but she didn't feel like she had the right to challenge them. She dated many women during her last two years of college and after graduation. She seldom brought her girlfriends home to meet her parents because she knew how bewildered they still were with a gay daughter. The only way she knew how to protect them was to keep her private life hidden.

Thea thought of resigning her position at the firm, but didn't because her friendship with Sara was so comforting and special. They spent most of their lunch hours sharing their personal stories. Sara worked part time in the Human Relations Department. She was a premed student when she met George, who had just completed his medical fellowship in Cardiology. He swept Sara off her feet. They married quickly and had their first child within a year. George and Sara agreed that she should be home with their children, so she withdrew from medical school after the wedding. Working fifteen hours each week was a compromise she and George struggled with for months.

Her first child, Ari, was born ten months after their marriage and Rennie, eighteen months later. Sara was so busy nursing, feeding and changing diapers that her personal needs were forgotten. Her love and dedication left her little time for herself. She adored being a mother, but was struggling in her relationship with George. He was a good man, but his entitlements overruled her need to be acknowledged. He worked hard and became successful quickly. His successes made her bow to his expectations and accept his absence as a necessity. He seemed to have no room in his life for intimacy. Thea encouraged Sara to go to therapy with George. After two sessions, he discontinued treatment, citing that it took too much time. Sara continued because she wanted to find a way to be happy with George.

One day, during the lunchtime discussions, Sara began to disclose what she was realizing. "Before I realized I had needs, I had no expectations of my husband to fill them," she said. "Sometimes when I try to talk to him, he will leave the house or say, 'you don't know what you're talking about.' I have accepted that. But now, as I allow my feeling to surface, I want him to acknowledge them too. It really doesn't matter what they are."

Sara wasn't sure why she was changing, but she felt good being more alive, more excited about life and less lonely. Sara was sure that she could make George come alive because she believed so completely in her love for him. As Thea listened, she admired her strength and commitment, but felt like a spectator who was lost and defeated.

Story of a Black Woman

"I KNEW MY MOTHER WAS COMPLETELY DEVOTED TO MY SISTER
AND ME ... BUT I ALSO KNEW THERE WAS MUCH MORE TO MY MOTHER
THAN THE LIFE SHE WAS LIVING."

The role my mother played in my life was meaningful, but complicated by the absence of my father and the many fathers of our extended family. Now that I think of it, our community was made up of mothers, grandmothers and boys too young to leave their families or too dysfunctional to find their own place in the world. In a way, I felt sorry for the sons of my mother's friends. They, like me, grew up fatherless and later struggling as black men for acceptance in a white world. They fought this difficult battle without anyone to show them the way or teach them self defense. In the days of slavery, black men who fathered children were not considered part of the family. A family was defined as a mother and her children. I saw each of them struggle to let go of their mothers in order to establish their manhood and then return to their mothers with contempt because they were aimless about their lives and dependent on her love.

Perhaps that mother/son conflict was due to inner-personal conflict and that is what destroyed my parent's marriage. Perhaps my father's confusion about his black manhood muddled his emotional strength and his determination to survive the social discrimination that waited to crush his spirit.

In all cultures and in every race, motherhood is a role simultaneously glorified and condemned. For black women, motherhood is a powerful demonstrator of her leadership. Historically, black women were considered founders or mothers of tribes and the primary carriers of the culture.

I knew my mother was completely devoted to my sister and me, but I also knew there was much more to my mother than the life she was living. She was creative, intelligent and yet all she did was housework and childcare for others. It was assumed that because she was a black woman, housekeeping came naturally to her. It was assumed that she was naturally a mother, because she was a black woman. No matter how well she handled the two responsibilities, she was still devalued. My mother explained to me that all black women of child-bearing age are referred to as mother, and as mothers, they are charged with the task of socializing their black children and becoming the core of their socio-emotional development.

My mother read books whenever she had a free moment. She read late into the night, especially on weekends. Like my great, great grandmother Tashi, she seemed to separate what she did in her life from who she really was deep within her soul. She took my sister and me to the public library to check out books because it was cheaper than buying them. I loved those trips because we took the bus to a special diner and had a big meal that ended with three scoops of ice cream. My mother was happy on those days. She was also determined to teach us the love of learning. Yet my mother's demeanor and her conversation seemed to hold another lesson. Now I realize she was teaching us how to live among white people without becoming like white people, and to mediate between two often conflicting cultures. It required me to develop an ability to be different people at different times, a duality of socialization, without losing the core sense of myself. The conflict was tricky at times. I resisted being friends with white children at school because I didn't know how to belong in interracial friendships. So I studied hard and achieved high honors. I gravitated toward other black students while I was there, but I couldn't wait to get home where I felt totally safe because my life was known and uncomplicated.

I felt powerful in my family. I could cut greens the way my grandmother showed me. I made a bed perfectly, pulling the sheets so tightly that you could almost use it as a trampoline. I cared for my sister when my grandmother needed a break; learned to figure out how to repair things like the toilet that wouldn't flush, or the drawer that wouldn't close. I didn't want anyone to notice that my father had abandoned us. The more competence I showed, the more things were asked of me. I was fighting a winning battle and I was proud. I was fully alive, fully responsible. I was the keeper of those I loved.

Story of a Woman ... Now Old

"No one asked us how we were feeling or how we were surviving."

As I feverishly addressed the needs of my brothers and sisters, I became more isolated. I was so exhausted at the end of each day that I usually went to sleep about 9 o'clock.

Marion slept with me. No one had a bed of their own. She clung to me day and night; hung onto my leg for security. She wanted to be with me all the time. In my devotion and desperation, I completely lost my privacy. Going to church on Sunday morning was the only thing I did alone. I walked to church alone. No one needed me, no one depended on me. I was able to be with myself. On my way to church, I passed the school. I glanced at the entrance with detachment now that my life held a higher purpose. As I walked through the door, the church's quiet and peace wrapped around me. It was as if my mother ordained it. During the Mass, we remembered and prayed for the dead. I prayed to my mother's soul that I carried within me. I asked God to comfort and care for her until we met again, my mother and me.

I had very little time for fun, but twice a month, my cousins from Utica rode a trolley to my small town. They slept over, so we had lots of time to talk and laugh.

Occasionally we would buy an ice cream cone. I took Marion with me no matter what we did. Eventually, they resented my little sister tagging along and told me that if I brought Marion along, I couldn't come with them. I gave up their company because leaving Marion behind was unthinkable.

For a year and forty days after my mother's death, I wore only black clothing. My brothers wore a black armband to honor her. Everyone in our small town knew my family. Even though so many people knew about my mother's death, no one spoke to us about her. No one asked us how we were feeling or how we were surviving. I thought it was strange that the single most significant loss in our lives went unacknowledged by everyone. It was as if her death didn't happen. Did they really think that silence made the feeling of loss go away? It made me feel lonely in my pain. It made it more difficult to understand death when it was not discussed. I have since grown to appreciate the richness of talking, asking and sharing.

Speaking is so important. My mother and I never spoke about how serious her condition was. We never spoke of death. We never said good-bye. She died alone.

Millions of times I replayed her death in my mind. I would be standing near her, holding her hand, stroking her forehead with a worn cloth, wetting her parched lips and massaging her feet. I would tell her that life after death would be better for her. I would give her hope and love. But my mother died without me and now, I am alone without her laughter, her guidance, her comfort.

DEVELOPING AWARENESS

——✺——

I will trust my own wisdom, because it is my greatest source of peace and personal power.

How We Think

"The challenge of our new future is learning to trust its uncertainty."

Throughout human history, women have been expected to endure. We accept endurance in the absence of choice. Have you ever asked yourself why you endure so much? Sometimes we need to endure for a short period of time, giving us time to create a new action. When we endure unhappiness for an extended period and go on giving, endurance becomes harmful; it silences our spirits. It is time to recognize that giving without considering our own needs is unhealthy because it ignores our identity, our importance, our presence and our value that yearns for expression. If this pattern persists, we disappear and could become depressed. It is time to grieve for the part of our lives we lost to unhealthy endurance. Grieving will call our attention to the price we have paid in the name of endurance.

We deserve personal freedom, recognition and respect, but until we appreciate and demand the presence of these precious qualities in our lives, they will remain a fantasy. Our emotional entitlement is an important part of our personal gain. By linking our feelings and our thoughts, we begin a process of holistic healing that focuses our energy. We become one body, one mind, one soul. Using the ancient, original definition of virgin, we become one-in-ourselves. The goddess-poet Sappho, twenty-five centuries ago, wrote of the independent, creative woman who is forever virgin. As we unveil the subtleties of socialization, we will hurt and heal simultaneously.

A women's journey of transformation is challenging. Through a spiritual life, we can generate faith in the process of healing. At this stage, it may be hard to believe that our spirit could be free. It may be hard to imagine the glory of our released Self. Our spiritual life generates hope because it links our present life with our transcendence. It puts us in touch with another reality that doesn't have to make sense out of everything. It helps us to see life not as isolated experiences, but as a flowing pattern created from a self in evolution. Spirituality is, at its root, a matter of seeing all of life from a different perspective. It is waking, sleeping, dreaming and anticipating newness in our lives. Our spiritual life is simply our life seen from the vantage point of our history, our mystery and our spirit. Our spirituality is a yearning to know the meaning of our lives and the art of creating wisdom from our experiences.

Our life will expand as we slowly come alive. At this stage, you are asked to consciously and boldly look at the extent of your loss, both specifically and universally. It would not be surprising if you resist the acknowledgement of loss. Denial keeps what we don't want to acknowledge obscured from our awareness because we fear that the awareness of loss will sweep us into a profound pit of sorrow from which we can't recover. It requires so much strength to merely live our everyday lives that when we begin to examine our loss it often appears that the loss far exceeds the strength we believe we possess. Remembering our losses can look and feel like death or failure. It is seldom linked to hope.

Facing death is unavoidable as we begin our spiritual life or at any stage of rebirthing. Death prepares us for a new birth into a higher consciousness. We may think of death as darkness, regression and emotional destabilization. Here we are speaking about death as self-initiation into the process of becoming whole. It involves knowing your entire life and valuing all the broken pieces because they belong to your journey. Here, death is the initiation of your becoming what you can be. In its darkness you will open to the life of the spirit and transform the culture into which you were born. This kind of death means that we are letting go of life as we knew it through socialization in order to gain access to another life where our participation in the sacred becomes possible. You may also learn that death is not as final as you once thought. Spiritual death is never final because the death we feel will redirect us into new life. It gives us the courage to face tough times, and this idea is destined to play an essential role in your ongoing journey. This paradoxical connection between death and life becomes the foundation of our transformation and spiritual awakening. It sends us searching for meaning in the pursuit of wisdom and wholeness. When you are in pain wisdom invites you to search for meaning. Your search will transform death into life. In this way death contains hope.

Did you know that the Goddesses of Destiny were spinners? Spinning began as a woman's craft connecting time and destiny. Now it is time for you to understand the life you have lived so that you will become the goddess of your own destiny.

How We Feel

"Our pain is not a mistake ... it is a messenger."

We may be tempted to justify the extraordinary sacrifices we have made. In pride we say: "There was no one else available." "I did what I had to do." Denial will surface in many forms with a variety of justifications. We may be hesitant about letting go of the feeling that the worlds of those we love will not fall into shambles if we trust them to make their own decisions. We may be apprehensive about the vacancy we feel in our identities. We may worry about lacking purpose or usefulness in our lives if we let go of this unhealthy altruism. It may feel disempowering. We may begin to think of resocialization as a feminist movement. We may be tempted to use this label as a way of abandoning the journey of change in order to return to life as usual, especially when others accuse us of behaving like a bitch, or worse. But if you have come this far, life will never be the same.

The acknowledgement that our lives have been unhealthy may feel like a mental revolution beyond anything we have ever experienced. We may find ourselves questioning the very way we think and feel. Don't be afraid of this uncertainty that questions what you thought was unquestionable. In the past we relied on outside authorities for clarity, but the power of others can never create our authenticity. The uncertainty you feel now is the fertile ground necessary for you to redesign your life slowly and consciously. Uncertainty is an opportunity for you to weave your life. Ancient weaving took place in special places where only women were allowed to go. Both young and old gathered to discuss the ways of women as their hands glided across the looms, tightening and adjusting the color and fabrics of their design. So find a special place for your fear and darkness to be safe and be comforted. Don't miss this opportunity to connect with other weavers. Reaching out for help is a tremendously creative act. It takes into account what you need and the potential of the giver. Therefore, it should not be seen as a weakness, but a conscious personal power that continually asks itself if the gifts given and shared have ongoing value in your life. Reaching out is not an act of dependency, but of inter-dependency that leads to connection. It builds around you a community of friends. It expands your capacity for relationships. Reaching out is an acknowledgement that our lives are always connected to and responsive to the presence of others who can assist and enhance our life. Anything can happen when we reach out. We might get our connection easily or we may have to continue our search for comfort. The fact that anything can happen is the surprise and beauty of your spiritual life. Because some persons cannot give us what we need, that does not mean that no one can give us what we need.

We may feel suspicious of the supportive care we are receiving from our resocialized sisters. To be cared for has always been our fondest dream and our deepest dread. Caring for others excessively can cause us to forget our personal needs. What happens to us when we ignore our personal needs for long periods of time is tragic. Even worse: believing that we're not supposed to have needs and that somehow we are supposed to be big enough to absorb the needs of others and only incidentally think about our own. If our needs are not addressed for a long time we begin to feel self-conscious about having them. When we are lost, our relationships become codependent because we actually come to feel that others depend on us so completely that our withdrawal from their care would be the destruction of the entire relationship.

Proclaiming your needs in a relationship is an act of resocialization for women and may cause conflict. When you ask for what you need, you are reclaiming, redefining and rediscovering who you are. You are allowing another person to know you intimately. You become somebody when you speak your mind even if others don't agree. Silence, avoidance and unassertive behavior make it difficult for us to enjoy our relationships. No one wins when we disappear. To think otherwise is to build our lives on a false illusion that is directly related to socialization. Any time we break the silence of our forgotten self, we are victorious. It may take us some time to feel the victory of openness because everyone associated with us must readjust their perception of who we are in their minds. Be committed to the non-negotiable truths you are learning about your life. Those truths are based on one constant truth: Your life belongs to you. Being cared for is calling us out of hiding. Women have always been creative about finding ways to gather and speak about their lives. In spite of modern inventions, post-war women have become busier, and the ever-increasing demands on our time as full-time employees, dual-income partners and single parents–result in women becoming more and more isolated from one another. This is a huge loss.

America's employment force is dominated by women. Companies that employ women have little consideration for their role as parents, and as women increasingly become single parents, their isolation also increases. This isolation limits their support system and consequently threatens their feelings of well-being. What is implied here is that women who are unable to share with other women the truth of their lives are deprived of a crucial component for possibilities of friendship and all of its gifts. Learning to be cared for in a conclave of our peers is new and may initially feel strange. We need to speak about this strangeness because it too becomes a sign of the distinct way socialization has kept us from one another. In our isolation, we may have come to believe that we are the givers of love but are not supposed to be the receivers of love. Learning to seek out and receive the gift of friendship from other women is the way we gift ourselves.

How We Are With Others

"Every relationship we have changes us in some way."

Your socialized mentality permeates all of your interpersonal relationships. Take a moment to list all your significant relationships. Examine how much of your energy is focused on one and whether that extension of energy is in your best interest. Your best interest can be defined as what you are getting from each relationship. What feelings are connected to these relationships? Discuss your relationships with a trusted friend. It can help you become more objective. A friend can help you find new boundaries that are realistic because they take into account your limitations and needs. Friends can help us be more creative with our boundaries and remind us of what we deserve.

Don't blame yourself for your poor relationships. Remember that relationships are fluid experiences. You can shape and reshape them according to your awareness. Every kind of relationship we have changes us in some way. Their influential powers in our lives are an important part of our becoming. Each person you know is part of your journey. That they have influenced you in some way is indicative of your aliveness and your participation in the relationship experience. Relationships are opportunities to learn about ourselves and to learn more about what relationship means.

We will experience many kinds of relationships during our lifetime. Some will be successful for a lifetime; others will end as our life changes. Yet their enduring effects will shape who we are forever. Women love to talk about their relationships because they struggle to understand them; because they're proud of them or just because relationships are often the most important part of their lives. Because we are so relational, we tend to blame ourselves when relationships struggle or terminate. We ask ourselves repeatedly, "What we could have done differently?" A more beneficial question is, "What did I learn from this failed relationship?" We carry a heavy amount of shame and guilt about relationships that fail. This self-blaming may be another form of mother blaming. We blame mother for everything that goes wrong in a family because we hold her ultimately responsible for family harmony. Because she is mother, it is believed that she is the only person in a family that can make the family work. Women take this unrealistic expectation seriously because it is one of the strongest messages of socialization: that because you are a woman, you are solely responsible for the relationships you enter. Since all women are expected to be motherly, motherliness and perfectionism get paired and become subconscious assumptions for everything a woman does. Resist believing that an undesirable outcome means you were not good enough or adequate enough to make a relationship work.

This personal internalization of responsibility is a trap for women. This term means that you have made yourself profoundly responsible for others. The guilt and shame that we carry when we believe that we are responsible for the behavior and destiny of others can cripple our emotional growth and destroy our peace. Learning to be gentle with you in relationships is an important step toward resocialization. Guilt and shame only take your power away from you and they misrepresent the extent of your personal power. They prevent you from learning the lessons you need to learn in relationships because you are wasting your energy overcoming self-incrimination. When we blame ourselves, we are like everyone else who blames us for the sole purpose of vindicating themselves from responsibility of loving, caring and relating. We must speak to ourselves in a different voice, one that is kind and compassionate.

Fight unrealistic expectations by talking to trusted friends and by facing the limitations of your power. Remind yourself over and over again that healthy love has boundaries. Boundaries and love can, and must, co-exist to ensure comfortable, healthy relationships.

Because we are so eager to love, we are inclined to feel that only we know about love. Resist deceiving yourself in this way. Any relationship you have is as much about the other as it is about you. In relationships you are a partner, not the director. Don't be conned into any other role. The role of partner in a relationship makes it easier for you to maintain your individuality while you love. Getting lost in love endangers us and those we love because it requires self-denunciation rather than self-actualization. The unhealthy application of this faulty principle weighs heavily on your life. Only you can bring yourself back to a reality that makes sense. It does not mean that you are less loving or less of a woman. It simply means that loving yourself must be a part of all love.

JOURNALING

1. As a result of socialization, we begin to think that we are only good when we are giving. Our goodness gets linked to how much we give. When we give without boundaries, parts of our own life get lost. Cultural myth is that a good woman loves without loving herself. Describe the losses in your life that were caused by your need to be a good woman. **Write!**

2. How did you experience each of these losses? Most women like to think that they are immune to the tragic effects of gender socialization. They do this by not acknowledging their experiences of loss. Did you hide from the pain of loss? Did you talk about it or remain silent? Did you behave as if it didn't matter? **Write!**

3. When we understand loss, we can also feel the emotional consequences of a forgotten Self. Socialization suddenly becomes real. Without experiencing pain, real healing does not happen. How do you recognize your pain? How do you feel it in your body and in your heart? Share a loss with an important friend after you have written about it. Think about how you can take command of pain by listing the steps that you can take to stop running away from it. **Write!**

4. Losses are hard to acknowledge if you have never thought about your possibilities. If you are having a difficult time completing these journaling assignments because you cannot identify your losses, then find a longtime friend with whom you feel safe. Ask her to help you note your losses. **Write!**

REFLECTIVE CINEMA

Movies that reinforce the themes of this stage recommended for viewing:

- Used People
- Tootsie
- Rabbit-Proof Fence
- White Oleander

STEPPING OUT

- How have you felt blamed in your life? Contact one of the blaming people and confront them about how damaging the blaming was to your life.
- Call a friend and ask for help with a project you are working on.
- Have a Goddess Party. Invite your friends to honor how wonderful they are. Tell them to bring pictures of their lives. Write a short story about their life to share with the group.
- Go shopping. Buy yourself a gift.

Story of a Married Woman

Most of the time she did not feel real; certainly not fully alive. She remembered that once Sue asked her in a half joking way, what she did for fun. What made her laugh out loud? Nina pondered, taking the question seriously, and then finally said that she was ticklish under her arm. She then quickly admitted that it had been years since anyone had found that spot. Nina realized that she and Sue were different, but couldn't identify why. She had tried for years to get her involved in a friendship on a much deeper and honest level, but quite frankly, Nina didn't know how to join her at that level. She felt an inadequacy and self consciousness that could only be protected by resistance. Had Sue seen more in Nina than Nina recognized in herself? Perhaps that is why she felt self-conscious around Sue.

Nina suddenly felt annoyed. How could Sue know more about her than she knew about herself? Nina had such ambivalent feelings. Mysteriously, she accepted most of Sue's invitations because some part of her was intrigued by this woman. Another part of her was upset by someone who wanted to change the only world she knew, the world she had sacrificed so much to create. Sue's knowing about Nina's life was not magical or presumptuous. It could not be ascribed to some supernatural powers that allow one human being to be insightful about another. What Sue recognized in Nina was a woman like herself. The woman she used to be. At that time, Sue had been forced to examine her life and that meant looking inward. It had taken a major crisis that she would never forget to set her on the path of reclaiming life. Sue had never shared with Nina the details of her personal pain; anguish so intense that she had been forced to walk in a darkness she had never known. Sue knew that Nina wasn't ready to hear about such deep brokenness and pain. But she also felt that Nina possessed the capacity for intimacy and eventually someday, they would be able to share all their thoughts and feelings. She too knew that the catalyst, the thing that would elevate their friendship to another level, may be sharing her personal pain with Nina. She waited patiently for the right moment.

Nina envied Sue. She envied the ease with which she spoke, the lack of restraint in discussing topics that were personal. Sue could laugh at things like her un-chic wardrobe, dismiss her weight and be totally happy with herself. She could easily glide from joy to anger, annoyance to peace, honesty to privacy. There were times when Sue seemed old and wise and other times when she was childlike. The agenda of her life was constantly changing and yet she moved from one event to another gracefully, as though it was expected. A few weeks after the meeting, on a cool October morning, they met at the community park to attempt a two-mile walk. The air was crisp; the park, quieter than usual. After one lap around the path Sue asked Nina to sit with her on a bench that faced a small lake. It was time, Sue felt, to stretch the intimacy level of their friendship. She sat facing Nina and related her story without shame or guilt. She explained to Nina that from the beginning of her marriage Erin was preoccupied with something, something that he couldn't or wouldn't share with his wife. She'd felt excluded, but did not understand from what. For years she felt uncomfortable questioning her husband. He sometimes left the house without telling her where he was going or where he had been. He woke very early, and while everyone still slept, worked on his computer. He stayed up late at night to watch television. He said he needed his own quiet time.

Their sex life, from the beginning of their relationship, was physically satisfying but emotionally disappointing. After sex, Sue usually felt good and close to Erin, but the feeling of closeness didn't last. She knew that he liked pornography and accidentally discovered his cache. She dismissed her discovery believing that most men needed to satisfy their oversexed nature. She'd never discussed it with him. After her two babies were born, Sue paid less attention to Erin's personal needs, especially his desire for privacy. She was so busy; she'd simply reconciled herself to his emotional unavailability. He helped her around the house and was willing to babysit. She was glad that she was at least free to develop her own interests. Besides, she'd rationalized Erin was good-natured and worked hard to support his family. In her heart, however, Sue knew that the relationship between them lacked something very substantial. Intimacy.

The years seemed to fly by. Then, one cold February day, Sue was presented with terrible news, she had breast cancer. She was shaken to her core. She remembered days when she'd actually held on to a wall or gate as she walked along the street, feeling so fearful and dizzy that she thought she'd pass out. Over the next few weeks, after the diagnosis, she began her painful adjustment to the reality that she might actually die. Everything in her life began to feel different. She told everyone in her family, including her two children about the prospects that faced her. As she tried to accept the possibility of imminent death, her fear subsided. Instead, a strange intensity emerged. Suddenly life seemed more precious. Not knowing how much time she had, Sue wanted to reclaim the part of herself she lost years before. She would not squander another day, another moment. After years of silence, she finally confronted her husband about his use of pornography. She wanted to know what he did on the computer during the wee hours of the morning. She told him of the space she felt between them, the unknown, the unsaid. Her loneliness screamed at him for truth not compliance; for a love she wanted and now demanded. Where did love go? Why did everything feel so wrong, when it seemed apparently right? What was his mystery?

After prolonged discussions, Erin finally told Sue about his private life, the one he had kept separate from her. He cried as he finally admitted the sexual addiction that had plagued him most of his life. As he confessed his shameful truths, Sue finally understood the secret and the mystery she'd always felt. For years during their marriage, Erin seemed emotionally detached, yet attentive to the children, sometimes in ways that made Sue feel uncomfortable because he gave the children the love she craved. Erin didn't seem sexually interested; their intimacy lacked tenderness. It lacked friendship. When she complained about being lonely in bed, he complained of restlessness. The discomfort she felt was vague at some times and poignant at others. When the family was all together, Sue felt that everything was okay, but when she and Erin were alone, their distance was unavoidable. However, she wanted to hope that there must be a way through this storm. As Sue told her story to Nina, she cried quietly. She told Nina the irony was that the thought of death forced her to find reasons to live. No longer could she justify or rationalize the dissatisfaction with her marriage. Erin was relieved, no longer torn apart by guilt and fear. In their darkest hour, their marriage was created. The tears they shed, the anguish they shared forced them to look within. Apart from the way they saw each other and their marriage, there was absolutely nothing to change. Nina listened with new respect to her friend. What should she say to Sue? She reached over, hugged her and whispered, "Thank you."

The breast cancer crisis had occurred five years earlier. At this point in the marriage, no visible remnants of those terrible days remained. Both Sue and Erin had been determined to not only stay in the marriage, but to make it better. Now, after years of therapy, there was complete truth and openness.

Nina walked with Sue to their cars, knowing that they made a great personal leap. Her friendship with Sue would never be the same. For the first time since she'd met Sue, Nina felt she could really call her a friend. Above and beyond her growing intimacy with Sue, something else had happened to Nina. She'd not only learned something about Sue, but about herself. What she'd learned did not yet have words, but it was lying there in her heart waiting to be named.

Story of a Lesbian Woman

"AS SHE SAID GOOD-BYE, SHE WAS CERTAIN THAT HER FRIENDSHIP
WITH SARA COULD NEVER INCLUDE GEORGE."

Thea's friendship with Sara was a gift she cherished. Gradually, Sara included her in outings to the park and luncheons at her home. Sometimes Thea helped feed the children and played with them. She never saw herself in a motherly role, nor did she ever believe that she could duplicate the love they shared with Sara. She offered them a different kind of love, one that was about being a friend. They welcomed what she offered freely. That she and Sara lived in separate worlds was very clear when she spent time with her and the children. She admired her ability to love in so many ways, even when she was exhausted. She couldn't understand George's emotional absence from a woman who was emotionally connected to every moment of his life. Nothing about Sara's life seemed alien except her tolerance of an unhappy marriage. Thea spoke openly with Sara about her life as a lesbian. She talked about her friends, her dates, her conflicts at work; her parent's lack of affirmation. It was refreshing to talk openly and not be judged. Sometimes Sara offered insights that Thea gratefully accepted.

As time passed, Thea felt like a permanent part of Sara's life. She held a sacred place in Thea's heart where no one else had ever been. They planned at least one weekend outing that always included the children. Thea began to realize that her life with Sara was her life. She dated other women and occasionally went to T-Dances on Sunday afternoons, but it wasn't as satisfying or as real as her time with Sara and the children. Most nights they spoke on the phone savoring every moment as they shared the history of their lives.

Thea knew Sara many months before she finally met George. He was a handsome man, but rigid and unwelcoming. He tried hard to be polite, but Thea could see that it seemed difficult. One Friday night she was invited for dinner. Everything went well until George noticed how much Thea helped Sara and how happy the children were around her. He made a strong attempt to distract his children from Thea's attention. She felt so ashamed that she wanted to run as fast as she could to distance herself from what was becoming a hostile gathering. Meeting George could be the end of the safest relationship she had even known. She could imagine George prohibiting Sara from seeing her. She feared the possible loss. A silent hush permeated the entire evening. Thea stayed only to please Sara and the children. As she said good-bye, she was certain that her friendship with Sara could never include George. He would not allow that to happen.

In late October, Sara invited Thea to go pumpkin hunting. She planned the carriage ride through a pumpkin field looking for just the right shape to carve. Thea refused the invitation. This was her first refusal. It had nothing to do with the pumpkins or Sara and the children. It was Thea's way of pulling back from the growing desire to want what she and Sara could never have. She didn't want to ruin what they had and did not want to agonize over a forbidden love. She could feel Sara's astonishment and hurt when she refused the invitation. Further discussion over the phone only became more unsatisfying. Thea would have to take a risk and tell Sara openly about her growing conflict. Maybe the power of her desire would be demystified if she talked openly. As Thea planned her conversation with Sara, she became clearer about what it mean to be lesbian. Her relationship with Sara actually expanded what lesbianism meant. When she first came out, it was a sexual discovery. Now it expanded to include a life with another woman, doing the everyday things any other couple would do as they journeyed through life. Her relationship with Sara made her realize the way she wanted to live. She wanted the fullness of life that came from life itself, as is lived and experienced in friendship and caring. Sex is the physical, sacred celebration of a life in union with another, but only part of this connection. Sex no longer depicted the only distinction that separated lesbians from all other women. As she went out with her friends that Saturday afternoon, her heart was heavy. The only comfort was her determination to talk with Sara.

Story of a Black Woman

"IN OUR HOUSEHOLD, FOOD WAS CELEBRATED ... USED TO COMFORT AND PLEASE US. MOST IMPORTANTLY, IT CONVEYED LOVE AND SURVIVAL."

My grandmother and my mother told me that black women are very familiar with oppression. They have been forced to cope with it for centuries. My mother made us read black history books and biographies of famous black women. I knew reading was more about inspiration than information. I was happy to read as many books as possible because it gave me a good reason to stay indoors where I was close to my grandmother and protected from the outside world.

The aromas from my grandmother's kitchen made my head spin. I would literally be right under my grandmother's apron and on weekends, when my mother was home, the kitchen was like a girl's club. "In our household, food was celebrated; used to comfort and please us. Most importantly, it conveyed love and survival." The kitchen was a place where I was always welcome, even expected, to shine. Good food has always taken us through the fire and sustained us in survival. We had to nurture our children and our men. We had to be strong for our men because being weak was not an option, at least not publicly. So, on whom do we lean when the world is so heavy on our shoulders and our backs are bowed? We rely on one another.

When I was young and living at home, we were not expected to be slim. It is only now that I am expected to compete with white women. Grandmother told me that her generation thought it was unhealthy for black women to be judged on a white woman's terms. She gave me a hard time when it became obvious that I was trying to control my weight. My struggle with my grandmother began during late adolescence because when I stepped outside of my own world, fat no longer made me feel strong, proud and fine. When I entered high school, others judged my full, strong body as out-of-control, uncared for, sloppy, dirty and low class. For many years food became my enemy. When I was eating alone, I used it to plug the holes within me that needed to be filled with love. My body carried my shame. In my dorm, food was my mama, my grandma and my lover. It never hurt me like my daddy, my classmates or the white world.

My mother and my grandmother were in conflict about my weight, but my mother won. My mother pictured me raising my wings and competing with whites at their level.

She knew a fat woman would never make it. She changed my diet dramatically. I hated the restrictions, but longed for the results. This pursuit of thinness seemed to put a strain on my relationship with my grandmother. She thought of my thinness as surrendering. My mother thought it was victory. I was ambivalent. It seemed I wasn't going to win this battle and this realization depressed me.

Because I was so intelligent, I went to a school outside of my community. A full scholarship was an honor, but it thrust me into a white world with no support. Being fat and black made me feel unlovable and shamed to my core. My sexuality terrified me. Sex became synonymous with fear and shame. My fat allowed me to avoid the issue completely until my sophomore year in college. That's I met Vance.

He must have noticed my naivety right away. He approached me with kindness and offered me friendship. I was flattered to have a male friend, but terrified at the same time. After two months of friendship, he asked me out on a real date. I was ready to have fun as a friend, but not as a lover. Vance had something else in mind. He presumed my willingness to be sexually active. All evening, I fought him off until his persistence created enough self-doubt that surrender was my only option. Now I felt shame was attacking another part of me, the part that wanted to say "no." The part that still wanted my body for me, that was afraid of not being good enough. My shame could not challenge his complete determination to grow me up! I felt violated and betrayed, not only by myself, but Vance. Did he see the holes inside of me from lack of love? Within our own community, sisters are looked at and treated as sex objects. What I wanted from Vance was love. What he wanted from me was sex. He used my body to prove his manhood. And I allowed him to.

Story of a Woman ... Now Old

During the two years that my father was gone, his children had become an independent family that no longer required parental guidance. My Uncle Moses lovingly watched over us without exerting his power to control our lives. He seemed to innately believe that we could find our way, and we did. I think he intuitively knew the enormous force of our love and loyalty to one another. I never tried to discipline any of my brothers or sisters. Loving and caring for them was my deepest concern. There was no energy to create rules or enforce them. We all seemed to know that our lives were indelibly bound by the death of our mother. As best we could, we parented each other. I was the hub of their unity, their care and of the family we had become. That position started before my mother's death and magnified profoundly after. To this day, that central role has never changed.

My father returned to the family as insensitively as he had left. After two and one half years, he walked through our door with Julia. I was sixteen. Julia was seventeen, the same age as my brother Eddie. We were shocked to see him and even more confused by this young woman who had become his new bride.

Like my mother, Anna, Julia's life was completely derailed because of my father's interest in her. From an early age, she wanted to become a nun in the Eastern Religion. Just as she was about to leave her family to enter the novitiate, her parents decided she should marry my father. She did not know him, and she certainly did not love him. She did not want him, but because her life was the property of her family, through an arranged marriage, she joined with my father in Lebanon. After two and one half years, she said good-bye to her parents and sailed to America, never seeing her parents again. She told me that she prayed the ship would sink before it reached America. How sad that she felt only death could save her from a life she did not choose.

*My father entered my bedroom one night, shortly after they arrived and announced that we should call Julia, "mother." I told him swiftly and directly that we would never do that. "We had one mother and she is dead," I said. "We will not have another." To my surprise, my father left my room quietly. I started calling Julia **Khalaty**, the Arabic word for maternal aunt, and so did my brothers and sisters.*

I could recognize the same sadness in Julia that I saw in my mother. She was trapped in a life and a relationship that had nothing to do with her own dreams. Her life had become a possession before she knew what life was about. Her spirit was dominated by sadness, lost hope and dreams.

Realizing My Losses

I will grieve personal losses as I remember all the people and causes I made more important than myself."

How We Think

"Now you must come to understand the time you have lived, to become the goddess of your own destiny."

Most of us feel that good communicators speak clearly and willingly about whatever is on their mind. We get so stuck on this idea that we often neglect to recognize listening as the other side of good communication. Communication gives us an opportunity to disclose ourselves in very important ways. But without a good listener who can receive our sharing, the experience is lame at best. Without a good listener we are echoing in a chamber of lost hope. Without a good listener, emotional vulnerability is uncomfortable. We all know the emptiness of being unacknowledged. One of the cruelties of abuse is being ignored; deliberately overlooked.

Because we are women, what we say is often disregarded as unimportant, unenlightened and lacking authority. For centuries the devaluing of our thoughts and contributions has been a legacy of loss for humankind. Whatever is feminine is devalued, and that is never more dramatically demonstrated than through our communication with others. This tragic result of socialization can cause us to doubt our own intelligence, our own wisdom, and stifle, in a dramatic way, the contributions of our creative energies. While we cannot reverse this cultural, prejudicial tragedy quickly, we can learn to respect our own voice and the voices of other women. Every act of listening and sharing changes the energy of this world in some way.

Not being listened to hurts us at a deeper level; the implication being that we are not important. Ignoring us erodes our self-opinion and belief in our personal power. Maybe that is why we use so much of our power to serve, rather than lead.

Many of us live in silence about our life experiences. We may think that no one wants to listen to the story of our insignificant lives. Women think that their lives are too private to share and too unimportant to be interesting. This is the same silence that kept their mothers from them. Now we must recognize and work to resolve this toxic silence. Most of us have not listened to our mothers discuss their lives. Unless we ask our mothers how they feel, what they dream of, and what they've missed, we may never know. They, like us, have fallen victim to this socialization of silence. What we don't know about our mothers and grandmothers are part of our lost Self.

So you can see that listening requires much more from us than our silence. The first acts of listening take place inside us. When we develop a profound respect for the lives that women lead, we want to listen. Listening begins when we are at peace with letting each woman's journey be uniquely and forever her own experience. Listening begins when we don't feel compelled to find solutions or give advice. Listening begins when we understand that we grow when we know, so we must listen to learn, not to win. Listening requires as much of us as sharing.

When we are listened to, the gift of true communication is realized. It is a gift appreciated and realized by everyone involved. It makes us feel noticed, understood, appreciated and taken seriously. Someone else is witnessing the way we are experiencing our lives. Listening to one another creates the opportunity to appreciate that person's life experiences. We help them feel accepted and shatter the isolation that silence creates.

So many women suffer privately, and the isolation of their suffering magnifies its destructive influence. Because we are practiced in private suffering, we are usually reluctant to seek out other women who are willing to help us by listening. We forget that our private suffering not only ensures that our isolation will continue, but withholds from other women the gift they would receive if we would allow them to be available to us. When we actively listen to another woman, we participate in their healing. Active listening is conscious listening. It involves being emotionally and mentally present to another woman as she unveils her story. Genuine listening means that we suspend memory, desire and judgment, and for a few moments, exist for another person. When the experience is sincere, the emphasis is on the other woman's words, tone, body language and feelings. As listeners, we hear our own stories echoed in another woman's life.

Don't resist the identification you feel, use it to develop empathy. As you listen, do not match her story with your own experiences. We have all had the experience of sharing something with another person and having that person respond with, "Oh, you think that's bad? Let me tell you what happened to me!" This type of response invalidates what has been shared with you. It is competitive in nature. The art of listening begins with an open heart. And by listening with an open heart, we learn how to give true comfort.

Make it a point to let your sister know that you have heard what she said without judgment. Offer words of empathy, encouragement, support, or simply be quiet with each other. Ask questions about what was not clear. Ask her to expand on the parts of her story that interest you. Thank her for trusting you with the sacredness of her life. Remember how privileged you are that another human being is showing you her inner life. Listening can transform your relationships in ways you can't imagine. Don't take listening for granted and don't overrate yourself as a good listener. It takes determination and practice to be a good listener.

As we learn to give comfort and to accept support, love and acceptance of other women, our selfhood will emerge. The connection with other women is a primary ingredient in self love. Loving ourselves is inseparable from loving the experiences of womanhood with all its variations. We are powerful when we listen, and it is important that we respect that kind of power.

How We Feel

"Your ability to listen indicates the level of peace you have attained."

Our lives are haunted by the constant specter of perfectionism. We compare ourselves to the myth of perfect as if perfection were real. We criticize ourselves and other woman for not being perfect enough, as if being perfect was possible. When things go wrong in our lives we consider the unfortunate event as evidence of our inadequacy, and so we hide in shame. The impossible dreams we hold inside have robbed us of our right to be human. As women we are expected to rise above our humanness instead of embracing it. Humanness requires the acceptance of fragility and error. Humanness includes the realization that we cannot control the destiny of others. It means that we can feel tired and that wecan say "no." It means that we are evolving. It means that we have the right to love ourselves in all circumstances. It means we have the right to make decisions about our behavior that are Self centered rather than other centered. Being Self centered affords us the human dignity of stopping long enough to think about how we feel and about the consequences of our behavior in our own lives.

How does perfectionism prohibit listening, you might ask? When a listener expects perfection, she is more likely to be critical, or even hyper-critical, than accepting. Judging is not listening. It is uninviting because it is emotionally unsafe. Perfectionism is destructive because it interrupts the spiritual flow of energy that creates interpersonal unions, which should be the objective of all communication! Instead, judging imposes an outside agenda on someone's life that has nothing to do with their real journey. Perfectionism creates an agenda of intolerance by demanding that its criteria be met for acceptance to be given. Thus, the agenda of perfectionism makes us feel ashamed of our humanness. We don't want anyone to hear our true story because we fear being measured against a myth of impossible dreams. Perfectionism holds women accountable to rigid codes that are manufactured by sexist beliefs about women. This may be why so many women, young and old, hesitate to discuss their lives. Perfectionism is the patriarchal notion of what women are supposed to be, causing them to feel inadequate when they do not measure up or when they stumble along the journey of life.

Women have been listeners who did not always respect one another. We made ourselves available to men and gave them unconditional positive regard because we were socialized to believe they deserved it, even when we didn't like what we heard. Resocialization invites you to regard all women respectfully and with a willingness to learn about the ingenious ways they survived their lives. Resocialization challenges you to listen without feeling that you must agree. Listening does not require agreement. However, it does require respect. One of the most important contributions of the feminist movement was inviting women to experience the rich rewards of gathering and listening to one another. It encouraged them to critically examine patriarchal ideals that dictated the course of their lives. They found a new ideal for human behavior that continues to create opportunities for women and balance for humanity. From the movement grew a whole body of information we now call the psychology of women. Women's organizations are creating special events throughout the world to encourage listening to one another and being inspired. But resocialization is your private transformation. Listening to yourself and other women is laying claim to your own fundamental right: to love the journey of your life.

Listening to one another creates a journey of hope for all women, especially you. Listening unites us and comforts us. The creativity of other women becomes your personal resource for change. Listening shatters our over-privatized lives by showing us that other women struggle, too. When they openly tell their stories, we can be encouraged to shake off the demonizing shame and guilt. Listening invites us to feel the peace of being with someone without being responsible for them. Learning to be supportive, and expressing that support, enables us to feel positive about ourselves. Listening is a positive use of our power. Listening to learn eliminates the power struggle of having to dominate. It puts you directly in touch with the diversity that exists in all relationships. It is an opportunity for you to be awed by the richness of diversity and to use it to expand your own awareness.

Because the sphere of women's power has been narrow, we cling to our rightness as a way of proving our worth. This struggle oftentimes makes mother-daughter relationships very tense. Without a doubt, mothers have authority over the lives of their daughters, but when that authority clings too rigidly to being right it alienates rather than integrates the relationship. Think about this: how much more expansive would our authority be if we could listen without feeling the need to be right? The healthy use of authority would mean the right to influence rather than dominate.

Your ability to listen indicates the level of peace you have attained. Your ability to listen indicates how resocialized you have become. Listening indicates your spiritual depth and makes you a creator of world harmony.

How We Are With Others

"One identity is forged by feeling unified with other women."

We will gain equality by changing our relationships with other women because it is with them that we can experience equality. The demands that absorb our lives often rob us of the rich and close connections we can have with other women. When we listen to one another, we drastically change our relationships. Our social isolation is broken when we are heard. Our support system becomes real when we listen and share the truth of our lives. Our support system is an essential component for change; it is our family of choice. We must build that support system with loving care and deliberateness. It is at this stage in our resocialization that we should be choosing a team of women who are also in transformation. They will become a meaningful reference group that will strengthen our efforts by providing encouragement and the sweet experience of being cared for and listened to.

Our identity is forged by feeling unified with other women. The weakness of our past association with womankind has created divisions among us and resulted in our political oppression. Unity will heal that fragmentation. It will couple our personal strength with the collective strength of women. In order for us to develop this identification, we must see ourselves in every woman. Our connection to one another will make us more alive in our living, more spontaneous in our loving and more zealous in our pursuit of justice. At age eighty, Elsa Gidlow authored *Creed For A Free Woman*. A passage from this poem defines our lives.

> "I AM CHILD OF EVERY MOTHER,
> MOTHER OF EVERY DAUGHTER,
> SISTER OF EVERY WOMAN,
> AND LOVER OF WHOM I CHOOSE OR CHOOSES ME."

Only women can truly understand the significance of being resocialized. By connecting with other women we allow ourselves the pleasure of a support system that knows us, understands our joy and pain, and has the kind of wisdom necessary to help us to continue to grow in resocialization. Our connection with other women should go beyond our personal lives. We should all consider and encourage relationships with women who play a part in our professional, medical, financial and spiritual well-being. Resocialization includes supporting and encouraging women who are willing to challenge the masculine culture that dominates the world and resists the integration of feminine qualities. A respect for what is feminine will balance the movement of medicine, politics and religion. It will ensure that women will be heard. It will close the divide between men and women.

Those of us who teach children can cultivate in them a respect for women. Every woman, upon the discovery she is pregnant, should take the following pledge: "If you are a boy, you will respect women. If you are a girl, you are definitely going to respect yourself."

Let your children listen to your voice. Tell stories about your life and the lives of their grandmothers. It is then that they will have an intimate knowledge of your life. They will come to better understand who you truly are and gain a deeper respect for your personal history. As they get older, they will expand their understanding of you and connect it to their own history. In this way, they will carry you and your feminine nature into their own future.

Because most women have a long history of not being listened to in relationships that they counted on for understanding, they may resist your interest in wanting to hear what they have to say. Our history of not being listened to has hurt us deeply because it compromised the power of our convictions. That means even when we have an opinion, we are timid about convincing others of what we believe. People who sense our lack of conviction don't listen to us. We may have cut ourselves off from others because the others of our childhood and early adulthood did not take us seriously enough to listen to us. Listening is the difference between feeling accepted and feeling isolated; it is a rich potential for women. The part of us that was never heard increases the gap between our true Self and our false Self. The part of us that is never heard discourages our creative Self. What conveys loving appreciation is being noticed, understood and taken seriously. Listening indicates your willingness to suspend your presumptions and instead, remain open to discovery. Listening is an open-ended experience that is designed by the speaker and listener. Your presence and emotional availability is the greatest proof of your sincerity. When we see sadness or depression in someone, we assume that something iswrong, that something has happened. Maybe that something is that nobody is listening.

129

JOURNALING

1. To sensitize you to what listening is all about, take ten minutes to listen to the sounds around you. Words, nature sounds, traffic, animals, house sounds etc.; tune your ear to their entering and leaving. Write about the experience. How do you connect to these sounds? Where does your body sense them? **WRITE!**

2. Find a woman friend who wants to share a troubling experience. Without interruption, sit and listen to her talk for at least ten minutes. Empty yourself in order to connect. Remind yourself of how capable she is of arriving at her own truth. Remind yourself that her pain, her boundaries, her problems are not your responsibility. Take note of her choice of words, the expressed emotions. Do the emotions match the words? Listen for what is not being said. Pay attention to the meaning of the words spoken as well as their sounds. If you are not comfortable with this or unable to find someone to do this with, attend an Alcoholics Anonymous meeting or that of some other co-dependency group where people share openly. **WRITE!**

3. How did you feel while listening to your friend? Did you feel empowered by listening to her? What truth have you discovered in your friend's reality? Tell her that you are grateful for her trust in you, that you appreciate her openness and that you respect her for it. Let her know that you are sorry that this painful experience happened, and that you are confident that she will be able to work through it. Let her know that you heard what she was saying and that you learned from her. Then write about the experience—what did you learn from her and about yourself? **WRITE!**

4. Take a sheet of paper. On the left side, list the women who have influenced you as a child, adolescent and teaching stage of your adulthood. On the right side, list a quality, attribute or wisdom that each woman represents. Review the list. Do you see any patterns? What have you learned from other women in your lifetime? **WRITE!**

REFLECTIVE CINEMA

Movies that reinforce the themes of this stage recommended for viewing:

- Bridges of Madison County
- Far From Heaven
- The Joy Luck Club
- Beaches

STEPPING OUT

- Have a listening party. Participants talk about their lives for five-minute intervals on any topic. Each person has four speaking sessions. No one can give advice. Listeners take one minute to thank the speaker for her sharing. Example: "Thank you for telling us about your mother's death."
- Ask a friend to make your favorite dessert.
- Say "no" to someone who requests something of you.
- Go dancing with your friends.

Story of a Married Woman

"SOMEWHERE ALONG THE WAY, THEY'D LOST THE ZEST FOR LIFE ...
THE JOY OF BEING A COUPLE."

After listening to Sue's story, Nina felt another emotional shift inside of herself. She was changed. It wasn't just about knowing Sue's story that caused this new awakening; it went much deeper than that. What was happening to her was not a conversion, but a conversation with herself to which she was listening.

Over the next few days as she went through her daily routine, one that no longer required her conscious attention, she thought about the possibility of change. Would she, could she ever possess the freedom Sue had found? It was attractive and desirable, but was it attainable? She had known freedom before, but was not certain she recognized or knew how to achieve it now. Freedom meant something different now because she was married with children. She wondered if she had the right to personal freedom. There were times in her childhood when she'd felt free enough to say what was on her mind, not worrying about anyone's approval. Between the ages of seven and ten, she'd been a tomboy and hung out with all of the neighborhood boys. She played their games and loved the competition. She wasn't shy and never held back from taking a dare or a risk. It was rare for her not to have scabs on her knees. Fear or self-consciousnesses did not govern her life then. How did she lose that precious freedom?

When had everything changed? Puberty! Her developing breasts had been a danger signal to her mother. Then, everything Nina did was examined and criticized. She was suddenly made to feel that the world had become a dangerous place for girls and her friendship with boys was tainted with suspicions and accusations. This sudden shift in her parent's attitude spoiled the way she related to boys. The equality they previously shared was strained with tension that felt unresolved. The worlds between girls and boys became separate without either group knowing why.

As Nina grew older, the separate worlds of the sexes became more apparent and it was taken for granted. Her love for men was expected simply because it was presumed that she was going to be a wife and mother. She loved her husband and children. That was never in doubt. Her love quickly became a pattern of shoulds and should nots. She fell into the trap of not questioning the reasons why her life felt out of her control; unauthentic.

Most people who knew Nina and Joe, or more accurately viewed their relationship from the outside, thought it was great. How could they know the lack of passion and communication that made Nina feel like they were strangers living under the same roof? Often, it felt like they were reading a script. It was not a romantic script. They rarely laughed and hardly ever smiled.

Somewhere along the way, they'd lost the zest for life, the joy of being a couple. Maybe it was unrealistic to expect life to always be a honeymoon, but what was supposed to come after? What was supposed to be there instead? Nina wondered if the answer could simply be that they both worked so hard at being married they forgot to be lovers. Whatever had caused it was not nearly as important as recognizing that something essential to her happiness was missing. Somewhere during the years they'd been together, Joe had become a stranger to Nina and Nina, a stranger to herself.

Sitting in the circle of women each month could lead her to places she never thought she'd see; revolutionize her life if she allowed herself to admit how much she longed for change. What would it cost? It could happen, if she could let go of her image of the perfect wife; the perfect daughter; and the perfect woman. But, to leave those roles, to shed the burden of their demands, would be like stripping naked. She knew that most things worth doing or having exacted a price. Was she willing to pay?

A lobster sheds its shell to grow a new one. During that time, the lobster is totally vulnerable. Yet, if it does not shed the shell, it never grows. Nina knew what she had to shed, but had no idea what would replace it. And, because of the fear, because she could not imagine what would replace her comfortable, numbed existence, she sadly admitted that it might require more than she could handle at this moment. She asked herself privately, over and over again, "Can I do this?" If she decided to exercise her right of choice, if she demanded some time and space for herself, it would cause conflict in the family. They were all comfortable with the way she was, a person who Nina did not even know. She was the person who was always there, the one that could always be counted on by everyone but herself. They depended on her and she allowed the constant dependency for so long. Everyone in this family was living a script that wasn't working, especially for her and Joe.

She both envied and respected Sue, who had dared to transform her relationship with Erin into something good. She had been strong enough to demand the change. She wanted a complete life and she got it. She must ask her, "How does one begin? What do you do? How do you start to find your way when you are so far off course?"

Nina felt lost and confused. Sue was her only role model for living a different way. What she'd seen her whole life was her mother being all the things her father and children needed her to be. Nina rolled her eyes, imagining her mother's reaction to her desire for inter-dependence. Could she relate to a daughter who wanted to be her own person? Nina wondered, Could it be that being a wife and mother was not enough? If this was true, what did it say about her mother's life? If Nina dared to change, if she found she needed more to be happy, wouldn't her mother see this deviation as a rejection of her own life? Could her mother approve of a less traditional life?

It was easier for her to imagine her mother's anger. She remembered how her mother gave constant and un-requested advice under the guise of support. Julia had always been a devoted mother, but Nina understood there were things about her mother that she might never know. She wondered if her mother ever knew herself. Did her mother also have dreams she had to put away? Was there ever a time that her mother enjoyed her dreams and danced in the moonlight? Thinking about her mother made Nina feel sad; it made her realize that she too had relinquished her own dreams. Now Nina knew she could not think of what was lost, but what she had to gain. She thought of how she might begin to reclaim herself.

That evening, after the children were in bed, she told Joe she was going to attend a woman's meeting each month. She told him he would have to help her out with dinner and the kids. She told him how important it was to her. He wasn't pleased. It made no sense to him; it was a waste of time. What he could not admit was the fear he felt because he sensed something different about Nina. He worried that any changes the group might encourage in Nina might require changes in him as well. "We're doing fine. The kids are happy. Their school work is outstanding. What more do you need? You always want more, Nina! More, more, more!" Joe protested.

Accusations like this diminished Nina's power . She'd start out feeling strong and confident about her needs, but he could so easily obliterate power, and guilt rushed in to take its place. After a long pause, she spoke, forcing the words, "Yes! I want more!" She went on to explain that more does not have to mean the destruction of what they already had. "It means I want to get to know me again. I don't even know who me is any more. That's all it means." Both were intelligent enough to know that Nina's changing would have a ripple effect on the entire family. She believed what they both needed now was to trust that their love would endure, no matter what changes might occur. Clearly,

Joe did not see this as a beginning of something better, and that put pressure on Nina. She had to rely on her own strength and faith without his approval. She knew she would put one foot in front of the other and proceed. She wished it were with his blessings because she still felt uneasy and uncomfortable when she went against his wishes. But she had made a choice and she would continue, and see where the road might take her. In order to do this, she would have to tolerate the distance this might cause between them. Unsure as to where it would lead, Nina took the first step onto an uncertain path.

Story of a Lesbian Woman

Thea realized that a lunch-hour conversation would be inadequate. She invited Sara to dinner knowing that it might cause problems at home. Without hesitation, Sara accepted. They met at a small, quiet Italian restaurant on the east side of Manhattan. Thea wasn't sure if they should talk before or after dinner, but ultimately decided to take her cues from Sara. She hoped that Sara could be as present to her anguish and tender feelings as she had always been in the past. Sara was always an audience to lesbian life. Over the months, she heard Thea's stories, but now, she was becoming part of her love and desire. Thea feared this could be the end of their friendship or a major change that would alter their connectedness.

Thea arrived early to prepare herself to reveal the emotional conflict she carried so deeply in her heart. After a short wait, Sara walked through the restaurant entrance like a princess: tall, slender and strong in every way. Clear about her beliefs, her sacrifices and her commitments, her power came from who she was. It was all of this, and so much more, that Thea adored about her.

They smiled at each other in a way that brought tranquility to their uncertain world. Sara ordered a glass of wine. They both knew that food was not nearly as important as the reasons they were there. After one sip of wine, Sara asked Thea to tell her what was troubling her. Thea's eyes immediately filled with tears. She began her story by telling Sara how deeply she had grown to love her and how much she had enriched her life. "My love for you is begging for an inclusion that will never happen; sexual union that is unthinkable and much more time together which is not possible," Thea explained. As she spoke, she felt the magnitude of her pain intensify as once again she felt the pain of separateness that made her feel like an outsider. She realized how angry she was that their worlds kept them from the kind of union that her love longed for. A relationship was not possible.

Only minutes into her story, she was silenced by Sara's tears. Why is she crying? Thea always presumed that Sara could handle every conflict as if it was a natural event. She assumed that this would merely be information to her. What was her emotional connection to what Thea was saying? Thea wanted to hold her, but dared not. Sara's tears created a deep silence between them.

Finally, Sara whispered, "I love you too, but I don't know what that means. I don't know what to do!" Did she love Thea as a friend? What was the depth of her love? Thea was afraid to ask. Although they were increasingly more physical and emotional with each other, it never occurred to Thea that Sara could be in love with her and struggled with that same deep yearning that could potentially unite their lives forever. The shocking possibility dismissed her tears. She was now focused on Sara's pain. She did not want Sara to be in pain. She didn't deserve it!

"Thea, I have never been in love with a woman before, but I want to share my life with you. I think about you all the time. I want us to be a family. To make that happen will take time, but right now, I only want to be with you. Let's leave!" Sara whispered. They stood up together, held hands and left the restaurant.

As they closed the car door, their passion exploded. It tore their lives apart and brought their lives together at the same time. On the way to Thea's home, they kissed, they cried, they laughed. The ride was surreal. Though pain awaited them, now only their love for each other mattered.

STAGE SIX

Story of a Black Woman

"I WANTED TO LOVE SOMEONE, BUT NOT LOVE THEM MORE THAN MYSELF."

I graduated college with honors and swiftly transitioned into my career as a journalist. My greatest accomplishment was using my darkness to redefine myself. I have learned that the key to self-acceptance is self-definition. I have accepted my full and wonderful body. It is exactly as it should be. I exercise to build my body and I exercise my heart to build the courage for intimacy. Now, cooking relaxes me and gives me a chance to unwind. I feel my mother and grandmother around me as I recreate the soul food that nourished me as a child.

My friends from college were marrying off quickly. I asked myself, what in the world was I waiting for? My friends and family asked me what I was waiting for, why I had not settled down. Was I defective in some way because I wasn't married or because I wasn't attracted to someone who could complete me? Ironically, for the first time, I felt complete when I was in my own private world. But, when I stepped outside of my world, my personal security didn't seem to matter. My grandmother reminded me that she was getting older and wanted a great grandchild. I told her to hang on; there was hope, but not immediately. My mother was less pushy about the grandchild thing. I wondered if she was afraid for me or was she afraid for herself?

I wanted to love someone, but not love them more than myself. I felt whole now, but my wholeness was untested by love. A wedding ring seemed to be the ultimate symbol of social acceptance. If I had one, it seemed to mean that I was a member of some sort of exclusive club of valued human beings. This subtle message made me feel uncomfortable, because it obscured my own value. How could a man make me feel more complete, when I felt complete already? I did want a love relationship, but wasn't sure how I would meet the kind of man that would complete my dreams.

I was hired to write for a small-town newspaper outside of Chicago. The pay was meager, but the position could become the springboard for other journalistic opportunities in the city. I was in charge of writing a weekly column about cultural diversity. The subject was vague, but I was determined to make it come alive by spicing it up with the cultural drama of real stories about ordinary people who were private heroes.

I went out into the community to interview common folk. I wrote the life stories of men, women and children; the young, the old and the infirmed. I listened to stories of heroism that were awesome. During one of those interviews, I met Donovan. He was young, handsome and articulate. As I interviewed his mother, he interjected memories of her that expanded my story. It was obvious that he was the center of his mother's life. Maybe they were two heroes living in the same house. His obvious love for his mother was like my love for my mother, but I admired his love more because he was a man. Donovan lived with his mother.

Two days after the interview, Donovan called me. After a friendly conversation, he invited me to lunch. Surprised, I accepted the invitation. I trusted him immediately because he was taking care of his mother. As I drove to the coffee café near my home to meet Donovan, I wondered, did I really need a man? Are there any brothers out there worth dealing with? The thought of male energy in my life seemed appealing. After all, I missed my father all of my life. Donovan was probably as fatherless as I was, and I wondered how our deprivation would collide. I am a black woman who avoided discrimination by avoiding life. He was a black man living in a world that is not counting on him to win and doesn't want him to. He turns on the television to see himself arrested. Too often he watches movies to see himself depicted as a greasy buffoon struggling through life aimlessly. I wanted to believe that Donovan was different.

Our introductory coffee began a steady ritual of getting together. He was pushy, and that flattered me. I met him at his mother's home many times, so my relationship with him grew very intimate and comforting. His mother cooked like my grandma, and best of all, she didn't mind me joining in. Donovan was excited about me being in his mother's home and cooking while he watched television. After two months of dating, our intimacy became physical. When I went that far, I thought I was putting an end to my single life. Without much discussion, we married. My marriage, one I'd prayed and hoped for after spending many years building my career, was brief and ended in divorce. I soon realized that in my desire to become a bride, I neglected to honor myself by allowing adequate time to make my decision. There is true value in waiting. It always reveals the true disposition of the heart. By not waiting, I left myself open to deception. That's what happened to me.

Story of a Woman ... Now Old

"I NEVER THOUGHT ABOUT GOING BACK TO SCHOOL BECAUSE
MY LIFE HAD CHANGED SO MUCH."

The unhappiness that I recognized in my mother's life, and now in Julia's, confused me. I watched Julia cry every day for a long time. She knew enough to grieve the life that was taken away from her. Was it a predicator of my own life, I wondered? At this point, I did not attach meaning to it because I felt I was a different kind of woman. The fury of my life didn't leave time to count the costs my history demanded. I was attached to my responsibilities, proud of my accomplishments and nurtured abundantly by my brothers and sisters. My life existed within this world of family.

Julia was strong and generous with her energies, quickly taking over most of the responsibilities. I helped her, but did not feel the same responsibility I had when my mother was alive. We frequently baked the family bread together. Like my mother, she spoke only Arabic and we communicated well. She never tried to discipline us. How could she? She was only a child herself. At first, I felt displaced by her competency but soon realized that our family status, among other families, was restored by her presence.

My father was mean to her in the same ways he was mean to my mother. He beat her for reasons that seemed trivial. I was even beaten by him on many occasions. I grew to hate the way he was with women. Like my mother, Julia's pregnancies followed one after the other. She gave birth to four children: Theresa, Junior, Gabriel and Freddie. Each time she became pregnant, I took over the family responsibilities. My father demanded that I be available to relieve his wives during pregnancy. Theresa was born while I was still home and I loved her so. Like Marion, she became attached to me, and I to her. I cared for her whenever I could.

Now that my brothers and sisters were all in school, the new babies Julia bore gave my life new meaning, a level of responsibility that I knew so well. I never thought about going back to school because my life had changed so much. My self-identity was so completely separated from being a child, from being free, from belonging and feeling a connection to my own dreams. School was unthinkable.

I was now a little freer. I started going out with my girlfriends. We played jump rope and kick the can. Simple pleasures were so appreciated. Even though I had grown into a beautiful young woman, in my heart, I was still a child. At nineteen years old, I had never worked outside of the home, shopped in a store, had my own money, dated or talked to any man outside of my family. I never read a book because I could not read. That shame reminded me of my loss.

GROWTH THROUGH LISTENING

*I will listen patiently to myself and other women as wisdom
shows me a better way to live my life.*

How We Think

*"For centuries, the devaluation of our thoughts and contributions
has been a legacy of loss for humankind."*

We have been working hard to understand our personal history. Now it is
time to add specificity to insight by recalling relationships that became
unbalanced. When we don't consider ourselves important, others automatically
dominate our consciousness. When we are unclear about our needs and
unassertive about asking for what we want, our Self becomes lost and forgotten
by those we love. Without a strong commitment to who we are, it will be
difficult for us to function in a relationship. Our self-doubting makes us servants
of any relationship, not participants. Any relationship can become unhealthy if
the people involved don't communicate. Communication is a process that
engages both parties to negotiate equally and sensitively in order to infuse life
into the mainstream of their relationship. Communication will change as a
relationship changes. Without effective communication, a relationship will
become a vacuum of forgotten dreams and unresolved conflicts.

The work we do during this stage will drastically change the way we perceive
power. It will clear up the boundaries between us and others. Instead of using
so much of our power over others, we will use power for self-determination. We
will need to slow down our use of power so that we can reflect on the
appropriateness of its use. The use of personal power has consequences that
must be considered in order to use it wisely. Use these questions to reflect on the
personal and interpersonal consequences of your power.

- Am I using my power?
- How will the use of my power affect me?
- How will it affect my relationship?
- Is my use of power respectful of the other person's right to govern
  their own life?

- How can I support others' use of power rather than usurping it?
- How does the other person feel about my use of power?
- Have I used the counsel of another person before taking action?
- How will the use of my power create a positive result? (Remember that a positive result may not be an idealistic result)

Nurturance, which is a product of our power, is not always appropriate. We are challenged to determine if nurturance is useful and what type of nurturance will best serve the relationship. Determining whether our use of power would be appropriate or inappropriate is sometimes a lonely decision, but it is a decision that we must make honestly. As we deliberate our actions a definition and refinement of our selfhood is born. Honest reflection about our behavior actually becomes therapeutic because the Self is born in consciousness that calls us into being.

The term honesty is used to imply an emotional cleansing that separates our true self from our false self. We can be honest to the degree that we are able to free ourselves from shame and guilt. Emotional honesty turns us to the real meaning of our life because it reflects how comfortable we are with humanness. Honesty is a quality of disclosure that combines our experience (what's happening to us and our behavior) with our emotions (how we feel about what has happened to us). This complete experience can effect a permanent change in our lives. Our personal truth telling is an expression of an authentic self because it is uncomplicated and direct. Honesty makes our inner life uncomplicated by uniting our intra-psychic experience with what is actually happening to us. When we are able to be honest we become whole.

We must grow to accept that we are the organizers of how much we love, who we love and how we express our love. We are the origin of all our actions. By acknowledging the inappropriate use of our power, we will separate our core self from the feelings that perpetuate this behavior. We may acknowledge that we have done for others, what they could have done for themselves. Have you ever done for others what you hoped someone would do for you? We have been the conscience of others as well because we lacked faith in their judgment. We have felt for others so passionately because we are compelled to protect them from pain. These excessive distortions obscured our selfhood and distract us from our inner messages.

How We Feel

"As we recall the parts of our lives we gave away, abandoned or lost because doing "good" was more important than feeling good, we will grieve."

We may, at this stage, have another wave of denial because what we do, we do lovingly. We may want to justify our over-indulgence in the lives of others. Our self-reflections and examination of relationships are very private processes. It is self-effacing because the ultimate truth is that love does not make us perfect, nor does it bring others to perfection.

Love is a powerful motivator. It is a master emotion because it influences how we think, how we feel, and how we are with others. Because our lives as women are wrapped around being loving we forget that love requires guidance. We forget that love is for us as well. Love is in union with all, especially you!

What we must reflect on now, is the expression of love. Love always needs expression. The expression of love must be as safe for the giver as for the receiver. Use these questions to guide your love.

- How do I feel about showing love?
- Why do I want to show love this way?
- Is this act of love going to compromise me or the person I love?
- Am I really comfortable loving this person, at this time, in this way?
- Am I as caring about myself as I am about the person I love?
- Do I expect anything in return?

These questions will help you recognize that love is not a simplistic experience. They will clear up the misconceptions that hold us captive in unhappy relationships. When we love in ways that are uncomfortable for us, we are contributing to that unhappiness. Whenever we compromise ourselves, we will feel an immediate discomfort come over us. Because we tend to be less empathetic toward ourselves, we endure discomfort in the name of love. Love is supposed to open us up to let in new experiences of who we are. When we are not open to ourselves while loving, our Self becomes lost. Retrieving our selfhood will require that we honestly evaluate our relationship styles and be willing to

145

discover how you stand on the sidelines. Because relationships are sacred territory for women, it may be hard for us to admit that the sidelines never make us happy.

We may actually experience relief as we acknowledge the inappropriate use of our love power. We will be released from the bondage of always having to be nice and always having to be right. We will be released from false beliefs about womanhood and feel unburdened by excessive demands on our time. We will defame the call to be perfect. We will release ourselves from the obligation of compulsory nurturance. Perhaps, for the first time, we will discover a new order in our lives.

Grieving is part of growing. As we recall the parts of our lives we gave away, abandoned or lost because doing good was more important than feeling good, we will grieve. We may even question the very purpose of our lives. We may feel the loss of our socialized self and the false security it brought us. We will learn to incorporate the inevitable process of loss and grieving into our program of recovery.

Even though grieving has been continually experienced throughout the stages, the intensity of its effect is never more poignant than now. Our feelings will encompass emotions of loss, sadness, anxiety, anger, regret, longing, frustration and hope. Grieving is a necessary part of our work because it allows us to surrender the past for a new future.

How We Are With Others

*"We must not lose our personal authority while in relationships or
we will lose our personal identity as well."*

Resocialization is about our personal and interpersonal freedom. Freedom does not mean we walk through life without emotional attachments. However, it does mean that our life is more about choices and less about obligations. Choice implies that we have made a reflective decision about our behavior and commitments. Choice implies that we want to live an authentic life with innate integrity and healthy boundaries. It means that we are comfortable with ourselves—comfortable enough to be sure and unsure. Choice implies that we consult with the facts about our decision and with our intuitive nature. Up to this point, our intuition was never lost. It was simply distrusted and ignored. We are reclaiming our intuitive life force because it is our deepest truth and our truest self. We reclaim our intuitive self because it is the birthplace of our real power.

We must not lose our personal authority while in relationships or we will lose our personal identity. No one, despite their willingness to try, should be able to take our authority from us. Our personal authority must have a place in every relationship. We must learn to trust our authority by using it. Our use of authority in no way takes another person's authority away. It is possible for two or more individuals to all use their personal authority simultaneously. Our unique opinion, intelligence, insight and creativity are born from the use of our authority. So, authority with others is beneficial because it is creatively intimate. It expands our individualism while it creates a bond among the individuals involved.

Everyone wins.

As we identify relationships from our past that were destructive, we must ask ourselves how we can learn new alternative behaviors by consulting with our recovering sisters. Remember, we are learning a new way to be. It is vital for us to employ the process of consulting with others, not as a substitute for our authority, but as an expansion of possibilities that could influence our ultimate decisions. Let the counsel of your sisters' stay with you as you determine, in each situation, what is good for you. Though you use their counsel to formulate insight, you must always remember that your own voice is your final voice. Trust your gut feelings about most situations. When your gut is telling you something is wrong, figure out the meaning of your uneasiness and do something about it. Your discomfort is your body telling you to pay attention to yourself. A stream of life has always flowed through us. Recognize it. Drink from it. Cleanse in it. That stream was never lost, it was simply unused. That stream of life is our precious self.

JOURNALING

1. How do you know when you are making someone more important than yourself? Read the following list of signs that indicate your inclination to over-prioritize others. Which ones have you experienced in your relationships with others? Can you add to this list of symptoms? **WRITE** your own list.

    - When you are afraid to say what you need from them or what you are uncomfortable with.
    - When you fear conflict.
    - When you surrender your own style of living to accommodate another person.
    - When you endure criticism without defending yourself.
    - When you are obedient because you are avoiding negotiation.
    - When you resist defining boundaries in new or ongoing relationships because it requires you to use your power.
    - When you avoid or deny your sexuality because it violates cultural expectations that you are heterosexual.
    - When you are unwilling to express anger toward others who do not want to consider your feelings.
    - When your behavior becomes too accommodating and you begin to feel uncomfortable.
    - When you feel frustrated most of the time because you expect others to know what you need.
    - When you give up your outside friendships to accommodate the insecurities of the person you love.
    - When you stop taking care of yourself because you think it's selfish.
    - When responsibilities become more important than joyful experiences.

2. On the left-hand side of a piece of paper, list all of the people you have made more important than yourself in your lifetime. On the right, list the attributes of that person that made them more important to you in your

eyes; refer to the list in the previous exercise. Is there a pattern? Which of those signs stand out as the main reason why you make a person better than you? What steps can you take to make equality a part of your relationships? **WRITE!**

3. Women grow up in a critical world. We learn to be critical of ourselves. Your inner critic can have a very loud voice. What does your inner critic say to you? Who does your inner critic act and look like? Are your parents' voices a part of her? Engage in dialogue with your inner critic to change her voice into positive affirmations. **WRITE!**

4. Women often undervalue their giftedness. Self-pride has given way to privatized shame. Shame can occur when we are laughed at, mocked, ridiculed, bullied, criticized and blamed. One of the ways we can throw off the shackles of shame is by reminding ourselves, over and over again, about our goodness and giftedness. Write a goodness list about yourself. Begin with: "I am a good person because _____." Then write, "I am a gifted person because _____." When you have finished, write a paragraph that describes your feelings as you wrote each list. **WRITE!**

REFLECTIVE CINEMA

Movies that reinforce the themes of this stage recommended for viewing:

- Steel Magnolias
- Rambling Rose
- The Reader
- The Whales of August

STEPPING OUT

- Share with a best friend how timid you are in the face of conflict. Try to tell her why you behave this way.
- If you have children, hire a babysitter and give yourself a few hours of free time.
- Watch one of the recommended movies alone. How did it demonstrate how powerful you can be in collaboration with another woman?
- Ask your spouse or partner to complete a household task that you ordinarily take care of alone. (Examples: grocery shopping, laundry, transporting children)

Story of a Married Woman

As long as she could remember, being in a relationship was the central part of her life because it added richness and purpose. It was where she experienced her highest highs, her lowest lows and sometimes bouts of depression. Clearly, she was most vulnerable in her romantic relationships with men, becoming so confused that setting boundaries was difficult and sometimes impossible. Whenever her romantic relationships with men did not work out, she struggled with self-blaming, even when she knew the failure was not her total responsibility.

Her emotional confusion in romantic relationships led her to a self-compromise that was out of control. Her decisions made no sense to her and even less to friends. It took her a long time to walk away from the hope of love and all of its promises, even when she recognized that it was hopeless.

Nina was clear that she wanted to live her life in relationship. It was the only way she could imagine living. She watched her mother both nurture and sustain all of her female friendships, the friendships that comforted her mother during lost time with her father.

It was expected that she would marry and that her husband would become the relationship above all others. It was also assumed that, as a woman, she was responsible for maintaining the marital relationship. It was as though being a woman meant that she, more than anyone else, had a secret power to create a marriage and sustain it, no matter what her partner was like, no matter the circumstance. Now, however, this personal omnipotence seemed both unrealistic and unfair to her. She was convinced of its illogic, but not free enough emotionally to rewrite the script of her own life.

Throughout her childhood, Nina adored her father. She wanted to become a strong, independent daughter to make him proud, while at the same time, she wanted to be Daddy's little girl. The contrast between these two competing needs made her feel divided within herself because they seemed irreconcilable. Now, she wondered if that split, that perceived inconsistency, molded her present confusion.

There was so much about her father-daughter relationship that she did not understand. Would she ever? Was it important? He'd been very successful. His position in the community made him seem larger-than-life in Nina's eyes. Whenever they were in social situations her father was the center of attention. And when she thought her pride could not be any stronger, he would tell everyone that Nina was his dream come true.

Nina loved to be with her father in social gatherings because it was there that she felt his love. He hugged her openly and laughed when he spoke of her. He seemed relaxed, alive and sensitive in the presence of others. However, often at home, a dark mood would take control. He became the private man who lived in the shadows of his own mystery. He became withdrawn and obsessed with his need for privacy. Her inner-child was frightened by his seclusion. Nina's mother trained Nina to be quiet when her father was home. She could remember playing in remote areas of the house and never inviting friends over when her father was at home. All her life, she watched her mother treat her father with privilege: the serf and the master. Her mother honored him, no matter how withdrawn or unappreciative he was to her. As a child, Nina assumed that the double standard in their household was automatically and simply established by the great divide of being male or female. She grew to want her father's status and cringed at the idea of her ever being in her mother's secondary position.

By the time she was ten or eleven, she understood why her father needed so much privacy. He was an active alcoholic. Once she realized this, Nina tried to justify and invent reasons for his nightly alcoholic rituals, the things that separated him from his family. On the rare instances when Nina would get his attention, she worked hard to maintain it, to deserve it, and regarded it as a sign of personal achievement.

She took her mother's attention for granted because she was always hovering over Nina. Nina's rebellion against her mother seemed to be an essential component for releasing herself from what her mother's life had become: a life filled with little joy and even less respect. Privately, she feared her mother's life because she thought she was destined to live it someday, no matter how she felt about it. It was a giant cloud that seemed to loom over Nina's head. A feeling that this will be your life!

Nina held the idea of masculine privilege as her personal ideal because it would be the recreation of her childhood. But as she matured, it became more and more difficult to believe in. Ironically, all of her relationships with men seemed to reiterate her secondary status, even when those men claimed to believe in equality. What was really equal did not seem to have anything to do with what felt normal in her relationships with men. It was as if they too were scripted by a power that they did not understand. They both seemed to be dancing to a tune that was all too familiar. No matter what they aspired to be, how much they both said they wanted equality, both she and her male partners, once in a relationship, automatically reverted to playing Mom and Dad. When she'd accepted Joe's marriage proposal, her determined independence seemed to disappear without her approval. Even when she was aware of it, she couldn't stop. Now she needed to understand why that had happened, as she now pondered how to make changes. Could it be that what she watched was more powerful than what she had mentally determined would be her life? Could she have absorbed, obviously without meaning to, all the subservience her mother had afforded her father? Had she caught that role model, even as she detested it? She wanted a new model for her marriage. Together she and Joe must create equality, more balance so that they both had privilege.

Story of a Lesbian Woman

"I'M GRIEVING THE LOST PRIVILEGE OF BEING A BRIDE;
A WIFE; THE RESPECTED DAUGHTER; THE DOCTOR'S WIFE."

There was novelty in their love for each of them. Thea yearned for, but never attained, the full life she shared with Sara. Once the love was acknowledged, it became an imperative that they be together. Thea felt the urgency, but consciously decided to let Sara set the pace for their transition. On many occasions, she apologized to Sara for breaking up her marriage. Sara emphatically set her straight. "You did NO such thing! Our marriage would never grow because George is not willing to change. I tried so hard not to know how much I loved you, but it wouldn't go away. I am unwilling to give up the promise of intimacy with no hope of getting it. I am proud of our love! It has awakened me!" She continued, "I will now face the harsh discrimination from family and friends that you once suffered. Be my support." Guilt never took possession of them again.

Initially George was enraged when Sara asked him for a divorce. He knew Thea was a bad influence. Lesbians just try to tear women away from men because they are man-haters. He didn't mention custody, but he was sure that two women raising his children was a bad idea. Sara assured him that they would work out a custody arrangement that kept him in the lives of his children. After a month of raging and accusing, George pleaded with Sara to talk to him about their problems. They both entered therapy as a way of healing from their disappointments.

In therapy, George was more open than she had ever known him to be. "Sara knew that we needed to talk, but I was in my own world. She pleaded with me to talk, but like always, trying to talk to me was frustrating as hell for her. I was brought up to keep my emotions in check, and I was a pro at that." He went on to say how down he was on himself now. "What is bothering me the most now is that she's doing what she wants, and I feel like I'm stuck. I'm jealous. I know it's my fault for not being able to communicate. She says she probably would have discovered her identity sooner or later anyway, but I wonder about that." The therapist listened in silence.

Sara was relieved, but dismayed by this part of George that she never knew. He went on. "I feel unhappy about myself. Frustrated, like I missed something my whole life and I don't know why. Basically, I've given up on everything. I'm lonely. I have no friends and have a hard time making new ones. I always expected Sara to take care of everything, even my social life."

Sara wondered where George found this new honesty. She was healed and comforted by it, but wanted him to know that it was too late for the marriage. Her only desire was to co-parent their children. Setting that boundary made George less willing to attend therapy with Sara. When they terminated, she knew it wasn't a perfect ending, but those three sessions made it easier for them to talk about the things they needed to discuss, their children.

Sara told her parents about the real reason she was ending her marriage, but they insisted that it was Thea's doing. "It is disgraceful!" they said. "What will we tell our friends? Divorce is bad enough, but our daughter is a lesbian?! How will we say those words?" they asked. Sara didn't answer. She was confident that they would find the words when they were ready.

Thea was anxious for them to live together, and sometimes her anxiety was apparent. During those times, Sara responded with anger, "I have to do this in my own time! When a married woman loves another woman, she leaves behind a whole world for which she had been prepared, one in which she believed; one that she wanted more earnestly than her own life." Sara's honesty brought Thea back to reality. She continued, "Sometimes I wonder about my decision. Then I remember how much I love you. The life I leave behind with George is the only life I thought I was entitled to call my own. I'm grieving the privilege of being heterosexual, a bride, a wife, the respected daughter, the doctor's wife. George and I are grieving together and striving to find a place where friendship can remain."

Thea knew all that she said was true. Sara's integrity made Thea love her even more, and when they touched, all the richness of communication transformed into bodily sensations that did not need words.

Story of a Black Woman

I became pregnant with my son Uzoma, almost as quickly as I got married. The pregnancy and birth of my son gave me hope and purpose. His sacred name, Uzoma, is Nigerian and it means "born during a journey." My pregnancy both scared and excited me. Donovan didn't want a divorce, yet he did not want to be a working partner, lover and father. When I stopped making excuses for him, I filed for divorce. My son was four years old. If you've heard that life begins at forty, believe it! During this time in a woman's life, she expands. It is a time of acceptance and the demystification of marriage. I traded uncertainty for clarity. What people thought of me was not nearly as important as it once was. My opinions counted more than anyone else's. Others didn't determine my worth, nor did they determine my role in humanity. I stepped away from all the myths that held me captive. Once again, I faced myself and loved my son.

My mother-in-law loved Uzoma and took care of him during the first four years of his life while I worked. He knew his father because his father was always with his mother. I knew she wasn't happy with Donovan's laziness, but she never challenged it. Indirectly she expressed her disrespect for him. "We women are the backbones of our families, you know?" she repeated. After our marriage, I discovered that Donavan had no real love for his mother, at least not the kind of love I thought he had when we first met. He used her helplessness, her age and her meager financial resources to sustain his aimless life. Simply because she feared her aloneness, no boundaries were set for fear that they would send him away. Her own social resources dwindled over the years until her small world consisted of only her and Donovan. Uzoma broke this isolation and she thrived during the first four years of his life. She walked him down the street as her prized possession.

I actually feel that Donovan was threatened by her love for Uzoma. When she needed diapers or food for Uzoma, Donovan conveniently forgot to buy them or neglected to tell me. Soon, she didn't even ask him anymore. She called me with her needs, and of course, I responded in gratitude.

When I decided to divorce Donovan, one of my main concerns was my mother-in-law. In order to break my connection with Donovan, she would suffer. She cried when I told her of my decision. My decision to divorce meant that I wanted to live near my mother and sister. I agonized about the loss that Uzoma and his grandmother would suffer. It seems that a woman's life is torn in so many directions, sometimes all at the same time. My mother and sister lived three hours away, not a great distance, but our moving would forever end the day-to-day contact they both enjoyed. If Uzoma saw his grandmother, it would be during his father's visitation. But was his father interested enough to claim his right to spend time with his son?

Knowing that Donovan had no respect for order, I agreed to a visitation schedule that was strict, but generous, I thought. I didn't trust him, but I did trust my mother-in-law. Undoubtedly, he had never been the caregiver. He fought for visitation with Uzoma because he saw it as his way of hurting me. It didn't matter to me what his motivations were, I just wanted my son to have access to his paternal grandmother. I agreed to drive half the distance twice a month for their reunion. I was named the custodial parent of my son. There is no course on how to be a single mother, but there is within me a natural instinct to love, protect and guide my son's young life. It was like having a second chance to live my life, but with all the wisdom of my mistakes minus the naivety. I consciously made decisions about his school, with whom he would play, who came to our house, whose house he was allowed to visit, who would babysit and what doctor would care for him. If he breathed, I knew about it. I listened when he thought I wasn't and heard when he thought I didn't. I had a new job, Uzoma had a new life and now we were both on a new journey.

Story of a Woman ... Now Old

I am twenty years old now. I have lived seven years without my mother. As my body changed, I tried to imagine what my mother would say about my womanhood. Would she approve of me? No one got excited about my changing body or my prospects for romance. I was becoming interested in boys, even though, I had no idea what boys and girls did together. Only my brothers' stories informed me about a world outside of my mother's kitchen. I saw that my cousins and friends had boyfriends. I wanted one, too. It was my first deep desire to belong to my peer group. My father's reaction was something I dreaded to face. He seemed to feel that he owned me as completely as he owned the women he married. He did own my life for the first twenty years, not because I gave conscious ownership, but because I was a woman and ownership was presumed.

My cousins told me about a thirty-three-year-old man named John. After several weeks of curiosity, his cousin finally introduced us. For one year, we met secretly to avoid my father's criticism. We usually went for a walk to the ice cream parlor in our small town. John was handsome and very quiet. He was mild-tempered and I grew to appreciate that about him. He was the oldest of eight children and the eldest son of an abusive father who abandoned his family for other women. I knew right away that he held a lot of anger inside but I felt I understood it, so I dismissed it. He hated his father because of the way he treated his mother. I wondered why I didn't hate my father. Perhaps hate was too heavy a burden and for it, there was no room in my heart. I tolerated my father by outgrowing him. He had so much control of my life, but my inner world was always mine. It was a field of flowers that I grew daily with acts of love for those I cherished.

One day, after our ice cream date, John asked me to marry him. He gave me a diamond surrounded by rubies. No one had ever given me a gift like this ever before, never! Our gifts were always simple: an apple, an orange, a small bag of nuts or a homemade cookie. Something as extravagant as jewelry was unthinkable. I was overwhelmed with excitement and couldn't wait to show my brothers and sisters this precious gift. It seemed to mark my passage into womanhood, personhood and, most especially, selfhood.

John's mother and siblings lived in Stafford Springs, Connecticut. His mother encouraged our marriage so much so that she purchased my wedding gown; a financial commitment that I'm sure was difficult for her to keep. I planned my wedding alone without much joy from my family because no one wanted me to leave. My father was furious and disapproving. Apparently, he thought being his daughter was an identity of a lifetime. Breaking away from his control was emotionally traumatic for obvious reasons, but less obvious reasons were far more significant. Those reasons were the final confrontation of my quest for personal freedom. I wanted to have an identity that was attached to my personal dreams. I wanted to be a bride and a mother. He wasn't going to stop me now. He planned his final rebellion by not attending my wedding, nor did he allow Julia to attend. But his rebellion didn't heed my resolve; I was determined to have my life. I had taken care of his children, loved his children and now, it was time for me to belong to myself.

CREATING HEALTHY BOUNDARIES

—⁂—

**I will create mature relationships by expressing
my personal needs, because love without boundaries
is emotionally paralyzing.**

How We Think

*"Creating equality is work because as we create it, we are simultaneously letting
go of gender oppression that we thought was normal."*

Stages seven and eight are closely linked because they direct recovery to relationship management. The idea that we must learn to manage our relationships rather than letting them manage us may be a novel concept. It takes us out of the victim role and expects us to be agents of change in our lives. Through this self-determination we gain visibility and speak in our own voice, and we use our voice to express the determination and inclination of our will. This use of our personal power will ultimately help us feel more authentic and more satisfied with our lives.

Those of us who have developed a sense of belonging to womankind will be powerful agents of change as well. Belonging to one another helps us to formulate new and free values. We can only expand our lives by selecting groups and individuals who can appreciate and celebrate the transformation of our identity. The resocialization process invites us into gatherings that are distinctly non-traditional. They are feminist.

Many years ago, the feminist movement called attention to the social discrimination that resulted from socialization. The intra-psychic vagueness that women felt was referred to by a famous author as "a problem without a name." Now, we have given this problem many names. In fact, we keep naming it throughout the stages of resocialization. We continually identify the destruction and sometimes madness that socialization has created in our lives. The feminist movement has always caused divisiveness within the women's community because some women feel the need to protect men who are threatened by the prospects of equality. The divisiveness within the women's community about feminist ideals has weakened the movement itself. The feminist movement threatens what we all believe: men and women are inherently different and their differences create an unequal world because we are inherently unequal. In many ways, it is thought of as a natural inequality that is predicated on the superiority of maleness, and the subordination of femaleness. Essentially, the feminist movement wants what is best for both men and women. It cries out for justice and equality. It cries out for freedom from the oppressive expectations that gender socialization demands. Feminism promotes the respect of women and men as equal partners in life. Resocialization is the new frontier of the feminist movement. The new frontier lies silently, and sometimes shamefully, in the hearts of contemporary women. It is concealed beneath her total dedication to be both modern and traditional at the same time. The contemporary woman may want to be professionally successful, but is personally powerless. She is exhausted with juggling the warring priorities of modern life. Resocialization is an invitation to women to understand and overcome the complexities of their lives.

Men can feel lost, angry and threatened by the changes women are creating because of resocialization. Because of their own socialization, they have counted on women to care for them in ways that they don't want to care for themselves. After years of doing just that, most women are not appreciated for assuming this oppressive responsibility. Rather than rewrite the internal script of their emotional and spiritual lives, women often disassociate from the feminist ideals. Concurrently, women may feel shame or guilt and disavow the ideals of feminism to escape the challenge they present. What a tragedy!

By understanding the meaning of feminism, we will grow to understand what it stands for: feminism began as a women's movement. Since that time, it has often been condemned by non-feminist men who cling to the idea of maleness more than the idea of justice. They see the movement as taking privilege away from them and using power against them. Non-feminist women are also afraid of the word, feminist. The reaction of fear that both men and women experience is understandable because they don't have a clear model of what an equal relationship is like. They have neither experienced nor been prepared to participate in relationships built on equality. Even more threatening is the fact that most men and women don't think in ways that help them create equality in their day-to-day lives. This is just as true of traditional lesbian and gay relationships because they too were subject to traditional socialization. All relationships are modeled on heterosexist ideals that promote the uneven distribution of power in relationships. Each partner is seen as an incomplete being in need of the other partner for completion.

In this system, men have power and are given privilege. They are excused from taking care of the emotional and spiritual needs of others, and they are judged harshly if they honor their own emotional and spiritual needs. As a result, men depend on women to take care of them. Women, on the other hand, are taught that caregiving is their most important role, and they are primed for this role throughout their lives. Giving care constitutes her ultimate fulfillment–or so women are taught. Women must seek and embrace the role of caregiver no matter the cost to their physical and emotional welfare. If this is the price they must pay for being in a relationship, they are willing because relationships are so important to them.

The compulsion we feel to need a relationship is one of the traps socialization creates for us. It leads us to believe that we are incomplete without them, and if they fail it is some kind of indictment of our inadequacies as a woman. This dangerous notion can promote desperation to remain in a relationship at all costs. Here are some radical, feminist notions that can counteract these feelings:

- We come into a relationship as a whole person.
- The gift of relational living is to enhance our wholeness.
- A relationship will enhance our wholeness when we are appreciated for our history, our vulnerabilities, striving, struggles, giftedness and our own ambitions.

We are loved for our being-ness and our becoming-ness. Consider these ideas of equality:

- Roles in relationships should be fluid so they reflect the needs of both partners.
- Different roles should not imply a difference in power between the partners.

- Traits that we call masculine and feminine are human traits and should be considered natural for men and women.
- Both father and mother are expected to nurture children. Both parents can be used by the male and female children as models for equality and love.
- Quality of life and environment are more important than the accumulation of wealth.

Our resolve to develop and maintain a feminist attitude will require constant vigilance because the scars and distortions of sexism are profound and subtle. Committing to this vigilance acknowledges just how deeply we have become immune to the inequality that has kept our lives captive for so long. Our commitment to resocialization is the systematic striving to identify all the ways we have internalized unhealthy attitudes about our lives. A subtle aspect of socialization that is not easy for us to acknowledge is our inclination to defend and protect the men in our lives from any accountability. We can be too willing to excuse the abandonment of our fathers or the emotional absence of our male partners. We protect them, as if they were children, and then criticize them because they are not answering our needs. When women protect men as if they were children, it is they who have lost track of their own worthiness. We become absorbed in our mothering role as if it was our ultimate purpose.

Feeling unworthy of equality is an impediment to gaining it. Maybe we can't even image it. We may feel guilty about changing the way we behave in relationships. If we have lived without our needs being met, without being listened to, being unappreciated, it may actually feel uncomfortable to want to be seen, to want to be known, and to want to be loved, because invisibility has been a way of life. This inner struggle can help us understand the depth of our socialization and the magnitude of our resocialization. Imagine how different our lives would be if we truly believed we were worthy of equality?

Our lives are surrounded by boundaries and because boundaries are so fundamentally important, it is imperative that we explore their meaning. There are external boundaries imposed on us by society. They are easier to manage because they are usually clear even when they don't make sense. Personal and interpersonal boundaries are far more complicated because they cause conflict and change as the relationship develops. They imply personal awareness and willingness to implement that awareness. The implementation of personal boundaries will put our lives in order and define what we stand for most clearly.

Throughout human history, women's boundaries have been violated. This worldwide trend has its insidious roots in the belief that women should not exercise their right of choice on their own behalf. We somehow internalized this gender-based message, and we put to sleep the healthy arrogance we need to take care of our own happiness. We must work hard to shatter this myth of silence and unworthiness that socialization promotes. Remember that socialization has no life of its own. It only exists if men and women believe it is true. Now is the time to stop being a believer of your own oppression. Our lives must belong to us in order for us to believe in ourselves.

The years we have spent trying to control and create the lives of others have prevented us from knowing and creating ourselves. How can we possibly feel any control over our own lives when all our energy is focused on directing the lives of others? When we live this way for long periods of time, our boundaries become unclear because we keep changing them, stretching them, or pretending they don't matter. We end up trying to live a workable life without boundaries of our own. We live by other people's boundaries when we don't create our own. The longer we do this, the more frustrated and lost we become, thus further contributing to the loss of self. We no longer recognize ourselves because there can be no individuality without choice. When for a long period we live in personal silence, we laugh less and cry privately. Sometimes, we cry silently because our emotions are shut down from lack of recognition and expression. We actually grow to be ashamed of our emotions because of the vulnerability conveyed. No matter how long it has been since you felt your feelings, they can always be awakened when you decide to live. True living must include our emotional life and the challenges of setting boundaries.

The correctness of our path lies in the joy of a healthy struggle. Prepare yourself for a rebirth of choice.

How We Feel

"The image of 'goodness' as the ideal 'self' makes it difficult for the
real 'self' to emerge and develop."

We may feel grief and anger as we relate our stories of love without boundaries. They are hard for us to recall because they imply inadequacy and weakness. We may relive the emotions that we repressed long ago. Expressing unresolved emotions is relearning the life spring within us from which new life springs up to blow like a fresh breeze within us. We need to grieve for ourselves. It may be our first act of self-love. We can employ memory, imagination and honesty to recount painful situations in life. If we tell our stories authentically, and with honesty, slowly we will regain the power we've lost.

This self-criticism emerges dramatically during our preadolescent and adolescent years. As our bodies become physiologically and sexually mature, we lose the luxury of imagining that we are free from being a sexual entity. At this time in our lives, our virginity matters. Who will we surrender it to as a token of our love and their possession? At this time in our lives, we are consciously aware that being a female demands that we be the object of someone's love. This obsession of worrying about whether we are good enough to be loved becomes a part of our identity that is particularly hard to overcome because it gets linked with crucial issues of approval, love and social acceptance. Unlike boys, our quietness, our unassuming manner, our obedience and our conformity are rewarded. We are less risky by adolescence because we feel the tentative nature of our acceptance. Our choices, which may include our careers, are subordinated to the ideal of belonging to someone else and that belonging becomes more important than our self actualization. Worst of all, it feels like it is our self-actualization. Our femininity comes to mean less-self. We begin to feel an uncomfortable split between our inner life and our outer conformity, and this becomes a private hell for many women.

As we mature, everyone is more critical of us because we are seen as candidates for romance instead of candidates for life. Our bodies, our behaviors, our dreams are all prerequisites for romantic love. The image of goodness as the ideal-Self makes it difficult for the real-Self to emerge and develop. We begin not knowing what we feel and not talking about what we know deep within to be true.

As we become women, our self-esteem is steeped in gender identity. It is dependent on the acceptance of our bodies because we know we are judged by body culture. Everyone is concerned about the rightness of our body, and we know it. What is upheld as an ideal body is not real, and they are not our bodies. Our body then becomes not good enough. A quiet disturbance gains control of our self-image, and we turn inward because there is nowhere else to go. We try to take control of the problem by controlling what we eat or what we keep of what we eat. If we lose weight, everyone is happy for us. But it doesn't work, because we are not happy with ourselves.

The dangerous discontent that becomes chronic in most aspects of our lives is directly related to our socialization. Our mothers can be crucial in counteracting these messages. She cannot save us totally because the institutions that govern our lives make it difficult to be rescued. If our mother never recognized her own social subjugation, then she cannot offer us any relief because she is not free herself.

Adolescence can be a time when we may feel so much despair and loneliness that we think about ending our life, and many of us try to do just that, generally with less violent attempts at suicide. Many more of us try than succeed. That we feel such shame at the dawn of our lives is tragic. That we seek our self-worth only through relationships creates for us false pride. It is during adolescence that the tragic effects of socialization show up in a big way. It indicates the loss of our internal locus of control which is a crucial part of our personal resilience.

We will revisit our adolescence. Our resocialization demands that we name every moment that we can recall; every persona that has played a part in the diminishment of our sacred Self. Painful as it may be, this recalling is the renaming of your life in your own terms. It won't be easy and it won't be fast, but as the journey proceeds, life will emerge. To regain your own reality is your ultimate victory.

We may be hesitant to discuss the feelings of envy, competition, abandonment, anger, guilt and betrayal that block our interactions with other women. They too may be a consequence of socialization and thus must be exposed. Honest communication will bring us closer and dispel the internal barriers that keep us from loving each other and prioritizing our relationships with one another. Our connectedness with other women is an essential part of our personal transformation.

As we allow ourselves to become close to other women, some of the struggles we had with our mothers will resurface. As we go back and remember conflicts in our childhood, we will be sad, angry or both. Much of the anger and resentment may be directed toward our mothers. We can use these opportunities to understand our mother's life, the life that was hidden from her that we now understand. We can use it as an opportunity to work through unresolved mother-daughter conflicts. Our relationship with our mother is intense and complicated, so it is not so easy to resolve. But in the resolution of each issue, we all know ourselves better and have the chance to emerge freed and less encumbered by unresolved anger. In the novelty of free expression, we connect the views of other women to our own knowledge and emotional history.

It is important to resist the feelings of shame that may result from realizing how profoundly socialization has victimized us. Shame is a difficult emotion to overcome because we believe in its false messages so completely during our childhood when there may have been no one to counteract the destructive beliefs we thought were true. Now, it is important to use healthy rebellion to silence shame. Shame can be replaced slowly with self forgiveness and healthy anger. There was no way, as a child, we could have known what we are now learning as adults. We are putting away our childhood naiveté and claiming our right to say who we are. This renewed self-assessment is precisely the beginning of real maturity. Maturity is not being led; it is leading, deciding, examining, changing, opening and reclaiming our lives.

The feelings of vagueness that often characterize how we feel will disappear as we, in a supportive environment, tell our stories of shame. This ongoing clarification gives birth to emotional freedom and healthy power. They become the fertile ground upon which to set your goals. New goal setting is important because it transfers emotional healing into behavioral change. Even if you alter them over time, make them anyway! Feelings of hopefulness and excitement are generated by our dreams.

How We Are With Others

"Our listening sisters are not there to judge or advise."

Although the true meaning of our lives is a very personal discovery, it happens while we are in close relationships. Relationships for both men and women should be fertile fields of spiritual and emotional prosperity. That is why our relationship skills should be consciously reevaluated and adjusted to reflect our changing awareness.

Friendships with other women who are committed to growth is the bridge over which we must pass in order to enter a fuller life. From our friendships, we gather self-respect and learn new options for relationships that are not oppressive. We can get our first taste of equality and understand the positive energy that equality creates. In healthy friendships, we are free to take care of ourselves.

Personal change will create healthier relationships. One huge change is using our conflicts as pathways to intimacy. Conflict is always a crisis and the purpose of crisis is development. Working out conflicts with our friends is a sign of maturity. If we disregard friendship without trying to work out our conflicts, we've lost an opportunity for development. Conflict invites us to utilize the insights we've gained in real circumstances. Without conflict, real growth is not internalized. The purpose of conflict is to lead us on to new and untrodden territory. It will be easier for us to engage in healthy conflict if we believe it has purpose. Reconciliation is finding a common ground where our differences are understood and forgiven. It invites us to create peace because we understand each other better. If we find ourselves in conflict with a friend who is not growing, we will need to decide how we are going to resolve this frustration. Do we want to speak? Do we want to be patient? Is there hope for our friendship? Do we need to let go? Most importantly, do not be discouraged because there are women who share your vision and ideals. They will be your new source of comfort.

In our relational environment resocialization takes place. Relationships with lovers, children, friends, family members, work associates, can all become places where we rediscover our lost voice and assert our new voice. To grow in relationships is complicated because as we uncover the insidious effects of socialization, at the same time, we must manage the relational changes that the insight is creating within us. Our temptation, of course, is to back away from conflict and the essential changes they demand. You now know that avoiding conflict does not work for us.

The true meaning of our lives is within us. Friendship with our recovering sisters, coupled with a spiritual life, will help us enjoy a unified self such as we have never known before. We have all maintained a secret dream of how we'd like our lives to be, and now that dream can be nurtured, affirmed, learned and encouraged by other women. At times, this liberated dream of ours may feel totally different from the everyday reality of our lives. We must not surrender to discouragement. Keep in mind that your dreams are a reality that is not yet accomplished.

During adolescence, relationships become the most dramatic event in our lives. All types of relationships accentuate our secondary status in dramatic ways. Gender socialization has pre-prescribed for both men and women this view of a woman's life in relationships. Even though we have been primed all of our lives for this entrapment, it is always a shocking reality to actually experience it. It feels so unrealistic and unfair, and it is. When we try to negotiate our way out we may be met with resistance, sometimes outrage, because our partners believe our subjugation is required in the relationship. If we become angry, everyone notices, and if we become lost, everyone believes that we have made a healthy adjustment. We slowly disappear.

Only our personal power can save us because it is our only source of personal determination. What is essential to our self-actualization may be viewed by others as shameful behavior. We fully choose not to identify with our powers to be accepted as a woman. Even the thought of power might be uncomfortable and embarrassing. The degree of your discomfort is a measure of how deeply and how much of yourself you've surrendered. During this time of your rebirthing remember the primal place that power should always have in your life. Power is your ability to influence others. Power is your right to own your life. Power is the projection of your emotions, your intellect, your creativity and your love. The use of your power is self-enhancing. The loss of power is depressive. In healthy relationships, power is required; no matter how complicated the use of power will be, because the belief that you deserve power, which is an intrinsic quality of your life, must precede your use of it.

A well-maintained myth within our culture is that women don't need, nor should they have, power. Our domestic use of power to help others is socially acceptable. Our use of power is viewed suspiciously by everyone when we step outside our front door. The use of our power is restricted to the family, homemaking and child rearing. Even when we work outside the home, our inclination is to define ourselves as wife, mother and lover, as if these roles were biologically determined. These roles and our willingness to pay deference to the needs of our male partner can be endless. Work outside the home is viewed as a personal choice, not an essential part of family survival. And because of this view, our work is not as financially rewarded as our male counterpart. Those of us who want to give one hundred percent no matter where we are may suffer from frustration, social isolation and deprivation of time alone. We can be angry with those who depend upon us because we feel trapped and deprived. While there are many social factors that disempowered women, none is more potent than social factors that teach us to disempower ourselves.

To be powerful is why we exist. It is the source of our becoming. We can't ignore the dominant position it holds in our personal survival. Our resocialization demands that we examine how we think about power, how we feel about power and how we use power in our relationships with others. Without it, we cannot enjoy who we are. Without power, we cannot become who we are. Discovering yourself will be the most exciting journey of your life. If you are afraid of what others might feel about your journey, just remember that they will have more of you if you have more of yourself!

You have used your power in a dramatic way simply by initiating your resocialization. I'm sure there were many times when you wanted to make other commitments more important than being with other women during supportive meetings. Every time you traveled to meet a friend, attended a Women's Journey meeting, wrote in your journal or phoned a friend in order to comfort yourself and learn a better way to live your life, you chose life. Maybe you never thought of your life as a choice. It is your greatest choice! We should view power reverently because it builds authentic connections between people and constitutes an essential connection with ourselves. We can become one with ourselves when we are powerful.

Each one of us has personal dreams and ambitions. Do we share them with trusted friends? Listening to each other talk about dreams helps dreams become real. Dreams are an extension of our true selves. The best way to make them a reality is by networking with others who can be excited with us and for us. Networking helps us to believe that our vision is attainable and friends can be a part of that attainment. It will happen when we join our aspirations with the talents, minds and hearts of other women.

As we disclose how out of control our lives have become, remember that those listening to us have experienced the same insanity. They have also struggled under the conspiracy of self-abandonment and self-denial. They will be comforted and validated by listening to us. Whatever stands in the way of feeling safe with other women must be confronted now because our honest disclosures with other women are an essential component of resocialization. It sets the stage for your recovery now and insures an on-going openness toward womankind.

Learning to understand and overcome the mistrust that women have for one another enhances our ability to appreciate the help and expertise they can offer us. At this stage, we reverse our socialization by accepting other women as experts about their lives. We realize that only other women can truly understand our struggles and offer the empathy we have always deserved. Now we can establish interdependent relationships with other women by negotiating and renegotiating our relationships with them. We do this in order to establish a relationship of mutual respect and personal justice.

It is important to relate our stories of interpersonal conflict and self a bandonment to many of our sisters. This openness to sharing is a powerful experience for everyone involved and for the entire resocialization movement. For each of us, it is an exercise in trust and power. We focus on our personal lives and feel the wonderful reward of being attended to by other women; we will become the heroines of our own lives. For the listener, it is an invitation to break the silence of her life in the presence of another woman. She has a chance to witness the coming together of a life that was nearly lost. They will share the gift of encouragement and belief. Both listener and speaker will begin to see how excessive cultural demands have kept them from enjoying the female world of

~

their birth. As we speak, we gain a new respect for ourselves and the history we've created. As we speak, our personal and interpersonal lives change because our conscious domain is pared down to its original truths. We will learn together how to use our power and respect our right of choice by using direct language. We will plan a social network for emotional and practical support. This state of wholeness we pursue, and eventually attain, is fluid, inclusive and interconnected.

JOURNALING

1. Boundaries are self-declarations about what is important to you. Some are negotiable, and others are not. List your firmest, non-negotiable boundaries, those that rest on your fundamental needs and values. Be specific: "I would never build a relationship with someone who abuses drugs." What boundary have you established for yourself that has given you the greatest inner-strength? Which of your boundaries are more flexible? **WRITE!**

2. When we do not spend time defining our boundaries or we are not assertive in protecting our boundaries, we get hurt. When is it difficult for you to protect your boundaries? Describe a relationship, past or present in which it was difficult for you to maintain boundaries. Were you vigilant or did the relationship test them to the point of breaking them down? If you had an opportunity to live the relationship over, what would you do differently? What lessons can you learn from the experience to help you in your journey to know Self? **WRITE!**

3. Have you ever felt trapped in a relationship? You may not have seen a way out. You may have felt paralyzed because you were afraid to make choices and moves on your own. You may have wanted a change but didn't know how to achieve it. Detail how you finally resolved the conflict. **WRITE!**

4. Shame and guilt weaken our boundaries. Because we internalize responsibility for too many problems and responsibilities, we are much more prone to unhealthy shame and paralyzing guilt. How does shame weaken you? How does guilt weaken you? Be specific. How can you resist shame and guilt? Create five statements that combat shame. Create five statements that combat guilt. **WRITE!**

REFLECTIVE CINEMA

Movies that reinforce the themes of this stage recommended for viewing:

- Precious
- Strangers in Good Company
- Moonstruck
- An Education

STEPPING OUT

- Attend at least one support group meeting for women somewhere in your community.
- Take yourself out to lunch.
- Take a hot bath or shower when no one is at home. Light candles and play music.
- Watch one of the recommended movies with a friend. Discuss how the female characters supported one another.

Story of a Married Woman

Her friendship with Sue was permanently changed. From the time Sue had shared the truth about her marriage, Nina felt much closer to her. Sue's honesty created a bond that Nina hadn't felt with anyone in a long time, if ever. She realized that all the pretenses, the masks she wore throughout her life, destroyed any hope of reality and true connection. How could anyone truly know me if the only thing I have shown them is a front, not my true self? Why is being real so hard for me? Can I actually become more real? Can I live in my reality? Nina was starting to realize that being real was the only real achievement in life, and it was an experience she did not want to eliminate because of fear. As she reflected on her life now with more clarity and honesty than she ever had, she saw that her life as a child, as a young woman, as a daughter, and now as mother and wife, lacked a fundamental connection with herself. What she thought was maturity, the guarding of her emotions, had required abandoning the parts of herself she enjoyed the most. She was starting to realize that becoming a real person, one with thoughts, opinions and needs, would not require her living a different life, but living her life differently. Her foray into realness would require a shift in attitude about herself and her value as a person. It would require that she honor her life, not as an impossible dream, but as a journey to be known and appreciated with all its events, each experience creating the foundation for the next wave of courage and wisdom.

One day, Nina was finally ready and told Sue about her personal struggles, her general confusion, her relationship with Joe, or more to the point, the lack of a real connection in her life. She shared her feelings of confusion, shame and frustration, and admitted with anger the impossible task of trying to be a perfect wife and mother. As she spoke, she felt a terrible pain, because in explaining her situation to another woman, she realized just how deep she had fallen into a pit of unhappiness and confusion. How did this happen? Why did it begin and how did it happen without her knowing? Sometimes, as she tried to communicate her feelings of obscurity, only her tears could tell the story. Nina and Joe made their own lives and too often went their separate ways, oftentimes avoiding each other devoting their real attention to work, to children and their families. Their utilitarian marriage was no longer good enough for Nina.

Nina shared without any solutions to her problems, and did not have great flashes of insight to share with Sue. She simply told the story of her life, the story of her feelings. Sue's patient acceptance was comforting. She listened with sensitivity because she saw herself in Nina's story, without knowing the details. Each of them spent a lifetime running from the frontier of their own identity. Nina felt relieved about not hearing advice. It helped her to stay inside of her own self-discovery. That afternoon a great friendship was born, and this time, Nina was an equal partner, not just the recipient of someone else's outreached hand. They both believed this new and stronger friendship would last a lifetime.

The close bond she had formed with Sue gave Nina a new energy. She felt less lonely and much more connected to everything she was doing. At the same time, it extenuated her separateness from Joe. She suspected that he too was feeling the emotional space between them.

She was sure she loved him, but was unable to love him the way she had and still be a person in her own right. It had taken her a very long time to understand that, but once she did, it was impossible to continue the same journey. She would need to be as committed to talking to him as she was to talking about him. She had to be willing to face his resistance consistently. If she didn't, the consequences would be grave. Their marriage had to change and the change needed to include him. In the past, her anxiety about his reactions to conflict kept her silent and complacent. She was committed to approaching him directly, but feared the results. She was committed to taking the plunge into uncertainty.

One Saturday night, while eating dinner at a favorite restaurant, Joe admitted how angry he was about her flip attitude. He accused "those libbers" of having changed her; causing a distance in her behavior. As an example, he pointed out her selfishness at having hired someone to clean the house. He was angry that these people charged so much; they moved his books and they were not in a financial position of affording such luxuries. He thought it was unjust to pay someone to do what she was free to do because she was not working. She was giving up her part of their agreement. He was much angrier than Nina was used to seeing him. Although the argument had started as a specific irritation about the house-cleaning people, it eventually became more personal. As the anger grew, it became more and more directed toward her as she questioned him. In trying to discover the real source of his anger, he became more threatened. He made it *clear that his anger was justified, but she wasn't. Feeling responsible for Joe's disappointment and anger, whenever he expressed it, was natural to Nina. To her, it was part of their relationship, just another way she protected him; loved him; and it rose up in her now like an unavoidable force.*

During his ranting, she avoided eye contact, and withdrew from her own anger which kept trying to surface. Instead, she used all her energy to focus on what he was saying. She found she had difficulty defending her decision to hire housekeepers. Once again, her powerlessness was overriding her thinking and judgment. How would she ever stop this nosedive into self-betrayal? She knew better, but felt helpless to rewrite her inner script to bring about a different and more authentic response. Her emotional stillness kept her locked inside. The evening ended badly, although Joe thought he had won because she had nothing substantial to say.

Nina got into bed that night but could not sleep. She kept going over the discussion they'd had during dinner, and grew angry for not being assertive. It was shocking how quickly she had reverted back to her old behaviors when challenged. Obviously, she and Joe were at odds over several vital issues. Their relationship could, if Nina allowed it, continue as it had always been, but she quickly rejected that idea as unthinkable. She did not want to go back to the boredom of a scripted woman. That was not an option. Their relationship would have to change and that change would perhaps include conflict. Her question now was, could she weather the storm? She wished there were an easier way, a kind of detour, but she understood that this was wishful thinking; an unrealistic dream.

She kept reminding herself how much they did love each other. She also knew that it was she who would have to be the protagonist; the one who was willing to initiate any struggle to make their relationship different. She believed it was essential for change and a critical part of creating equality between them.

When they made their original agreement about postponing her career and he being the wage earner, Nina thought that was an equal partnership. Wasn't she always supposed to want to be married and to want to have children? What she didn't understand then was what would happen to her because what she was supposed to contribute was without value and generated little respect. She pulled the covers over her shoulders and turned away from him to create a necessary separateness she hoped would give her strength. He let her be separate. That was a beginning. She was unable to defend her rights to relationship privacy, but in her head she knew that she deserved that freedom. She deserved the right to be free enough from domestic responsibilities if she wanted to study and develop her own professional interests. She deserved the right to be included in financial decisions, even if she was not contributing to the household finances. She deserved whatever she felt was critical to being whole and happy with her personal life. She deserved the time and energy it took to explore her wants and needs. She deserved to be, within the framework of the marriage relationship, a separate and complete individual. She wanted to be loved for being an individual and not simply as an adjunct to everyone else's life.

Sunday morning's breakfast was special because Joe prepared it. As he cooked, the kids made toast and set the table. Nina prepared coffee for the adults and cocoa for the kids. Everyone had their hands in the feast. Maybe that is why Sunday morning breakfast was so special. Symbolically, it was the beauty of this family ritual that let Nina understand that her family could work together and share. If they could do it Sundays, they could do it other times. She asked Joe to take a walk in the park after breakfast. She wanted to talk. He accepted the invitation and seemed to be relieved that she'd asked. She felt anxious about what she had to say, but hopeful that their relationship could endure the change and be better for it.

MONDAY MORNING

They walked briskly through the park passing anyone who got in their way. Conversation flowed easily now. Nina felt released from the resistance she once brought into the friendship, so saying whatever was on her mind was easier. Sometimes her openness made her feel uncomfortable, as if it were betraying Joe, her parents and her life. She was aware that having this friendship with Sue was a great leap forward into the uncertainties she had to face.

Simply not taking responsibility for Joe's resentment of Sue was a leap forward. Now it seemed so ridiculous to surrender so much to someone else's insecurities. Even love did not make such a sacrifice noble. Perhaps he may be feeling an exclusion and helplessness because he doesn't know how to fit himself into my life, my friendships, my career, my needs. Joe had many superficial friends.

Relationships of substance seemed to be Nina's job, a position she cherished but did not want exclusively. He spent a great deal of time and energy doing manly things with his friends, but she wondered if anyone really knew him deeply. She could not help him be known, even though in her heart she felt responsible for his happiness. Nina was quickly learning the complexities of owning her own life. She always loved being a woman at every stage of her life, but being a loved-woman seemed to require that she become completely available to everyone she loved. She watched her own mother live in a state of personal surrender. Not until after her father's death did she realize that her mother actually knew how to run her life. Only then did she witness her mother making decisions based on her personal choices. She sold the family home and bought a new one in the part of town she always wanted to live; she traded in both cars to buy the car of her dreams and she traveled with her friends. She even dated casually only those men who agreed to a romantic friendship. What that meant to her was fun without self-surrender.

After two years of retirement, her father, at the young age of sixty-four, died unexpectedly. He died alone in his study, where he had spent so many drunken moments. After his retirement, he did not know how to live, so alcohol became deadly part of his sanctuary. Nina was angry that she never got a chance to care for him or say good-bye. The shock of his death left her feeling disoriented for several weeks. She grieved openly with Sue as she related the frustration, the lack of resolution that accompanied her father's death. Even though she watched him decline, she never imagined that they would never have a chance to be close. His death made her realize the long, dark shadow he had cast over her life. Perhaps in his absence she could see him more clearly. One thing she was certain of and must sadly acknowledge: her father died without knowing his daughter. In profound ways, his emotional absence affected her life. Her relationship with Joe must not end so tragically. She committed herself to realness and demanded the same of Joe. She wanted to share a real relationship with him and that could only happen if she were alive enough to struggle for intimacy, open enough to listen for truth, loving enough to be patient, focused enough not to compromise important parts of her identity and determined enough to be real.

Story of a Lesbian Woman

"... THEA RESPECTED SARA'S DIRECTNESS AND DEVOTION
TO THE CHILDREN."

After several months of arguing with George, Sara and the children temporarily moved into Thea's home. She had a shared custody arrangement with George allowing him alone time with the children on a weekly basis. Sara found her separation from the them difficult to bear. She continued her part-time job at the firm, but after leaving work, her longing for the children seemed unbearable on days they were not home when she walked through the door. She found it difficult to have fun when she and Thea had free weekends. To be so free from mothering, caregiving and attachment was foreign to her. It was the hardest adjustment she ever made... harder than enduring her parent's disapproval. Her preoccupation and longing for the children had nothing to do with her relationship with Thea, but it affected Thea personally. She wanted Sara to trust George's parenting so completely that she could be emotionally present when they were alone. At times she grew to be impatient with Sara's inability to let go and relax. Sara was aware of how her internal conflict was affecting the relationship. When the pain was unbearable, she would be angry at Thea for expecting too much of her. At times she questioned her decision to be divorced and in a gay relationship. When Sara was silent, Thea intuitively sensed her agonizing spirit and drifted away to respect her privacy. She struggled not to take responsibility for Sara's sadness, but love connects in all matters, and they knew that all too well. When Sara spoke of her conflict, Thea reassured her of their father's love. Sara clung to Thea's firm foundation as the only lifeline of hope.

The children adjusted very well to the separation of their parents because George and Sara were both committed to their care and emotional well-being. That was a responsibility that kept them friendly and it motivated George to manage his anger respectfully.

In spite of Sara's inner conflict, her love for Thea grew. Their relationship became a constant adventure. Occasionally her confidence was shattered by her inexperience about what being a gay woman meant. Being a daughter, a wife and a mother were the only expectations that felt normal. How did she fit being gay into her identity? Was it a total separation from what she knew or a gradual blending of gay identity into her life as

183

woman, daughter, mother, and now, lover? Sara was open to learning about this ever-expanding new world. Her love for Thea gave her confidence when she felt insecure and out-of-place. At times she needed to retreat from the newness to catch her breath.

She met Thea's friends. They were gracious and supportive of their relationship. All of them were working hard, paying bills, prospering, and for the most part, loving life like most couples she had known while being married to George. The absence of men seemed strange at first, but she eventually learned that gay women manifested various power styles, bringing normalcy to every phase of their lives.

Thea always imagined the love of her life in every romantic way; romantic evenings, travel, the freedom of spontaneous sexuality and the privacy to be fully satisfied by one true love. She never imagined that she would become an instant co-parent. She was now faced with the new and unexpected conflict of joining Sara in parenting the children and wanting Sara all to herself. Emotions of jealousy secretly and shamefully interrupted her peace. She witnessed Sara's devotion to her children. When she was with them she was absorbed, and Thea did not know how to fit into that love. Her neediness and vulnerability made her feel like a child herself. She managed to conceal her insecurities for many months. Sometimes she found herself starting conflicts as a way of redirecting Sara's attention to her and intimating that she needed to choose between her and the children. She hated herself for these emotions, but they would not be denied. When she isolated herself in the study, she felt even more miserable. When Sara finally asked what was really bothering her, Thea avoided an honest discussion because she couldn't admit her immaturity. Sara wanted to understand Thea's struggle, but without an honest disclosure it was difficult to resolve the problem. She told Thea, lovingly and directly, that she could never be torn between her love for the children and her love for her. "The children need me in ways that you don't and unless you join me in their care, we will always be divided as a couple," Sara explained.

From the first day of their meeting, Thea respected Sara's directness and her devotion to the children. She always knew that the solution to her inner conflict was for her to become a deeper part of their lives than she was before their union. They must become her children, too. That was challenging for many reasons. Although she was childlike in many ways, Thea never had close relationships with children. Until she met Sara, her life was childless. She would have to trust that this new fusion would be good for her and a necessary adjustment in their relationship. Now she had to decide if she was going to sit on the sidelines or play on the frontline. This unexpected challenge forced her to find a solution, and the solution would change her life forever.

Both Sara and Thea were experiencing their relationship differently. Thea hardly had time to think about herself anymore. Oftentimes she brushed her teeth and drank her coffee in the company of the children. She tripped over things as she walked through the living room on her way to work. She had to remember to bring childcare supplies wherever she went. Car seats were now standard equipment in her SUV, and worst of all, Sara was often too tired for intimacy at the end of a busy day. Thea held her, wishing for more, but understood her exhaustion because she too was among the ranks of burned-out parents. She was learning how exhausting love could be, particularly when raising children.

Because Thea had no legal rights to the children, her presence in their lives had to be an emotional experience. She wanted the children to be comfortable in their home and know that comfort could only be achieved if the children felt secure and loved by both her and Sara. She would trust love as never before. Did she need to love the children as she loved their mother? If that is what it took, Thea would willingly open her heart in new ways to surrender to the demands of love.

Thea wanted Sara to return to medical school to complete her degree. Sara was in agreement, but couldn't figure out when she would find the time or how she could endure the time away from the children. Relying on a nanny, for Sara, was not a comfortable idea. After weeks of discussion, Thea and Sara decided that the children would be enrolled full time in school. It was agreed that Thea would drive the children to school every morning and the nanny would pick them up in the afternoon and stay until bedtime. Three years into their relationship, both Thea and Sara knew with certainty the strength of their love. For each of them, their relationship presented a life different than the life they presumed they would live. For Sara, it satisfied her need for authenticity and adventure. Thea woke every morning believing in Sara's love for her.

Story of a Black Woman

"MY GRANDMOTHER USE TO SAY THAT SHE SPENT HER
WHOLE LIFE FEEDING PEOPLE..."

For years after our divorce, Donovan tried to shame me back into the marriage. His son needs him fulltime, I wasn't being an effective parent, Our son needed a father figure to be a strong man, His mother missed Uzoma, My ass was so big no sensible black man would ever love me, I never remarried, so why couldn't he be my man? The insults were endless and so was my resistance.

My vigilant mothering and advancing professional career left me little time for myself. Through the years of Uzoma's high school and college, I was intent on creating a successful human being. From time to time, I realized my resolve was to make my son a different kind of man than the other men in my life. Sometimes he rebelled against the pressure of my personal dreams for him. I spent twenty-one years dreaming him a life, and now, it was time to dream a little for myself. I hardly knew where to begin.

Uzoma graduated college when I was fifty years old. The time had come for me to step back. Abdicating my mother throne was a bittersweet experience. I had to leave behind the know-all-be-all mom because I had created a human being who was now thinking on his own and making his own choices. Some mothers do this without much trouble, while the rest of us have to learn painfully. I learned that Uzoma was God's gift to me, and I to him. As I experienced the demolition of my motherhood, I learned that my son's life that I touched, guided and directed was just a moment in time. He now had the right to control his own destiny and that's what I wanted for him.

A month after graduation, Uzoma married Liana, who graduated as a biology major and wanted to resume her graduate studies in California. Uzoma began working as a civil servant in child protective services. He was accepted into a psychology program that led him into his doctoral training. It sounded like a lot of responsibility for both of them, but I didn't interfere. I must admit that California seemed millions of miles away. He knew, without a doubt, that I would never abandon him. Now I have to believe that he was not abandoning me.

My grandmother used to say that she spent her whole life feeding people. The white people she cooked for, her fellow church members, people who just happened to stop in at dinner time and of course, our family. Although I've always been a working mother, cooking has been a unifying experience for me and those I love. I cooked for my grandmother and mother as they aged. Our house was the hub of good food for Uzoma and his friends. I cooked my whole life and only now was I faced with a new challenge: cooking for myself.

Because eating food is more about nourishing our souls than our bodies, more about the good times when we're all together, about telling others that you love them, it has become the tool of matriarchal power. Now I wander through the grocery store wondering what I would like to eat. Soulful cooking for me didn't feel right. More times than I care to admit, I found myself sitting in a restaurant alone. After a few months of this mindless eating, I began to invite friends for dinner. I began to shop with me in mind. I reminded myself that what was good for others would be just as good for me. I always prepared food with love, whether it was a breakfast of ham, eggs and grits or a bowl of oatmeal. This soul food tradition has been an emotional experience and it has everything to do with loving myself.

As I settled into my new aloneness, I began to recognize so many ways that I had become lost to myself in my absorption with serving others. I thought I knew the difference between caring for others and loving them, but in most situations that involved others closest to me, my personal needs vanished. Did I think others were helpless and incompetent? Did I feel that I had a higher wisdom about how their lives should be? Was I so out of touch with my own self that others became a substitution for my personal emptiness? What was it?

From where did this struggle come? My father, my co-workers, my own son did not seem to struggle with this problem. I can remember so much conflict about simple things like whether to buy myself a new coat that I needed or buy my son a new coat that he didn't need. During the prolonged illness of my beloved grandmother, I traveled every weekend to help care for her. After her death, I continued traveling to comfort my mother's grieving soul. The stack of unread books on my end table became a memorial of my forgotten self.

I contemplated visiting my mother or spending the weekend reading. I visited my mother. I never resented my decision, but neither did I experience the sweet joy of self-nurturance. Choice didn't seem to enter my mind. If I imagined that others needed something from me, choice was not an option. I never remembered resenting what I gave or the time I sacrificed, but what I didn't recognize was how silently I slipped away without a whimper of protest.

If I thought I had choices, I didn't seem to believe that I had the right to exercise them. As I listen to many of my friends, I realized that many black women live with a divided self. Our talents and our dreams are stacked away like a shameful possession that competes with our cultural prescription: exist to serve, exist to care for others, exist to carry the legacy for our mothers and grandmothers, exist as the backbone of our family's economic responsibility and survival. Now I realize that real oppression is the absence of choice. It is our obstinate strength and the ability to survive that makes a black woman a distinctive force of feminine power.

Now that I enter the more mature years of my life, I will reclaim myself. I will learn how to awaken from this lost dream and be me again.

Story of a Woman ... Now Old

"IS IT POSSIBLE THAT I COULD HAVE GIVEN SO MUCH OF MYSELF AWAY
THAT MY SELF COULD NEVER BE MINE, COMPLETELY?"

My wedding day was sad, not because of my father's disapproval, but because I was leaving my brothers and sisters. They wanted to be completely happy for me, but couldn't. Marion crawled under the kitchen table and cried for hours. Tommy came running into my room as I was getting dressed and asked me to help him find his shoes. Ellen stood by and watched me dress with tears running down her face. As I saw their grief, my heart was torn. My life was spent protecting them from pain, and now I was the cause of it. Is it possible that I could have given so much of myself away that my Self could never again be mine, completely? I was torn in so many directions. Immediately after our marriage, we were moving to John's family home in Connecticut. I was excited about traveling. Believe it or not, this was my first trip! I was excited about being a bride and having everyone stand in my honor; to have music played in my honor; to have a meal prepared by other women in my honor. Today, I was honored and that protected me from the pain of leaving my cherished others.

Immediately after the wedding, John and I, along with our wedding party, sat down to a pork-chop dinner. The food was delicious but the atmosphere was chaotic. There was no reception; no wedding cake; no one caught my bouquet; no one slipped off my garter. Still wearing my wedding gown and veil, we packed ourselves into a car and drove three and one half hours to meet my in-laws. When we arrived, John got out of the car quickly and went into the house. He seemed to forget his bride. My mother-in-law, Anna, asked where I was and admonished him for not being attentive. Anna welcomed me warmly and so did all of John's siblings.

John did not have a job, and of course, I had never worked outside the home. So we lived with my in-laws the first year we were married. My mother-in-law was comforting to me, but she became irritable as the months passed and we were not contributing financially to the household expenses. The concern about money was a new experience for me. For the first time I realized that money had never been a part of my life. In my father's family we always had what we needed. I helped my mother-in-law as much as I could, with hopes that it would compensate for the burden of our presence. John, who never worked very much, seemed less concerned about our financial dependence.

At the end of the first year, I got a job in the knitting mill because I realized that John alone was unable to support our family. For our financial survival, I had to earn money. We moved downstairs into a small apartment. I worked nights and John worked days. Not only was I employed, but pregnant with my first child. I adjusted quickly to the mill job. Although it was hard work, I enjoyed the liberation from household tasks. From that point in my marriage, I worked until the age of sixty-two.

My first two years of marriage were a difficult adjustment for me. Being away from my family was a huge loss. I worried about my brothers and sisters every day, but was reluctant to speak about my concerns because I might have appeared ungrateful for the new family John brought into my life. John was kind, but his kindness could not dismiss my longings. I visited my brothers and sisters every few months until I began to work in the knitting mill. Working in the mill was foreign. Managing money was foreign. Having a child of my own was foreign. I had been a mother all of my life, but mothering my own child was unchartered territory. I was happy, and yet aware of my inner exhaustion.

MY LIFE IS MINE

——⊶⊷——

**I will protect the ownership of my life by
avoiding unhealthy compromises.**

How We Think
"If you are unsure of your power, you will lose it."

In a world where change happens rapidly, it is challenging to accept the
slow, methodical process of reinventing our lives. It is only possible to do so if
we continue to accept the magnitude of socialization. Acceptance will come in
waves of insight gained through self-reflection and by listening to other women.
Resocialization is not a momentary experience, but a lifelong journey. It is a
process of becoming, realizing, birthing, struggling and learning to enjoy our
personal existence. This type of honesty is one of the toughest challenges we
face. Sometimes, after experiencing a serious illness, we become much more
honest because we are forced into a vulnerability that peels away our defenses. In
this way, illness can make us who we are. Sadly, for some of us, a medical crisis
is the only thing that can spur us to search for our true self. But you can make
this shift to honesty now by simply acknowledging how inconspicuously your
life was compromised by socialization.

We need to recognize that simply being ourselves should be much more
natural. What is natural, however, gets redefined by cultural attitudes that have
nothing to do with our real self. At birth, our lives were wrapped around
attitudes, beliefs and emotions that were not good for us. We didn't have a choice
then, but we do now. We learned to take our behavior seriously so we could
survive in a critical, watching world. The terrible trap that paralyzes the Self
makes us think that we are responsible for the behaviors of others. We made
ourselves fully available to the needs of others by creating permeable boundaries
alterable at a moment's notice. We have taken our caring so seriously that
we forgot that we deserve care. We experience caring as a one-way street.
Caring, loving, serving, adjusting and denying became more important than
being ourselves.

Change can only happen over a long period of time because resocialization involves untangling a complex web of emotions and beliefs amassed over a lifetime. Resocialization is a process of self-knowledge, which means, discovering the self that is all-embracing. The beliefs we try to shed are also held by the people who touch our lives. Their expectation is that we should carry on the legacy of submissiveness, deference and compulsive altruism. Their expectations complicate our journey. Our growing awareness and new changes may actually stagnate our existing relationships into silence or inflame them into power struggles. If you are unsure of your power, you will lose it. If you are comfortable with your power, you will gain self-assurance through conflict because you'll be forced to stand up for yourself and define what you believe in without fear. Being sure of our power creates an inner peace that is undaunted in the face of conflict. This kind of honesty has its own beauty. Those who struggle for power with us are threatened by who we've become. Life was easier for them when we were less interested in ourselves. They may feel unsure of their own existence if they are unable to control ours. They may try to use the treachery of shame and guilt to restore life as they knew it. Negotiate a new relationship without falling victim to the compromising emotions of unhealthy guilt and shame. Be confident in your conviction that love can exist and flourish without control. Love can only flourish when you are flourishing with it. Love, in any relationship, is a call to self-unity.

At this stage, conflicts become inevitable. Use them and accept them as an essential component of personal growth. You must be unwilling to let conflicts distract you from your power. Your disturbance is a sign that you are living in crisis and the purpose of crisis is development. Understand that when a conflict is resolved, we can be closer to others. If it is not resolved, we will be burdened with unhealthy relationships for a lifetime. We will have lost an opportunity for intimacy. Keep these guidelines in mind when faced with conflict:

- View the conflict as a passage to intimacy. We should not condemn ourselves; condemnation yields weakness.
- Understand that avoiding conflict will make us sick and unhappy. Facing conflict will make us self-assured.

- Resolution of conflict will illuminate the real meaning of life's existence and brings us much closer to those we love or eliminate unloving relationships.

Our families will bring about the greatest crisis because they are the closest to us. The term family is used here to mean all types of gatherings in which the members are striving to love and care for one another. Any type of extreme behavior means there is a problem. We experience so much of our personal well-being, and the fundamental way in which we know ourselves, with our family.

Some family members will protest our changes. We should view that as a sign of their resistance to change. They may use actions and words to cast doubt on our efforts toward emotional liberation. They may question the quality of our mothering or our devotion to the family. They may discourage outside relationships with good female friends. They may joke about our changes, making them seem trivial. They may use irritability, criticism or manipulation to contaminate your resolve to change your life. We can face the problem squarely by employing all of our resources, most especially, our courage, patience and persistence. We must stay focused during these turbulent times and utilize the networking system we have created to manage loneliness, sadness and anger in our struggle to maintain our dreams. We need other positive and encouraging voices in our lives to drown out the angry voices of those who would have us remain as we have always been. Coping with intra-familial conflict without alienating its members takes strength and patience. It will demand adjustment and a healthy love where each member is regarded with personal dignity. Sometimes this takes time. We must be patient and continue on our journey. Very often the angriest of family members eventually catches up with us and comes to accept our new Self. If we can resolve conflict with them, we are pulled into our journey to wholeness. Every conflict is both a challenge and an opportunity.

Until our families adjust, we will need the support of our family of recovering friends. Remember that your friends are the family you choose. It is important to shift our emotional support to them until our families adjust their expectations to our new identities. When they respect our personal boundaries, honor our considerations, share our responsibilities and stop demanding that we answer to all their needs, they have made an important adjustment. As we turn inward, we release anyone who does not respect our transformation. We oppose any attempts at minimization.

Once we have firmly established our determination to change, our family relationships can begin to rebuild a system of love based on equality. The adjustment of our families and friends will happen in their time, not ours. Practice patience. Their eventual adjustment will not only enhance our recovery, it will bring them to a new level of psychological health. Like socialization, resocialization can also spiral through our social system. This time, however, it will be a healthy positive spirit whose benefits will have a rippling effect.

How We Feel

"Anger is the vigilant master of selfhood."

Any change in our lives is accompanied by emotional upheaval. We are flooded with emotions that change from minute to minute. It is this constant emotional fluctuation that makes us feel unstable, insecure and fearful during transitions. It is important that we give ourselves permission to experience our discomfort because it is our pain that motivates us to learn how to care for our hurting Self. The lessons we learn as we walk through our valley of pain usually become a permanent part of our lives.

When the people we love express opposition to the changes we are making, we may feel alienated and afraid. Bonding with our recovering sisters will keep us focused on our purpose. It is important for us to trust that they can give us the support we need. This period of alienation can become an opportunity to strengthen our resolve to be free. Remember that great achievements usually include struggle. Alienation will teach us to rely on ourselves. We will learn, out of necessity, that caring for ourselves must be a priority. Alienation will force us to realize a selfhood that we have long forgotten or never knew.

When the people we love fail to give back the loving and caring we have given them, we may feel abandoned, disappointed, frustrated and doubtful about the effectiveness of love. We may be tormented by doubts about our relationships that sound like this:

- Why don't they recognize my pain when I am so cognizant of theirs?
- Why don't they realize what I need when they never had to ask me to fill theirs?
- Why didn't they notice that I was tired from the effort of protecting them from the burdens of living?
- Why didn't they see that I was bored and lost while I worked so hard to make their lives progressive and interesting?

At times we may feel cheated and disregarded by others, especially those we care for without hesitation. We may question our self-worth, our purpose in life or even if we are worthy of love. These depressing emotions may lead us to a behavioral impasse and internal turmoil. We face a tremendous dilemma: we have grown too much to accept traditional values and we are too disappointed in the reactions of others to believe in liberation. Patience will help us cope with this inner turbulence. Learning how to channel our anger into conscience living will restore our peace and accelerate growth. Believing in the journey of transformation is as important as the transformation itself. The magnitude of our life is reflected by our dreams and beliefs.

However, being patient at this stage does not mean repressing our anger. Anger is an emotion that is directly linked to our self-love. Anger is an expression of power and self-respect. It has been prohibited for women far too long. The repression of anger has hurt us deeply.

Traditional definitions of women have removed anger as a right in order to keep women in a minority status. A self that cannot be empowered to be angry is a self that does not matter. When we are accused of being an angry woman, remind your accuser that you are a woman who can become angry. Being called an angry woman generates shame; being a woman who can become angry is powerful and purposeful. Don't allow anger to shame you, it is our right; essential to our self-preservation. Think of anger as a positive emotion. Don't apologize for it, as we often do. We must speak of our anger, not to change others but to heal ourselves. Anger is used to acknowledge our hurt, our need and our truth, not to punish others who fail to do so. Anger will become the emotional mediator that will distinguish our forgotten selves from our renewed self.

Anger is a vigilant master of selfhood. It signals our internal discomfort by triggering fear and anxiety in its purest form. At first, we may not be certain of why we are angry. We don't need to know our anger immediately. We can be with it, by feeling it. We don't need to connect it with other parts of our history. Until we accept our anger, we cannot grow from it. It demands new levels of consciousness about who we are and what we stand for.

Anger is a signal of discomfort that will demand our recognition because it points to an incongruity with our emerging, renewed self. We must, therefore, employ all of our wisdom and skills to resolve the anger in a way that will protect our dignity. Acts of self protection become indicators of self proclamation. Anger establishes clear boundaries between us and others. Although we are initially uncomfortable, ultimately the expression of anger brings order and emotional peace into our lives.

How We Are With Others

"We won't be so serious, tired, angry, or burdened if we stay focused on loving ourselves while loving others."

We have been with others in every imaginable way. Our challenge now is to be with ourselves while being with others.

In our families, we learned the unrealistic ideals of being a woman without boundaries. Most families generate tremendous neediness within its ranks that are supposed to be satisfied by the mother, who is usually the silent head of household. Family life has brought abuse and depression to women for centuries. Family life, as it is traditionally defined, has been unhealthy for women. Women have suffered from abuse of every kind within the family. Her role as mother is not respected by institutions that employ her or the governments that are suppose to protect her. As individuals, women must divest themselves of traditional, unworkable and unrealistic expectations regarding their lives. The concept of family is changing. Mother will not be seen as the resting or blaming place for family members. She must step down from the sacrificial pedestal and be counted as a family member of equal standing, like all others.

Changing how we are with others is also going to alter the meaning of family. To be relational means giving ourselves an opportunity to connect spiritually with the lives of many people. Some of the people we connect with may not be members of our biological family. They become family to us because we have grown to love them. They have become part of our being-ness. This means they are part of our emotional preferences, our consciousness and our love. These connections add meaning to our lives by making it possible to experience the many facets of our personalities. They challenge us and help us become who we really are. Our relational self must be able to manage being with others while we are being with ourselves. Relationships, by their very nature, should become opportunities for visibility, not invisibility. Learning the skills to negotiate selfhood in relationships will make the experience of relationships expansive and unifying. We won't be so serious, tired, angry, or burdened if we stay focused on loving ourselves while loving others. We will find ourselves running toward others, rather than away.

As we change our lives, opportunities for selfhood open up for our daughters and granddaughters who witness our renewal. We are modeling an integration of femininity and masculinity, one which was previously unknown and is not socially appreciated. We are demonstrating a life characterized by flexibility, one which gives equal rights to ourselves and to generations of women to come. In so doing, our personal self has become spiritual and more political. Women who have become the bride-of-their-own-life teach the world that they belong to their own destiny first and all other relationships must serve this ultimate purpose.

JOURNALING

1. Ownership of your life implies protection of or having power over who you are and want to become. It implies taking responsibility for you. How dedicated are you to the ownership of your life? What do you think this term means? How do you feel about it? Have you protected and promoted your uniqueness? Have you been too absorbed in the identity of others? Have you allowed past experiences, family expectations and self doubt to erode ownership of your life? Evaluate yourself honestly. Be with yourself. **Write!**

2. In the center of a sheet of paper, write the words: self-responsibility. Draw a circle around it. On the circle, write down what you hold yourself responsible for. Write quickly and freely. Circle each separate thought and connect it back to the core word, self-responsibility. Do these for three to five minutes, then write for five minutes about the insights you gained. **Write!**

3. Women often fantasize about being loved, but are timid about asking for the love they need. How would you like to be loved? Be concrete about your loving suggestions. Go into your fantasies. They will become more real as you write. Write fifty acts of love you want to be a part of your life. **Write!**

4. Loving must always include loving yourself. The way you love can also help you to love yourself if it reflects your choices. In what unique ways do you enjoy loving? Write ten ways you love others that help you to feel empowered and beautiful. Next to each way, write what this loving act does for you. **Write!**

REFLECTIVE CINEMA

Movies that reinforce the themes of this stage recommended for viewing:

- Erin Brockovich
- White Palace
- My Big Fat Greek Wedding
- Like Water for Chocolate

STEPPING OUT

- Tell a member of your family how unhappy you are with one certain aspect of their behavior.
- Talk to your father about his life before his marriage and after your birth.
- If they are still with you, ask your mother or father what they argue about and how they resolve their conflict.
- Tell your family how much you appreciate what they do for you. Address each member. Be specific about your appreciation.

Story of a Married Woman

"ONLY HIS FAITH IN THEIR LOVE FOR ONE ANOTHER COMFORTED HIM."

Nina walked into the crowded room of women a lot more self-assured than she had been a year ago. She knew that sitting in this circle of women each month was an essential part of her healing. She was not sure how it worked, but she knew that she felt freer and closer to herself. Only now could she look back and realize how wounded she had been. Without knowing it, she brought her wounded-ness into all of her relationships, with hopes that these relationships would save her from herself. Now she was becoming a self she could enjoy. Throughout the past year she allowed herself to openly grieve the painful losses that were waiting for discovery. She recognized and accepted her survival as a victory. Like an eternal journey, she was discovering how history and significant people touched her life. She was becoming real, not by judging the world, but by loving it.

Before Nina left the house that evening she had a conversation with Joe that marked a transition in their relationship. It was real rather than reactive. In the privacy of their bedroom, they sat together. She looked at him intensely as her eyes filled with tears. For a brief moment, her emotions seized her being so completely that to say a word would have seemed like a violation. She began, "Joe, I married you without hesitation or reflection, I denied myself those rights. I never regretted our marriage even when I felt like I was dying inside. I thought that marriage would elevate my life to its highest purpose. It has certainly given my life purpose, but not my highest purpose. Only I can do that."

Joe listened without interruption or judgment. He never stopped looking at her as if he knew that what she had to say was as important for him to hear as it was for her to tell. Nina had changed. Sometimes it scared him. Sometimes it angered him because he did not know if her changes were a rejection of him. Only his faith in their love for one another comforted him.

"I was my father's daughter, Joe. I was a Daddy's girl; I idolized him and rejected my mother. He was my hero and I wanted to be just like him. I was determined to make him proud. I was so enraptured by his perfection that I excused his flaws. I grew up favoring men and their values, dismissing women as inferior. It was my divided-self that surrendered my dreams without considering their worth. It was my divided-self that wanted you to be all the things my father was, and more. I put pressure on you to be the *ultimate male so that I could feel like the privileged female. Because you were sober and my father was not, I worked even harder for your love. In some mysterious way, I felt it my obligation to reward your goodness with my life, my life the way you wanted it. Now, I must tell you that you can share my life the way I want to share it with you. I need time to return to a self that I can believe in, and our relationship will be better for it. Be patient with me. I love you."*

Surprisingly, Joe said nothing. No competition, no correcting, no resistance. He thanked her for finally initiating a conversation that brought him into her renewed life. After hugging her for a long time, he pulled away and said, "Nina, I've had so many emotions during the past year I could not begin to name them. Your insight threatens me. Your realness threatens me even though I know how committed you are to me and our family. Let's keep talking. I need to find some friends that want to do more than fish and hit golf balls."

She whispered back, "Grow with me Joe, it is our only hope for real happiness. The uncertainty of our future can be comforted by our love." He did not agree, but he listened. They walked into the family room where the kids were totally drawn into the action of computer competition. Everything seemed the same, but they both felt a difference that was exciting and frightening at the same moment.

On Monday morning, Nina sent her resume to five financial firms and researched the availability of a part-time nanny. She told the kids about her plans. They thought it was COOL!

Story of a Lesbian Woman

"THEA KNEW IF SHE WASN'T A WHOLE PARENT, SHE WOULD
FEEL LIKE AN OUTSIDER."

Five years into their relationship, Sara graduated from medical school. The excitement of her graduation and the celebrations that followed seemed to eradicate the last existing barriers within their families. This accomplishment made the families realize how powerful and functional their love was. For the first time, the children had a unique opportunity to witness genuine acceptance from both families. Sara's parents thanked Thea for helping their daughter. "Your daughter is my life," she replied. "No thanks necessary." Did they believe her? It didn't matter. Maybe in time, they would know that gay love, like all love, is only as real as the lovers themselves.

Before Sara started her residency, she and Thea took a two-week vacation in Europe. Sara was more comfortable now leaving the children with her parents and Thea's parents. Both Ari and Rennie looked forward to grandparents who honored their every need and desire. Ari learned woodworking from Thea's dad and Rennie bonded with Thea's mother with a vengeance. She watched her parent's happiness as they bragged to their friends about their grandchildren. Thea insisted early in their relationship that the children be a part of her family. Both she and Sara realized they were breaking new ground in family traditions so every boundary was well thought out. Sometimes, after long conflicts, eventually they arrived at a place where both of their needs were answered. At first, Sara resisted allowing the children to be disciplined by Thea. But, Thea fought back because she knew if she wasn't a whole parent, she would feel like an outsider.

Telling the children about their love relationship was a major accomplishment for them. Thea insisted that they be told shortly after Sara moved into her home because she knew firsthand how destructive it was to practice duplicity when honesty was require. They had ears to hear and eyes to see, and not telling the truth would do more damage than talking about it. Sara was resistant because she thought the children needed to be older to understand their relationship. Thea refused to live in shame and mystery. The disclosure was difficult because it forced Sara to face her own homophobic fears. They both realized that their story would be introduced when they were young, but would need to be retold differently and more deeply as the children matured. They bought books and sought professional guidance as they began the resocialization of their children.

How do you tell the big story of honoring another person's life, when they chose a life that is radically different than the norms deemed acceptable for human choices? As Thea and Sara began to face the challenge of "coming out" to their children, both of them realized that they were teaching life lessons about respect for life, as it is created by one's choices. Every day the children were surrounded by loud and powerful messages that prescribed a normal life for boys and girls. It told them about the future. Each day after school, the children came home to two mothers. Would Rennie miss not having a father to be a friend? Would Ari miss not having a father to be a buddy? These questions tormented them. Both Sara and Thea realized the enormous task that lie before them.

Sara resisted telling the children until one day while at the bookstore Ari saw a display for Gay Pride Month. He said, "Oh, this is a lesbian book." Sara was frozen by his openness. As they drove home, she asked, "Do you know what a lesbian is?"

"No, but you are one!"

"How do you know?" Sara asked.

"Because you live with Thea."

"Oh, yeah! Well, what do you think the word lesbian means?" Sara watched her son intently.

"Maybe women who like to march in Washington."

"A good guess, but you're still not right," she replied.

"Well, what, is it?"

"A lesbian is a woman who is in love with another woman instead of being in love with a man. Or she might be in love with a man too, but the point is, she can be in love with a woman."

"Oh, weird."

"You think so? Some people do think it's a little weird. But I think it's pretty great," Sara said, surprised by her own honesty.

After a long pause, Ari asked, "Well, what woman do you love?" he asked.

"I love Thea," she replied without hesitation.

"I've always known that," he said. This brief conversation broke the longest silence.

Before moving to Seattle for Sara's residency program, they searched for Seattle's gay community. They made contact with other families through Joseph, a gay realtor, who later became their best friend. Joseph and his partner, Nathan, had a son and daughter. They introduced their family to a gay parenting group, so Ari and Rennie would know other children with gay parents. They participated in community gatherings. They selected schools only after questioning the school's positions on gay rights. Ordinary decisions were not easily made because discrimination was a fact of life.

The move to Seattle brought blessings and losses. They no longer had grandparents close by, so they needed to rely on their community of friends for support. They bought a house that was large enough for family visitors and hoped the family would take advantage of their hospitality. The children spent holidays and part of every summer with their father.

Sara worked long hours, so Thea became more in charge of the children. For the first time in her life, she was deeply parental. The children accepted her expanded parental role without a lot of resistance because they loved her so much and had grown to trust and respect her. They seemed to know that it was part of a bigger plan for their family. Thea didn't work for the first year in Seattle. She took on the domestic management with great dedication and purpose. Sara loved her for it. She spent her free time getting involved in political issues that were affecting the gay community. The combination of domesticity and politics made Thea wonder how she ever had time to work.

At the end of her professional sabbatical, Thea decided to open her own business. It would keep her out of the uncomfortable corporate life and give her the flexible hours she needed to care for their children, who were now ready for junior high school.

Thea opened a coffee-house in downtown Seattle that offered the most extraordinary coffees from all over the world; pastries, soups and sandwiches lovingly prepared by Mia, an older German woman, who loved to be creative with food. Thea used her personality and artistic talent to make the café a gathering place for food lovers and thinkers. In a very short time, it became a huge success.

Thea wrote a monthly newsletter, Out of the Box, for Seattle's gay community. It explained the importance of the socialization for men and women and it also educated the heterosexual community about gay life. It invited them to challenge barriers that kept them separate and unequal. It told stories of real people suffering real loss because they live in a divided world. It proposed solutions that expressed equality. Finally, Thea found a way to convert her personal suffering into positive change; it prepared her to teach a divided world that there is another way to live.

Story of a Black Woman

I know it sounds crazy, but one of the hardest things I've ever had to do in my life is to believe in and love myself. As a little girl, I was shy. I wanted to blend in, but didn't know how. There was subliminal message inside of me: "If you were light-skinned, your life would be easier."

The death of my grandmother, and then my mother five years later, made me confront the reality of death. As I walked away from my mother's gravesite, it occurred to me that death was not unfamiliar territory. I'd been facing death for as long as I could remember and its image had been nothing less than terrifying to me. It took my breath away, made my heart beat irregularly and forced me to work hard in order to construct a life-style that was supposedly risk-free. The fear of death made me run fast to be perfect. So, yes death has been chasing me for a long time. Not a physical death, but something that is even more debilitating. A slow, torturous spiritual death.

During my younger years, I hid from the world in shame. I made myself unavailable. I hid from the challengers and thought I was safe. I imagined the world as evil. Time moved me along when I would have been happy standing still. I became a wife without being emotionally ready to choose a suitable husband. Miraculously, becoming a mother seemed natural and normal, like readiness was in place. My son, my new legitimate escape, became life. Now, in my aloneness, I must face the world that I avoided squarely in the face. I embraced the challenge. I decided to find ways to unleash the powers within me.

After many attempts to create my new life alone, I joined a support group for women of color in my church. I prayed with them in a way that I never prayed before. I prayed to the black Madonna, Isis. Isis sent a message to her devotees: "I am black and beautiful." The Great Goddess, Isis, was the feminine life force that I needed to reclaim parts of myself that were cloaked in shame. I needed a divine energy that knew me before I existed because she was in the cotton fields, because she had her children taken from her, because she was summoned by a master who she didn't love and a life she didn't choose. I needed a divine energy that knew my mother and my grandmother who always felt beautiful. I needed a divine energy that cooked in my mother's kitchen and blessed my grandmother's food. The one-in-herself-ness of Isis that sought quiet tranquility in order to bring forth what was meaningful made me want to know all that I could about her.

My hunger to know her sent me to the library for goddess information. What I learned deepened my appreciation of womanhood. I learned about the collective consciousness that is part of every woman. They are the patterns we all share. I learned that Europe's first civilization, Old Europe, was a peaceful, sedentary, art-loving, earth and sea-bound culture that worshipped the great goddess. She was worshipped as the force deeply connected to nature and her fertility was responsible both for creating and destroying life. The great goddess was immortal, changeless and omnipotent. She took lovers for pleasure. Before fatherhood, before male gods, the great goddess was the feminine life force. When the conquerors that invaded Europe imposed their patriarchal principles on the people, and insisted upon the observance of their rules, the Great Goddess became subservient. The complete dethronement of the great goddess was finally accomplished by the Hebrew, Christian and Moslem religions centuries ago. As the female goddess faded into the background, male deities took her place. I realize that I carry within myself my own glory and repression. To realize that once there was a god that looked like me, made me determined to find her, live her, be her.

Finally looking for me as a woman, grand-daughter, daughter, mother, friend and professional was like being the anthropologist of my own journey. There were so many questions I wanted to ask my mother and grandmother now that I was motivated by this hunger to know. I pulled out of storage the few letters and cards they had written to me. I was angry with myself for not asking questions and angry at them for not writing more. They had both taken with them into death a huge part of my personal history. I wept privately and sometimes sobbed about the closeness I missed with them. It relieved some of my tension, but I knew the tears would not wipe out my loss.

I wanted myth and reality to merge in me. I wanted to know from whom I came, what blood was running through my veins. I wanted to live consciously, to rid myself of the vagueness and confusion cluttering my mind. I wanted to be real. One night, during our discussion group, I was asked to recall my anger toward my mother. The thought of being angry with my mother was close to sacrilegious. How could I? "I'm not angry at her," I said firmly. It didn't work. The other women pursued my honesty like a vulture seeking its prey. I wanted to leave immediately, but knew how immature that would seem. So I became silent. That defense silenced the group. And I became angry with all of them for doing so. How dare they use that defense against me!

After a ten-minute silence, which seemed like ten hours, I began to open up about my mother. I didn't know why this challenge was so important to them, but something inside of me said: "Trust them! Being rooted in life means being rooted in all of reality." Slowly, I began to articulate things that were hard for me to admit, even to myself. I had been disappointed in my mother. I didn't expect her to be a queen, but at least, a vibrant, creative woman! I wanted her to be less defeated, someone who had willed herself to be more protective of her own personal life. I wanted her to be outraged by my father's abandonment. I wanted my mother's pride in being a black woman to be demonstrated wherever she went. I wanted her to struggle less. I wanted some man to make love to her into the night. I wanted him to help her and cherish her. I wanted my father to weep for her as she lay in her dying bed. I sobbed as I released pain that lay dormant most of my life. I mourned my mother's life more profoundly than her death. I cried for the child in me that always missed Daddy.

The silence of the sisters that surrounded me became my invitation to be released from every pain that held me captive. I was released from myself. Others came to me with hugs that made me feel my mother's closeness.

Story of a Woman ... Now Old

During my second pregnancy, my mother-in-law died from liver cancer. During her short illness, everyone surrounded her with care. My daughter, Ann, who was three years old, was confused by her illness and even more confused by her death. She wandered around the house for weeks looking for her Honey. She opened closets and closed doors while calling her name. I told her Honey was in heaven. "Where is heaven?" she asked. "I want to go there." In some way, I understood her confusion about a loss her heart didn't understand.

Soon, my second daughter, Diane, was born. I labored for days giving birth to a nine-pound, eight-ounce baby. I was worn out. Now, I completely understood my mother's exhaustion which had come with every birth. Our experiences as women bring us together in a way that nothing else can. The only way you can believe this truth is by living it.

John and I, along with our two daughters, moved back to Clark Mills. I was so excited to be living close to my family again. Our closeness was an essential part of my happiness. I knew my daughters would be enriched by the nearness of their aunts, uncles and cousins. We continued to struggle financially, but the comfort of my family made all concerns seem trivial and resolvable. I began working at Oneida, Ltd. Silversmiths as an inspector of finished flatware. I prided myself on being the fastest inspector in our unit. My hands were amazing. Their strength and efficiency never failed me. No one knew how many years of practice they had following the dictates of my determinations. I rose before dawn and returned home late in the afternoon. I prepared food and cleaned the house before I left each day. My routine hardly ever changed until I retired at the age of sixty-two.

As the years passed, I buried all of my brothers and two of my sisters. Each of them wanted me to be with them during their illnesses. I made every effort to satisfy their hunger for my presence. I cooked their favorite foods, and until they drew their last breath, I was both their mother and sis. Losing my sister Marion was the hardest loss of all. The cancer that consumed her body never obscured her mind. She talked to me about her feelings, her fears and her hopes of seeing our mother again. In heaven they would get to know each other for the first time. Marian loved me as her mother once, but she always yearned to know our biological mother. As I saw her slip away from the life we shared, I felt a part of me leave as well. Could either of us ever totally recover from her death? She promised to welcome me when I joined my heavenly family. "Everyone will be there to meet you, Bebe. Heaven was made for you!" Marion said. I was seventy-five years old when I kissed my little sister Marion good-bye.

My retirement years were more than welcome. At first, I didn't know how to slow down. My life was always dictated by all the responsibilities that I thought were more important than myself. It was during those years that I lost my husband, John, while living in Florida. It was a sudden death that liberated me into my own existence. After his burial, I moved back to Clark Mills, where my life began again; where it flourished. It was the place in which my life had meaning. My house on the corner welcomed me. My family embraced me. I still live in that house for which John and I paid $5,500 so many years ago. It is both my home and resting place.

HONORING WHO I AM

—ഞ—

I will improve the quality of my life by honoring who I am and spiritually connecting with humankind.

How We Think

"Every time you express who you are or what you think, you become who you were supposed to be. Yes ... you create your own 'becoming' over and over again."

Our lives have been influenced by two forces: the political force which we have defined as social expectations, and the personal force which is the uniqueness of our personality with all its gifts, talents and personal inclinations. Before we began the journey of resocialization, we may have thought they were one in the same. We made that mistake because we were unaware of how completely social conditioning obscured our primal selves. We have tried to recall our unremembered selves, the self we left behind because pleasing others--whether individuals, institutions, groups or cultures--became more important than pleasing ourselves. As our true selves emerge, it will be difficult to deny who we really are. The pathway to our realness lies within us.

Our subconscious lives must become part of our conscious awareness so it can redirect our behavior one day at a time. As we learn to honor our selfhood, in all of its manifestations, we will marvel at how powerful we are. Our primary source of strength will no longer be subject to the whim of others. Our primary source of strength will be our inner life. We must keep reflecting on our inner life as the source of truth. We will learn that it is more powerful than the external power sources we usually relied upon. It is a power limited by ourselves alone. This healthy narcissism will bring us into a new era of self-appreciation. We should delight in both our freedom to accomplish and to make mistakes. We should eliminate the word perfect from our expectations. Perfect is not an experience of this lifetime and we can stop enslaving ourselves to this myth.

Now is the time to rewrite the scripts of our lives. We can do this by freeing ourselves from a fundamental error that makes us and our bodies the scapegoats for cultural immaturity. We will strive to become fully functioning women, able to access our talents and strengths, meet our needs without shame and vigilantly keep meaningful relationships balanced.

⌢

Self-conversion is not about destroying what is bad, but identifying the good within us. It is characterized by these qualities:

- Feeling good about ourselves; – enjoying more sophisticated self-awareness,
- Being unafraid to be vulnerable because it offers us an opportunity to look into the window of our own souls and to acknowledge our humanness,
- Loving ourselves and the lives we live exactly as life happens,
- Realizing that we are more than the sum of our past and greater than our present existence, and
- Recognizing that we are always becoming ourselves through our ongoing history.

This restoration of internal unity is making peace with our true self and the social evolution that is constantly swirling around our lives. As we find ourselves, we take our place in politics, economic advancements, social reform and interpersonal connectedness. Our self-reconciliation comes from the harmonious self-image that can make peace with conflict while holding onto our personal integrity. We can add meaning to our lives by redirecting our personal journey of self-discovery, self-appreciation and ultimately, a self unafraid-of life.

How We Feel

"We need to grieve for ourselves. It may be our first act of self-love."

In the past, fears, anxiety, interpersonal tension and unhealthy modesty has prevented us from enjoying our authenticity. Now we can convert fears into actions, anxieties into courage and interpersonal tension into predictors of growth. We have rethought our lives and set aside childhood lessons that no longer hold value. We are more willing to express healthy arrogance. Healthy arrogance is feeling confident with our emotions and opinions. We share them openly and without an agenda of control or superiority.

At this stage, we can experience our feelings in their purest form without censoring them through the wants and expectations of those around us. We accept them as messengers of growth. We are less prone to defend ourselves. We are less consumed with being perfect. We see ourselves as people first. We are bolder in negotiating relationships that support our conversion and ending those that don't. We have learned to give ourselves time and the right of separation in order to access internal wisdom. We seek out new ways to integrate our brave new selves as we create a brave new world.

Perhaps for the first time in our lives, we enjoy a sense of well-being that comes from knowing that we can determine the direction of our lives. We realize that our lives are manageable when our choices are within the scope of our own power. We enjoy a real sense of purpose because we are more focused on our own goals, which requires letting go of being responsible for the goals of others. A new calmness overtakes us. By now we realize that we can do what we once thought unthinkable: – we can make sense of our lives. We can call into question what doesn't feel good; whatever is obsolete, whatever is toxic. We can change what needs to be changed for the rest of our lives, and we don't need anyone's permission to do so. Slowly, we have put to sleep the illusions of womanhood and awakened strength, peace and self-pride.

How We Are With Others

"We now understand that self-love must be the premise of all love."

Personal transformation cannot be accomplished alone. Forming friendships with other recovering women and supportive men accelerates our dreams. We should, by this time, have formed at least one personal friendship with another woman that is deep enough to discuss our most intimate concerns. Friendship is the highest form of interpersonal love. It expands our personal power. It is not supplemental, but essential. A friend is an integral part of our happiness; a resting place, a challenging place, an exciting venture that refreshes us by existing outside the routine of our lives. In this age of technology, maintaining connections is made easier. Within your community, wherever you are, there are women who have lost their voice and want to find it. Reach out to them as an extension of your commitment to yourself.

How we negotiate our friendships and intimate relationships is a strong indication of how resocialized we've become. When we can watch our friends struggle and have enough faith in them to know that they will find their own solutions, we know how resocialized we've become. When we can become awed by the wisdom of our friend's life journey without feeling that we must direct it, take glory from it or compromise it, we know how resocialized we've become. When we can protect and cherish our friend's right of choice, no matter who protests, we will know how resocialized we've become. When we feel lighter and freer, we'll recognize the depth of our resocialization. When we are motivated to continually examine the divisions of our spirit in order to reach new levels of psychic unity in our life, we will recognize the powerful effects of resocialization. When being the bride of your own life is your deepest passion, you are resocialized. When you grieve for women who suffer silently, violently and unrecognizably from the results of socialization, without being lost in your grief, you know what resocialization means. Life may seem the same for you. You will perform many of the same activities. You may have the same friends and the same job, but you are different because you have learned to see everything from a self that is whole. Now you can be open without being possessed. You genuinely care about your life and believe that protecting it is your privilege.

Healthy caring about others reflects love and concern and is always possible to achieve if you are vigilant about your motives. Caring about others is an expression of support and encouragement. It gives guidance without assuming responsibility. It recognizes that the others will learn to care for themselves when they need to and when they are ready for change. Healthy caring controls the degree to which we internalize the suffering and needs of others. It preserves our energy for personal accomplishments while emphatically linking us to the people we care about. Healthy caring is genuine concern. It is a skill we need to cultivate and believe in to maintain a primary focus on our own well-being. We now understand that self-love must be the premise of all love. It helps reconcile the concept of nurturance with our emerging self. We learn to defer or share caregiving with others. And in these situations we are facilitators of care, without actually performing the care-giving ourselves. Our personal needs cannot be forgotten as we care for others even when it complicates our caring. Healthy caring protects us from becoming drained or depleted. This balanced approach to caring allows us to share who and what we are with the world.

Our gradual separation from compulsory altruism will alter the way we see ourselves in the world. Caregiving will be seen as community rather than a feminine responsibility. Our new vision will demand that social and economic systems find new ways to provide care that is universal. We will deepen our understanding of the distinction between choice and conformity. Caring about others as we care about ourselves is far different than a woman's assigned role of caring without reservation. In this stage we say, "No more." Our giving is now determined by what we are comfortable with. We will never again put aside our own needs because now we know they matter.

JOURNALING

1. Women are honored when they become a bride and a mother. After these monumental passages, women are seldom honored. Imagine yourself being honored for the many important contributions you make to your children, your partner, your family and your work. For each of these parts of your life, write the reasons for which you should be honored. Start with: "I should be honored because _____." After each person, write six honoring statements. **WRITE!**

2. Women honor the people they love and serve in so many ways. Honoring yourself is also your privilege and responsibility. Write a list of 100 ways you honor, or could honor, you. Put a star next to the ones that mean the most to you. Why do they mean so much to you? **WRITE!**

3. Create a ritual for celebrating yourself. How would you begin and end your ceremony? Where would you celebrate your ritual? Who would you invite? What music would you play and how would you use it to celebrate your authentic persona? What instruments would you incorporate? What sacred objects from your life would be a part of the ceremony? What sacred memories, prayers, songs, poems, etc. would become a part of the ceremony? Write a prayer or poem honoring the spiritual being you are and your universal connection to others. Share this creation with a friend. Use it to celebrate your next birthday. **WRITE!**

4. Celebrating who you are gives your life a sense of transcendence that you are somehow connected to an ultimate purpose for humankind. What do you sense is your ultimate connection or purpose in this world? What do you want people to remember about you after your death? What will be your legacy as a female spirit who spent time on the planet? **WRITE!**

REFLECTIVE CINEMA

Movies that reinforce the themes of this stage recommended for viewing:

- One True Thing
- North Country
- Little Miss Sunshine
- Amelia

STEPPING OUT

- Ask a friend to prepare for you a favorite food. Tell them why you're asking and how it feels to ask.
- On your busiest day, STOP to make yourself a cup of coffee or tea. As you drink, do nothing. Just be with yourself.
- Wear a tight outfit revealing your body's wonderful curves. And go out shopping!
- Tell a friend about a story in your life that you have kept in shame-- a story that is about your humanness.

Story of a Married Woman

"For the first time, Nina knew her mother and felt a
deep sadness for the years that she had not known this
magnificent woman she called, 'Mom'"

Nina's life seemed unchanged as she prepared breakfast, tossed a load of laundry in the washer and helped her children pack their lunches. Only she knew how different she had become. It had taken her a long time to recognize that being real meant trusting herself without judging her life's experiences. She had come to know and appreciate her life history and how it shaped the person she'd become.

Slowly, Nina was mourning what she had lived through. Whenever she had private conversations with her mother, she asked questions about her mother's life before marriage. She learned that her mother left her dream of becoming a fashion designer behind to be her father's wife. One day she pulled from the attic a full portfolio of designs she had created forty years earlier. The paper was dry and brittle, still they retained the grace and creativity of her mother's imagination. Nina was in awe. "Why did you give up on your dreams, Mom?" she asked.

"Your father thought there was not enough time for me to be an artist and a wife. Since I never really tried it, I could not refute his position. So every now and then, when no one was home, I would come to the attic to look at my drawings. As the years went on, especially after you were born, I forgot they were there."

Nina said softly, "Yes, I guess that's what happens." Then she added, "But Mom, I decided to give my life another chance. Joe and I are struggling with the transition of our marriage. I want it to be different." Her mother admitted that she was worried about Joe and Nina's marriage, but she would trust Nina's judgment. Her words were a transformational moment in their relationship.

For the first time, Nina knew her mother and felt a deep sadness for the years that she had not known this magnificent woman she called "Mom." As Nina recreated her life, she missed her father more than ever. She longed for the opportunity to simply have it out with him and finally know the mysteries that were buried deep inside of him. She could no longer argue her case or hope for change. His dreams for her were frozen in her memory. They were sexist and outdated, yet its effect had some insidious control of her life. They seemed magnified by his death, and she knew it would take years to creep out of his shadow and find the warmth and happiness that gave her full ownership of her life. She found that peace-making with her father would be more difficult because there were few memories she could recall of a healthy attachment to him. She knew he would hate the kind of feminist she had become, but that may have been because her father had no idea what feminism really was or its full implications. She was trying not to hold on so tightly to what she imagined her father wanted for her because those ideals were unrealistic and detached from any relationship they might have shared; those ideals were immature. They lacked the honesty, reality and intimacy she craved. The peace she made with her father now would take a long time to create because she had so much to forgive him for.

She realized how relieved her father had been when she married Joe because now she had someone to care for her, as if Joe was an extension of her father's care. Maybe, she too bought into that bond of dependence and that was why she accepted marriage so swiftly. She now rejected that idea totally. Hanging on to a regimented relationship with Joe was an unhealthy way to memorialize her father. Maybe he was not sober and conscious enough to re-pattern his marriage, but she would not fall into that hopeless trap. She could imagine that he would want a better life for her, resurrecting earlier memories in which he was supportive of her achievements and involved in her interests. That's the father she loved. It was her struggle to connect with her father spiritually and that gave her a real sense of what spirituality was about. It was not about ritual, it was about finding meaning in the events in her life; loving her history but growing beyond the patterns she learned as a child. She created her own peace by forgiving her mother's dependence and her father's addiction. Her spirituality was her life, the life she remembered, the life she yearned for, the life she missed out on, the life that made her sad and the life that made her proud.

As she drove the kids to school that morning, a time she treasured, her daughter read her a poem she had written for the school paper:

> "MY LIFE IS A JOURNEY I CANNOT DENY
> EACH STEP OF THE WAY
> EACH MOMENT I LIVE
> ARE HOLY MEMORIES I TREASURE
> THEY GIVE TO MYSELF AND OTHERS
> THE GROOVY PERSON I'VE COME TO BE."

Signed: Allison, daughter of Nina and Joseph.

224

Story of a Lesbian Woman

"EACH OF THEM HAD THEIR OWN STORY TO TELL FROM
BROKEN DREAMS TO PERSONAL PEACE."

After fifteen years of life together, big struggles and adjustments were more a source of wisdom than a daily challenge. Sara grew to realize that Thea was a true love in her life, one willing and thoroughly capable of being an emotional partner. Thea learned that she had more of Sara when she was more available to her needs. Thea was a mother who organized her life to be available to the children she had grown to love so deeply. She was direct with them, but also inspiring. She wanted to know where they were even when they thought they were old enough not to have to tell.

Sara was comfortable sharing her parental responsibilities with Thea. She became involved in the lesbian community of friends that she and Thea created. Even when it was a strain, she rearranged her medical practice to be a part of their active social life. Living in Seattle was important for the entire family; it became the birthplace of their individual transformation and their family cohesiveness.

The children integrated their friends into their family life. Their home had become the teen hangout. Oftentimes they had discussions about being gay with a gang of teens around their kitchen table. They encouraged and fostered childhood friends in their home because they knew that changing a prejudiced world is more realistic if the feared, despised and misunderstood world was known up close. They could never foresee the kind of honesty these gatherings required. The honest conversations released them from the last segments of shame they harbored. Most of the time, Thea faced the deluge of questions that were poignant and provocative. The experience forced her and Sara to investigate the meaning of their lives in ways they couldn't imagine. In the beginning of this personal invasion, Sara felt threatened and resisted by conveniently disappearing. She and Thea struggled over how much to share and how in love they appeared to be in front of the children and their friends. Thea fought against shrouding their relationship in behaviors of platonic friendship. She always remembered the loneliness of shame that haunted her for so many years. She insisted that exposure and information was not a campaign of conversion, but rather, a way of acknowledging the diverse world in which we live and the many roads to life and love that are available to all of us. Sara loved and respected Thea's diligent adherence to truth. After much resistance, she allowed herself to be influenced by the messenger.

On this Monday evening, their entire family sat at the head of an assembly of parents from their local high school. Ari was now a senior and his sister, a junior. Their family was invited to discuss what it was like growing up with same-sex parents and what it was like for Thea and Sara to be parents in a heterosexual community that may have seen them as a threat. As they gazed out on a sea of about 150 parents, they wondered how many were there to learn and how many were there to challenge. Was challenging part of learning? Certainly, each of them had struggled with the prejudice and suspicion of being gay; prejudice is the part of life we all would like to deny.

Sara understood the apprehension and resistance of some parents, even after she committed to Thea. She grew up believing that her sexuality was set in stone, but life taught her that it can evolve according to personal circumstances. Her life grew out of her love for Thea. She wanted to turn away many times, but her love for Thea, and the support Thea gave her as she faced the kaleidoscope of emotions bombarding her each day made turning away unthinkable. The acceptance of being identified as a gay woman took her a long time to acknowledge proudly.

Each of them had their own story to tell from broken dreams to personal peace. They accepted the invitation to speak without a lot of struggle or preparation. They had grown to trust each other, as their love was tested in so many ways. They had grown to know each other because their conflict demanded communication and their communication pushed through internal barriers they didn't even know existed. They could now stand together in their differences, and as a family that stood for tolerance.

At age thirteen, Ari had a difficult time deciding whether to stay with his mother and Thea or to live with his father. His father wanted him to move to New York with his new family. It was difficult not to give into his father's needs because Ari felt like his father was a martyr who spent most of his life taking care of his patients and his family. "We were his life!" Ari shouted out one day. "He has no friends." The compulsion and responsibility to protect his father was overwhelming until therapy changed his way of thinking. Finally, Ari realized that it was his father, not him, who was responsible for the choices made. His father accused him of being gay after he decided to stay in Washington. "How can he learn to be man being brought up by two women?" his father protested. He ultimately decided being a person was more important than being a man.

Ari loved and respected his father, but his sense of self was very different than his father's. He firmly believed that it took as much courage for him to be a whole man as it took for his mother to be a lesbian woman. After graduation, he decided to enroll in NYU so that he could see his father more often.

Rennie struggled with the fear of being gay herself because she grew up with gay women. Is it inherited? Is it catchy? She forced herself to be interested in boys before she was ready to confront her fear. Even though the family had open dialogue about sexuality, Rennie harbored this fear for a long time. Her father also seemed eager for her to date. Maybe he too was afraid of her being gay. After many struggles with her mother during her freshman year, she finally, without ever intended to do so, exposed her fears.

Thea was supposed to pick her up in front of her high school after a class trip. One hour before Thea's arrival, Rennie called her to say she was getting a ride with her friend's mother. Thea was puzzled, but agreeable. She thought it was encouraging that Rennie was making friends so quickly at her new high school. The family giving her the ride was not a family that Thea or Sara knew, and that made Thea uncomfortable. That day, she arrived home on time, but the driver was not a parent, but Jonathan, a high school senior. She was grounded for the weekend for lying.

In the months that followed, Rennie became more distant from everyone in the household. In late March, she showed signs of weight gain and an unexplained illness every morning. She resisted going to school or participating in family get-togethers. Thea and Sara were consumed with anxiety, but nothing they did seemed to penetrate the wall of privacy Rennie had created around herself. Finally Sara insisted they visit their family physician. Nothing could have prepared her for his diagnosis: pregnancy.

In a rage of anxiety and sadness, Rennie screamed out her fears, "Well, at least I'm not gay!" It never occurred to Sara that either of her children would think of her lifestyle as a curse to avoid, even to the point of self-destruction. She was always worried most about Ari, but he seemed comfortable in his own skin. No problem seemed to alter his certainty. Now Sara bore the guilt of her daughter's pain and confusion. Her grieving was uncontrollable for several days. Thea was silenced by the shock, but knew a decision about the pregnancy needed to be made soon. She also knew the decision would alter Rennie's life forever, especially if she carried the pregnancy to term. Sara was always politically pro-choice, but now, the choice would affect her daughter's life and that of her unborn fetus. It's ironic how reality and philosophy can be strangers.

After a week of seclusion, confusion and grieving, it was clear that Rennie had no attachment to the idea of giving birth to a child while she was still birthing her own life. After hours of talking with her mother, they both realized and agreed that an abortion was the best conclusion to this terrible pain.

After the abortion, Sara and Rennie went into therapy for several months. Thea and Ari joined them for several sessions. Each of them was angry at Rennie for not trusting them enough to talk about her fear. She accepted their anger honestly and ultimately asked for their forgiveness. The depth of her sorrow generated a new maturity in Rennie. She willingly discontinued her relationship with Jonathan and focused on her life.

Could she be brave enough to tell this story tonight? Only time would tell the extent of her honesty. Two years had passed and it all seemed like a nightmare now, but she knew it was real because it made her grow up like nothing else could!

For each of them, the journey to peace had been long and hard. They each felt the darkness of not knowing where the end would lead them. Only love guided and motivated them to keep going; to stay close to each other and hope that a brighter day would emerge. The future was not a dream for which they had prepared. It was a dream they were forced to create from their love for life and their desire for a peace that made sense. Indeed, their family was a new reality.

Story of a Black Woman

"MY LIFE IS SPIRITUALLY CONNECT TO THEM, AND YET, DISTINCTIVELY MY OWN."

Throughout my life, I pondered the meaning of identity. Folks throw it around like we're supposed to know what it is and how to find it. When I didn't have one, I wasn't consciously aware of missing it. Perhaps it's the vagueness of real identity that sends women into frenzy to look good at any price. Far too many of my friends, who felt disadvantaged from birth, thought identity was fighting back because their skin was too dark, their families too poor, their thighs too big and on and on.

After many years of journeying, I've come to realize that identity is not one thing, but rather a collection of my personal history and the relationship I have with my heritage. My biological and historical roots, as well as my immediate life history, are my identity. One is insufficient without the other. Now, I would say, that if I'm to be born again, I must carve out a new identity distinct from the one society assigned me. I need to take the night journey believing that it will lead to the morning light.

I am now the grandmother of Asha and Rashidi. They live in California, so far from me. I speak to them many times a week to keep them close. After Asha was born, I wanted to visit often. My archetypical mother wanted to move to California to cook for my son and his family. It felt so unnatural to be so far away. It felt unnatural knowing they didn't need me the way my mother needed my grandmother. What was my place in their lives? Did I even have a place in their lives? This dramatic change in my life became a private conflict between the mother and grandmother I experienced and the mother I was. All of the mothering I knew was based on love and the desperation of not wanting to be alone. My son and his wife shared a more balanced and cooperative union. As I watched, I felt admiration and disbelief. Thank goodness these self-doubts were quickly extinguished by an inner peace that always led me back to my core self. There I remembered what was important. I listened to my son's love. I remembered the foundation of our relationship planted so firmly when he was a child. These spiritual memories gave me peace when I was challenged by a changing world.

My life is spiritually connected to them, and yet, distinctively my own. I can't tell you where the road turned. I can't tell you the exact day or time my life became my own sanctuary.

During holidays and birthdays, I travel to see my precious family. I awaken early each morning to prepare a breakfast menu which consists of grandma's cornbread, bacon, eggs and grits. I shop in the open market for fresh vegetables for dinner. We all take time out of our distinctive and busy lives to reenact the rituals of love our family accumulated over the years. I taught my grandchildren how to make Mama's extraordinary pie crust. We stuffed those pies with everything under the sun. Asha's favorite was stuffing an open crust with bananas and cream. Rashidi liked rolling the crust so he always made double-crusted pies. What he put in the center was not nearly as important as repeatedly rolling the dough.

My daughter-in-law at first seemed overwhelmed by the energy I brought into their home. I was challenged to ingratiate myself to her. I wanted her to truly be my daughter, but I came to realize that could only be done by sharing experiences. My desire to care for her was as sincere as it was to care for my son. I viewed her as an extension of him, but always her own person. Perhaps it was her strength and clarity that challenged me the most. She seemed to already have what it took me a lifetime to realize. Her background was more privileged and far less traditional. In our private moments, I invited her to tell me about her family and her life. She was generous with her disclosures. Coming from an intact family, both her parents were college educated and actively involved in their professional lives. She did not know her grandparents, which to me seemed such a loss; a loss she didn't seem aware of as she spoke. Like my son, she was an only child. Throughout her life, she took dancing lessons so, many of our meals ended in the family room with her and the children dancing to music I didn't know. Occasionally, I was pulled into the rhythmic trio and did my best. We all worked hard to fit into each other's lives because love was more important than the differences that challenged each of us. After each visit, I returned to my own life, satisfied with what we shared and accomplished as a family. As I walked through the door of my home, I realized so clearly that love was never supposed to be about the annihilation of myself. My confusion about love was created because I didn't know where I fit in. The worries of my childhood were so all-consuming that I had no time to discover the genuine me. I have come to realize that true love is about the giving of you to yourself.

As I prepare for my retirement, I recall journeying through racism, sexism and classism. Like all black women, I faced them all within the black and white community. I have watched both black and white men with less experience and skill be promoted over me. When I was denied entrance into Harvard's masters program because I lacked courses they thought were essential, I attended night classes at New York University. I graduated valedictorian of my journalism class at the ripe age of fifty-five. Black women don't have time to be quiet and discouraged. We must be dedicated to making our way by charting a new path. We must expect obstacles and not let them take us away from our dreams. My firm resolve counteracted the racism, sexism and classism that confronted me every day. On many occasions, I remember being followed by secret shoppers as I walked around a department store or guards making me check my bag when everyone else in the store carried back-packs. The only way I could make peace with the insult was to ignore the interference. When I shopped for my new home in a white community, small-minded whites became blinded by their classist and racist views. They couldn't figure out how this "nigger bitch" could afford a home as good as or better than theirs. Again, I ignored their resistance. I knew who I was, getting through the -isms by not paying attention to them. What we pay attention to is our intelligence, our spirituality, our peace.

On a recent trip, a woman told me a secret to aging: "Mark your birthday with milestones. Reinvent yourself. Think of all the things you want to be and start accomplishing them. The promise of life is real! I have made it through the rough times. There has not been much rest, but the Great Goddess has blessed me through every passage. She has blessed me with experience, knowledge and insight. She has been my energy. There were days I didn't know whether I could make it out my front door or how I was going to pay my bills, but I made it. The promise of life is real! My rebirth has been better than my life before. Now my life is evenly yoked and it feels damn good to be me again!

Story of a Woman ... Now Old

I just celebrated my ninety-first birthday with a small gathering of my family around me. Sometimes I wonder how I could have lived so long when my own mother died so young and when so many of my younger brothers and sisters died as well. Death keeps challenging me to find a new peace. Peace empowers me. It connects my loss with the life I've shared with each of my loved ones. My life with each of them resurrects tranquility after I have grieved. My grieving has always been true and deep, and it too is a part of my life. I can't really say that I had a plan for my life. While I was so very young, life swept me away. I surrendered to its force because it felt meaningful. If I were to live my life again, I would alter only one experience: I would want to read and write.

The inability to read and write has limited me in so many ways, even to this very day. When I was 32, I wanted to drive a car, but I couldn't take the written examination. My father said, "I will help you to get your license without a written exam because it's my fault that this has happened to you." He did help me through his political connections, but even more so, his gesture made me realize that my father was more appreciative and sensitive to my life than I ever thought. His help healed and reestablished our connection.

I love to cook, but could not read recipe books to duplicate new foods. In more recent history, the cooking show on television has helped me. I watch it every day trying desperately to remember the recipes. When I grocery shop, I'm unable to read labels or try new products unless someone is with me.

My inability to read and write has been the worst social embarrassment. People were always shoving papers in my face to read and sign. These experiences terrify me. My standard excuse is, "I forgot my glasses," as I work hard to hide my shame. As my daughters grew up, they protected me in unimaginable ways by arranging my banking, buying me what I needed, arranging for repairs of my home and taking care of legal transactions. The list goes on and on during the years of my life. My daughters are my loving protectors. My inability to read and write has kept me dependent on others when I didn't want to be dependent at all. It is a constant reminder of my loss. The dependence bothered me more than anything because by nature, I am self-reliant. I love my self-reliance, my competence and my determination to live life as I insist. As the years passed, I made some peace with this crippling disability by employing the same creativity and determination that characterized all other parts of my life: I memorized and preplanned events, kept a network of close friends and family who knew of my special needs. Even at age 91, my memory is still strong and clear.

What more can I tell you about my ninety-one years of life? I often think that how we remember is as important as what we remember. Love and connection is what my memory stores like priceless jewels. My style of remembering is the way I have lived. As a child, my mother and siblings needed me. My love for my mother and for each of them expanded my life into a fusion of meaning that will undoubtedly memorialize it. It was not what I planned, it was what I lived. I don't drive any more. I gave up my car several years ago because it seemed senseless to spend my limited income on a car I didn't need. My friends and family take me where I want to go. I still cook every day. Food becomes the messenger of my love. It exhausts me to have small parties at my home, but I still do it occasionally. Everyone knows that I'm the cook so they clean in exchange for my nurturance. I love to create new ways of preparing foods that are strictly my culinary inspiration. I pick wild grape leaves out in the surrounding fields to preserve them for stuffing. I make my own cheese and yogurt. I raise my own herbs and hang my clothes outdoors to grab the fresh air of spring and summer. My life in some ways is smaller now, but every bit as connected and meaningful as it was when I was a child. Now that I think about it, I am still a child in my soul because every thought about life excites me and engages me. I am outrageous in my thoughts, free in my loving, powerful in my opinions and liberated from the traditional demands of a woman's life. I am the goddess of my life and the bride of my destiny!

Peace with Myself

———— ∞ ————

Now I can inspire others to find personal peace because my life is unified.

How We Think
"We can love being women because it includes what we love most about ourselves."
"Finally, we are the brides of whatever we love."

We have been developing spirituality at every stage of our resocialization. As we regain our sense of self, we also regain inclusion in the world and indeed the universe. We take our place in the circle of life. Spirituality walks with peace. Once we make peace with the conflicts of our personal history, we gain a new sense of respect for our lives. Spirituality is developing a relationship with ourselves primarily and with the world in which we live. We can never truly separate these two components of spirituality because to do so would invalidate the implication of its oneness.

Spirituality is living life from the inside out. It is our strengthened disposition that helps us focus on our beliefs, our feelings and our needs; the things that comprise our inner truth. It gives us the courage to respect our emotions and fantasies, however objectionable they may seem to others. We grow to trust the constant unfolding of our ultimate truth. Spirituality awakens our sleeping Self by giving us the ability to visualize what our life could become and the courage to go for it. Spirituality is not a way of being released from the troubles and pain of our lives; it invites us to embrace them. It is not concerned with being perfect or living perfectly, it is an invitation to enjoy our humanness. Spirituality gives us depth to be grounded in our own reality, even when we're uncertain.

How do we know when we have developed a spiritual life? We have a spiritual life when love becomes more important than winning. We know we are spiritually in tune when we feel attached to the world and the people around us; when matters of the heart are truly an expression of our core. We know we have developed spirituality when we feel pleasures passionately and experience our pain patiently; when we can free ourselves from the complexities and confusions that once paralyzed us. We know we are spiritual when we are empathic, when compassion takes the place of ignorance, distrust and fear. We know we are spiritual when we appreciate the richness of culture and utilize the diversity it offers to expand our consciousness. Differences become opportunities for learning, not excuses to separate. We know that we are spiritual when the peace we hold inside of us is undaunted by conflict, transition or death. When we are spiritual, we acknowledge aspects of our lives that we don't fully understand, without offering apology. We become a healer of others when we are spiritual because we are free. We know we are spiritual when we have taken back the parts of ourselves that were lost or disowned. Most importantly, we help and heal others not by what we do or say, but by who we are. A whole, complete, spiritual, person, at peace with herself, does more to inspire growth than any amount of proselytizing ever will.

While we are changed forever we must remember that change is not a state of completion. It is an evolutionary process. We may still suffer with the uncertainty change brings into our lives. We know, however, that stagnation results from too much certainty. Spirituality makes change less threatening because we've become more comfortable with our becoming. Spirituality makes our lives an I'm-evolving experience rather than an I've-arrived experience. We therefore accept uncertainty and manage it with grace because we are now resocialized women.

Our spirituality connects our lives with the global movement of humanity toward new and higher levels of maturity. This connection makes it easier to endure our struggles because we see ourselves as world citizens. We bring new wisdom to the world. This unifying vision helps protect our inner peace from unhealthy intrusive social discrimination. We can join men who are feminists and encourage those who are not. In this way, we bring our recently created new life into the community of nations devoted to equality.

We now bring the message of resocialization to others because we understand how dangerous social conditioning is. We are examples in both instructional and unintentional ways through the quality of our lives. At the beginning of our resocialization, we needed separation to learn to refocus on our lives. The exclusion of others was symbolic of shedding the myths of femininity that paralyzed us. We may never before have believed that we could stand on our own and thrive. Separation uncomplicated our lives so we could grasp the fact that there was a self separate from them. Now we know that we can share with others without abandoning ourselves. We are strong enough to be separate and confident enough to be united. We can give without losing our identity. This is a wonderful place to be.

Resocialization has peeled away the destructive layers of sexism that numbed our souls. As reclaimed women, it is easier to speak about our truth because we know what our truth is. We have woven the pure, creative energy of our childhood with the strength of our mature and world-wise adulthood. Now we can ask questions without embarrassment. We can play without guilt. We can feel without shame. We can be without being perfect; seek education as a means of empowerment; change without being defensive; be creative and believe in the uniqueness of our contribution. We will challenge without fear any power that attempts to entrap us because we have confidence in our true selves. We can passionately make our lives our own. We have become the bride of our destiny.

We blend the best of ourselves with the best of society. Our personal revolution has joined the universal revolution toward spirituality, equality, justice and human dignity. Based on our new understanding of personal relationships, we will create a different world by being different. We will infiltrate political systems with a spiritual vision of the correct use of power.

Now we can love being women because it includes what we love most about ourselves. Most importantly, and finally, we are the brides of whatever we love.

How We Feel

"We feel the certainty of a 'new bride' because our psychology and our spirituality have become one."

Our search for a new reality in our lives has moved in countless directions. It encompasses our fears and hopes, our joys and sorrows. We have begun an endless quest, not merely with our minds, but with our whole being. Our spirituality has connected us with what we love and made us proud of what we have survived. Because we are feeling more whole, we can celebrate what we have learned and where we are going. We have the certainty of a New Bride because the stuff of our life is finally known and embraced. Our psychology and our spirituality have become one. We are now freer from myths of femininity and masculinity and this has cleared the path to internalized equality. Our unified self has laid the foundation of our spirituality because we now know who we are. We are in touch with our worth. We have claimed the tremendous gifts of creativity we hold inside of us. This sacred journey has led us to our sacred Self.

This is an endless journey because as long as we live we will learn the wonder of being who we are: women, mothers, daughters, grandmothers, sisters, friends, lovers, managers, artists and employees--on and on. We won't want it to end because the excitement of discovery generates a longing for more life. It is the Yellow Brick Road with more adventures and discoveries at every turn.

The creation and the discovery of our Self run parallel paths that are blended into our spirituality. Spirituality is not a resting or a hiding place, but the ongoing challenge to connect with our life emotionally. It means we appreciate the processes and possibilities available to us in every challenge we face. We face life with optimism.

We may have begun this journey of self-discovery with a very vague idea about spirituality. Confusing it with religion may have kept us angry, especially if we've had negative religious experiences. All religions are both human and mystical at the same time. Human because the mystical message is organized and managed by individuals that have all the same limitations each of us struggles with daily. This anger toward organized religion can thwart our spiritual progress because it cuts us off from the possible contribution of religion in our lives. Religion can serve as a path to developing our spirituality. However, the patriarchal nature of most religions makes them a foreign land to women. Religion should always be viewed as the servant of spirituality. It could offer us gifts that are difficult for many of us to duplicate on our own. It could put us in touch with a community of people who may have similar goals. It ritualizes in celebration and rites, transitions in our lives and instructs us about spiritual matters on a consistent basis. It can challenge our spiritual complacency and remind us of our transcendent nature.

In the formation of your new spirituality, religion may or may not have a place. Those of us who have personal conflicts about religion could find someone who can help us identify the source of those conflicts. Creating your own spirituality may include resolving religious anger that goes as far back as your childhood. Most of us were taught that religion would make us and keep us good. Remind yourself over and over again that you are innately good. We may have been taught that these rituals contained the power to make us good. We were vulnerable to this kind of literal, simplistic thinking during our childhood, but as adult women, we are challenged to define our own spirituality and to internalize rather than externalize the meaning and style of our beliefs. Your adult spirituality must have everything to do with the journey of your life. As you have journeyed back into your past, through the dark moments, the empty spots, the jungle of oppression, you will name your spirituality by realizing how you survived and what you learned. Your wisdom is the story of your survival and youthful insight.

How We Are With Others

"When we hear our own voice in the voices of other women, we will feel a deep peace."

When we began this journey, our spirituality was centered in others, meaning other people and other institutions which chartered the course of our personal identity. We have now created our own spirituality because we love, respect and cherish our own lives. Spirituality calls us to another level of consciousness that is based on loving who we are rather than who we are supposed to be. Our spirituality is connected with our continual evolvement. It honors how we think. It honors how we feel. It protects our sense of self in all our relationships. It does not mean we are so self-centered that the concerns of others and institutions don't matter to us. It means they don't have ultimate authority over us. It means that self-loyalty is a part of all loyalty. The spirituality of the New Bride makes her less likely to waste her energy worrying about the opinions or judgments of others because she is at peace with herself. Her own journey has helped her develop a broad empathic understanding of others; even when she is being challenged.

Our inner voice has been released from the bondage of socialization. We are free to be heard and we must be heard if true equality will ever be realized. Although we have liberated our inner world, we must acknowledge that world cultures still thrive on inequality. Desiring equality, defining it and envisioning its implications is our difficult task because many problems unique to women remain unsolved. Our spirituality challenges us to identify those problems and join others who work toward a solution. Our spirituality leads us toward taking an active role in righting the wrongs that still remain because of socialization and protect the gains we have already achieved.

Bonding with women will provide a surge of positive feminine identification. As our lives unfold, we will feel the splendor of owning our own life. When we connect our passage with the lives of other women, we are more content and comforted. As women, we are connected to each other in all phases of our lives. Unity empowers us. When we hear our own voices in the voices of other women we will feel a very deep peace. To be truly free is to remain in the state of becoming and never again be willing to be an accomplice in our own oppression.

Feminist men and feminist women will come together for change when they share on a spiritual level. This one-world ideal is an essential component of peace and intimacy between the sexes. We need to belong to the same world so that the world we live in will be a better reflection of our infinite possibilities. When men and women stand side-by-side supporting each other because they both know how destructive gendering has been, they will create a profound intimacy and a new level of respect in their relationships.

Spirituality is about choosing rather than being chosen. It is about achieving success through initiative rather than through enduring discomfort. It is about defining ourselves for ourselves, not to exclude others, but to integrate a genuine reconciliation in which all women accept their inner Self and recognize that self to be an integral part of an expanding universe.

JOURNALING

1. Congratulations! You have completed a wonderful journey that has begun to remake your life, for the journey to self is never ending. What has your journey done for you? How has your life changed? Do you believe your life has a message that can only be conveyed through your living? **WRITE!**

2. Are you inspired to encourage other women to reclaim their lives? As you do so, remember how afraid they will be of this momentous task. Recall your own fears now. Recall the fears you have silenced with your courage. **WRITE!**

3. In what ways can you personally inspire others? Writing? Painting? Public speaking? Teaching? In answering this question, think about what motivated you to complete this journey. **WRITE!**

4. What does spirituality mean to you? How do you experience spirituality in your life? How does it strengthen and heal you? In what ways can you experience your spiritual connection with others? **WRITE!**

5. Completing any act of healing is cause for celebration. Celebrate yourself! How can you celebrate your own accomplishment at the completion of this program? Involve yourself and other women who are important to you. **WRITE!**

REFLECTIVE CINEMA

Movies that reinforce the themes of this stage recommended for viewing:

- What's Love Got To Do With It?
- Bright Star
- Whale Rider
- Eleanor Roosevelt (PBS)

STEPPING OUT

- Invite a circle of friends to your home for a spiritual party. Have each woman bring a picture of herself as a child and tell her story.
- Join an organization with the specific purpose of helping to further the search for equality. Get involved with doing the work of that organization.
- Participate in some kind of spiritual activity with others; drumming, a retreat, a religious experience, cooking food with others for the poor; cleaning the beaches or parks and countless others which could certainly fill this page.
- Buy a book on goddess spirituality. Read short passages everyday for five days. Feel the results.

I have known good and evil,
sin and virtue, right and wrong;
I have judged and been judged;
I have passed through birth and death,
joy and sorrow, heaven and hell;
and in the end I realized
that I am in everything
and everything is in me.

Taken From: The Healing Power of Illness
(Thozwald Dethlefsen and Ridiges Dahlke, M.D.)

WOMEN'S JOURNEY

OUR PURPOSE

As women, we are ready to consciously determine who we are, what we deserve and what we want. Giving to others must include giving to ourselves. Knowing ourselves is our source of empowerment.

Women's Journey is a progressive program of recovery from the social pressures that restrict us in our search to reach our full human potential. It is a program that provides all women a free and safe place to learn, understand, listen and share the complexities of our lives with one another. In our sharing, we are informed and refreshed, comforted and liberated from the loneliness of being lost to our authentic self.

The purpose of Women's Journey is to make it possible for women to see their hopes and dreams made real. We stand for a safe world for women, regardless of race, creed or sexual orientation, in which they can carve out a clear sense of self. We are committed to the hope that every woman will experience the love and support of other women in her journey to self-liberation. We hold each woman's sharing as a sacred trust and pledge to maintain that trust in complete confidence. All of those who wish to participate in Women's Journey are welcome and are invited to join other women in their quest for self-assurance and empowerment. This invitation is extended to all women who want their lives to make a difference.

Women's Journey, Inc. is a non-profit corporation that offers women monthly gatherings to discuss their "Journey to Resocialization." For a schedule of meetings and themes, visit:
http://womensjourney.org

To contact Ann Mody Lewis, Ph.D.
Email: alewis4390@aol.com

CPSIA information can be obtained at www.ICGtesting.com
Printed in the USA
LVOW070710231112

308336LV00002B/36/P